Sleeping Beauty

Vampire Slayer

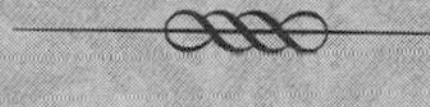

Maureen McGowan

San Diego, California

Silver Dolphin Books
An imprint of the Baker & Taylor Publishing Group
10350 Barnes Canyon Road, San Diego, CA 92121
www.silverdolphinbooks.com

Interior and cover design by Pauline Molinari.
Cover art by Mike Heath.

Library of Congress Cataloging-in-Publication Data

McGowan, Maureen.
Sleeping Beauty : vampire slayer / Maureen McGowan.
p. cm.
Summary: In this twist on the Sleeping Beauty fairy tale, Princess Lucette, cursed as a baby by her evil vampire aunt, discovers as she grows older that the only way to protect herself and her kingdom is to train as a vampire slayer. The reader is given chances throughout the text to choose the direction of the plot.
ISBN-13: 978-1-60710-256-4
ISBN-10: 1-60710-256-0
1. Plot-your-own stories. [1. Princesses--Fiction. 2. Vampires--Fiction. 3. Fairy tales. 4. Plot-your-own stories.] I. Title.
PZ8.M1761Sl 2011
[Fic]--dc22

2010039737

Printed in the United States

1 2 3 4 5 15 14 13 12 11

For Sinead Murphy and Molly O'Keefe,
who've pulled me in off the proverbial ledge
too many times to count.

Table of Contents

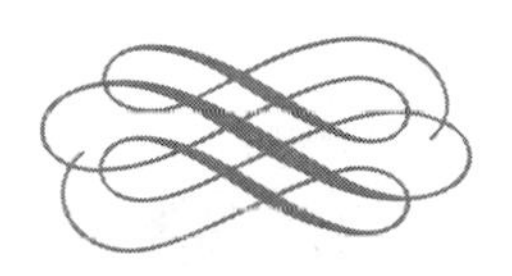

How This Book Works

Sleeping Beauty: Vampire Slayer is a different sort of fairy tale that's twisted two ways. First, it's full of adventure for our Sleeping Beauty Lucette, loaded with danger, and heaped with action—not to mention vampires. Second, you get to control what happens.

At three dramatic turning points in the story, you'll get a chance to put yourself into Lucette's shoes and decide what you'd do next.

There are no right or wrong decisions, just different ones. As you'll soon discover, Lucette's a pretty special girl. She's strong and smart and brave, and she needs to learn how to stop blaming herself for things she can't control, including whatever challenges you throw her way.

When you decide which path to take, you simply flip to the relevant page. When you reach the end of any section, there will be a guidepost to tell you which page to turn to.

The best part is you can read this book over and over. In total, there are eight different routes through this book, which means eight stories in one! After you're done, see if you can figure out all the possible routes.

Prologue

Sunlight streamed through the floor-to-ceiling windows lining the western-facing wall of the palace's reception room. On a raised platform at its north end, Queen Catia of Xandra, two months shy of her eighteenth birthday, sat on her throne with her husband, King Stefan. Between them, their baby girl lay asleep in her fur-lined glass cradle.

Since the baby's birth, the palace staff had worked around the clock to make the room beautiful for the princess's naming ceremony. Bright tapestries and banners decorated the glistening marble and glass walls. Ribbons of silver and gold hung from the vaulted ceiling, waving and dancing in the light summer breeze blowing in from the open skylights. The royal guard, in their scarlet, gold, and blue uniforms, lined the room—no fewer than ten on the throne platform alone.

Yet the young queen's shoulders were as tense as a mountain lion ready to pounce. *At least there were no vampires,* she said to herself.

Diplomacy demanded that the queen of Xandra entertain the leaders of other kingdoms, but all those assembled could sense the young queen's discomfort.

The queen turned to her sweet, raven-haired baby girl, who so clearly took after her tall and extravagantly handsome father. Even at this young age, the princess's cheekbones were sharp, and her jaw defiant. Her big, electric-blue eyes flashed intelligence and mischief from under long, dark lashes and strong brows that commanded attention.

The fairy delegation hovered near the platform, their translucent wings acting like prisms as they passed through beams of sunlight. The fairies would grant a wish for the newborn based on what their queen saw in the child's future. They'd been known to grant wondrous gifts, but they'd also been known to bestow gifts more akin to a curse.

The fairy queen, the smallest of the group and dressed in a shimmering ice-blue dress, flew forward until she was hovering over the cradle. Holding her hands over the baby's head, the fairy queen closed her eyes and nodded, seemingly in a trance, and her entire body sparkled even more than it had before.

Suddenly, the fairy queen flew back from the cradle so quickly that a rush of air caught the tendrils of Queen Catia's hair.

Everyone gasped, and Catia's eyes widened in fear.

King Stefan leaped from his throne and strode down the steps toward the fairy queen. "What is it? Tell me, what did you see?"

Still hovering in the air, the fairy queen's body paled to the point where she was nearly translucent, then she laid her hands on his shoulders. "Stefan, king of Xandra, my friend and descendant of my old friends now passed, I see many shadows in your young daughter's future. Loneliness, darkness, and danger."

Queen Catia rose, lifted her baby from the cradle, and, holding her tightly, went to stand at her husband's side. "Darkness? Danger? What do you mean?"

Color had returned to the fairy's skin and she radiated pale blue.

"My young queen, the danger's source isn't clear, nor its duration." She turned to the king. "I was planning to grant this child grace of movement, but I'm changing my gift." The fairy raised her hands above the baby.

"To symbolize light," the fairy said, "I grant this baby girl the name Lucette. May this name lead the princess out of the darkness she will encounter."

Queen Catia pulled the baby back from the fairy queen. "We're naming her Rose." Rose, for Catia's favorite flower. Rose, for the acres of gardens her husband had planted as a wedding gift last year. Rose because it was a beautiful bloom that could also protect and defend itself. Given the name Rose, her daughter would be both beautiful and strong.

King Stefan laid his hand on his wife's arm. "Darling, Lucette is a lovely name." He leaned down and whispered, "And it's not smart to decline a fairy queen's gift." Growing up in the country, his young queen had much to learn about other cultures.

The queen opened her mouth to protest, but before she could speak, a shadow fell, as if the sun had been covered by storm clouds, and an icy cold rushed into the room. The king wrapped his arms around his wife and child.

One of the floor-to-ceiling windows at the side of the reception hall shattered.

Everyone screamed and ducked as shards of glass burst into the room. Natasha, newly crowned as the queen of the vampires, flew into the room through the broken window. Nearly six feet tall, the vampire queen's rich red hair flowed and her skin shone as if it were cast from porcelain, providing a stark contrast to the shiny black stone that hung at her throat. Turning toward the royal couple, her yellow-flecked eyes flashed hatred. Crossing the room, Natasha's hair flowed around her, as if she held the wind at her command.

"But—it's daytime," Queen Catia blurted. "How can this vile creature walk in the daylight?"

What Catia did not know was that the black stone at the vampire's throat was magic and granted its wearer many powers beyond those of a normal vampire. The vampires of Sanguinia had stolen the Stone of Supremacy from the fairies over a thousand years ago.

Queen Natasha stepped forward and her red satin dress swished around her legs, flowing over the floor like pools of blood spreading across the marble. "Handsome as ever, Stefan," she said to the king, tracing a red-tipped fingernail down his arm.

"Hello, Natasha," King Stefan said. "I was saddened by the news of Vlad's death." King Vladimir had mysteriously died just weeks earlier, many suspected at his own wife's hand.

"Thank you, Stefan," the vampire queen said. "I wanted to invite you all to the funeral." She gestured around the room. "But in deep mourning, I couldn't bring myself to entertain guests." The vampire stepped up and leaned in to embrace him, peering over the king's shoulder toward his young wife. She bared her fangs dangerously close to the king's neck, but instead of biting, she turned and kissed King Stefan on the mouth. A small cry burst from his young wife, who remained frozen in fear.

Natasha stepped away from the king and leered at Queen Catia, her eyes filled with hatred.

"Go away!" Catia yelled. "You're not welcome here! You weren't invited!"

King Stefan spun toward his wife. "Catia?" The king's shock and hurt were obvious in his voice and expression. His wife had lied and claimed the vampire delegation from Sanguinia had declined to attend, when in fact she'd burned their invitations.

"Please accept my apology, Natasha," King Stefan said. "I'm sure it was an oversight." He looked at his wife with pain in his eyes, then turned back to the vampire and continued, "But how fortuitous you arrived before the naming ceremony. We were just about to begin."

"Lovely." Queen Natasha smiled, her fangs showing between blood-red lips. "But not before I offer my gift."

"No need for a gift." The king's voice was strong and deep. "Especially not after your invitation failed to arrive."

"Do you think me that petty?" the vampire queen inquired. "It is tradition for all reigning monarchs to offer gifts to new members of the other royal families, is it not?"

"You are most gracious," King Stefan said.

Catia tensed, because she knew the vampire queen was not gracious at all. More like vengeful and desperate for power.

"What are you naming the child?" Natasha asked.

"Rose," Catia blurted before her husband could speak.

"What a fitting name." Natasha stepped back, her skirts swirling around her. "A flower with fangs. I like that. Now, if you will hand me the babe"—she bared her fangs—"I will bestow my gift."

"Never!" Catia retreated, hugging the baby to her chest. "I will never let you touch my child."

With a growl, Natasha snatched the baby from the young queen's arms and leaped to the empty orchestra balcony, high above the room. The assembled crowd screamed in shock.

The iron- and protein-rich vampire diet made vampires notoriously strong, but no one had seen a vampire jump so high.

"Get her!" Catia screamed. "Someone! Save my baby!" The guards raced for the stairs.

Stefan stepped forward and called up. "Natasha, what are you doing? Please don't hurt my daughter."

"Hurt her?" The vampire queen held the child high above her head. A stream of sunlight burst through the darkness and struck the baby. "Nonsense. I'm only offering my gift."

She set the baby down on a planter of flowers on the balcony railing, then addressed the crowd. "To punish her rude mother, this child's blood will bring a curse upon the kingdom of Xandra."

The entire room gasped. Such words could lead to war between Sanguinia and Xandra after so many centuries of peace—so many years during which the necks of the Xandrans had not been at risk of vampire bites.

"Here is my gift." Natasha glared down at the assembled crowd of royalty and other dignitaries. "One day, the princess will prick her finger, and the instant her blood is shed, she shall never again wake while the sun is in the sky. Every morning, as the sun breaks above the horizon, the princess will fall into a deep sleep, waking only as night falls." The vampire queen smiled. "And every other citizen of Xandra will suffer the opposite fate. They will fall asleep each night at dusk, leaving the princess alone in the darkness."

The vampire queen picked up the princess, and Queen Catia screamed, "Save my baby!" The guards raced to the balcony, but the vampire queen leaped onto the railing, balancing on the toes of her black stilettos.

She expelled a cackle that filled the room and shook the crystal chandeliers. "This child and the people of Xandra will pay for their young queen's rudeness and deceit!" She licked her lips, flew into the air, and vanished.

Sunlight once again streamed through the windows, and everyone shaded their eyes against the sudden onslaught of brightness.

"My baby!" Catia ran toward the window as soon as she could squint her eyes open. "She's taken my baby!"

"No, she's here!" Stefan yelled.

The queen turned to see her husband standing next to the cradle between their thrones. When he picked up the child, her little hand poked out from her blanket and her tiny fingers wiggled.

Catia ran to join her husband and fell into his arms. "I've changed my mind," she cried. "Our daughter will need all the light in her life we can offer. Let's accept the fairies' gift. We'll name her Lucette."

After the other guests had gone home, Queen Catia dropped to her knees in front of the fairy delegation. "Please, you have magic. There must be something you can do." Suddenly the young girl, who'd grown up with her heart full of distrust for creatures such as fairies, was asking for favors.

The fairy queen placed her hands on the sides of the queen's face and looked directly into her eyes. "Today marked the first day in centuries that a monarch of Sanguinia used the Stone of Supremacy outside their own kingdom. The stone has very powerful magic, and a curse offered under its domain cannot easily be lifted."

Catia looked up. "Please! I'll give my own life. Transfer the curse to me. Anything!"

"Give me a moment with my circle." The fairies circled around their queen and shimmering light flooded the floor beneath them.

"Darling." Stefan put his hand on Catia's shoulder where she knelt, and she pressed her forehead against his thigh. "I'm sure they can do something," he said. "If not, we'll keep her safe. We'll make sure her finger is never pricked."

Still on her knees, Catia lifted her face toward him, tears streaming down her cheeks. "But how? How can our daughter go through life never pricking her finger?"

He took her hands and pulled her to her feet. "I will protect her. I will protect you both."

Given the day's events, Catia did not find her husband's assurances convincing. "I told you vampires were evil," she spat.

"Catia." Stefan shook his head. "You know that's not true. Vampire bites are extremely rare. Sanguinia and Xandra are at peace." But Stefan frowned. In the two weeks since King Vladimir's death, seven vampire attacks had been reported.

Catia thumped her hand against Stefan's chest. "How could you have let this happen?"

He took her wrist. "Me?" His face reddened. "Me? I trusted you with the guest list. When I questioned the daylight timing of the ceremony, you expressly lied. You told me she'd declined our invitation and no one from Sanguinia would attend. How could you possibly blame this on me?"

He dropped her hands, and Catia backed away from her husband, afraid, for it was the first time she'd seen him angry. She stepped toward him, softening her expression, hoping to regain his favor, yearning to see the love and admiration ever present in his eyes when he looked into hers. His eyes were blank.

The fairy circle broke and their queen floated back toward the royal couple. The king took his queen's hand, but a sense of coldness filled the space between them.

"Can you lift the curse?" he asked the fairy queen.

"No, but we can lessen its impact," she replied. "First, we can protect the princess while she's a child. The curse will not fall until after the princess turns sixteen."

Catia felt some relief, which soon dissipated and her body tensed again. "But when Natasha finds out you've changed her curse, she'll kill us all."

The fairy queen paled, then shook her head. "We will cast a barrier spell. If the vampire queen crosses the border into Xandra before the curse lifts, all the magic in the Stone of Supremacy will vanish. She'll still be a vampire, but with no special powers."

Catia's relief was once again short-lived as she considered the curse. "But after my daughter turns sixteen, she'll spend the rest of her days alone in the darkness?" The fairies' protection would do nothing to keep away *other* vampires.

"We can bestow one final gift upon your daughter," the fairy queen said. "Once the princess proves she has found true love, the curse will be lifted."

Catia dropped to her knees. This past year, she'd thought her dreams had come true—becoming queen and having a beautiful princess daughter—then within a moment, her dreams had turned into a nightmare. "How will my daughter find true love if the young men only wake while she is asleep?"

Section 1

Cursed

1

Lucette woke in the middle of the night to the sound of shouting. She slipped out of the golden four-poster canopy bed she shared with her mother, Queen Catia, and tiptoed to the dark window of her castle bedroom. Pushing aside the heavy brocade curtains, her reflection confronted her in the glass, and she crossed her arms over her tall, skinny form.

Her mother had insisted that her thirteen-year-old body would soon sport womanly curves, but that was difficult to imagine. She might be ahead of her classmates Gloria and Heather in their studies, but the daughters of her ladies-in-waiting were far ahead in bodily development. Their figures seemed to change daily.

Lucette had long ago shed her resentment over the fact that her teachers could sit close and help Gloria and Heather with their work, and actually touch them. Or that they got to write with pencils and beautiful quill pens, while she was permitted only wax crayons and chalk. Now, however, she couldn't help but resent her classmates' curves. Lucette's body had merely stretched up—she was five foot seven . . . and counting—and her height exaggerated her flat chest, slim hips, gangly limbs, and lack of a defined waist.

But her body wasn't the worst of it. Everyone said she took after her handsome father, but she'd trade her big blue eyes, bony cheeks, heavy lashes, and stark black hair for her mother's softer, prettier blonde features any day. As far as she could tell, the main way in which she took after her father was that, if it weren't for her long hair, she'd look like a boy.

The winter chill penetrated the stone floor in her room. Putting one of her cold feet on top of the other, Lucette scolded herself for not grabbing her slippers or throwing on a warm robe over her long flannel nightdress. And if her father knew she had gotten out of bed without her gloves on, he'd confine her to her bedchamber for weeks. He didn't even know her mother let her sleep without them. But the noise she heard in the courtyard held priority, and it had seemed close.

Her breath fogged the window as she leaned to press her forehead against the cold glass and shield her view with her hands.

Through the window, she saw vampires. Three big ones. But they were outnumbered by the team of six slayers dropping down from the edges of the courtyard.

A tall slayer—dressed in black from head to toe, and barely visible in the moonlight—pulled out a long stake, spun around, and thrust it through the heart of the tallest vampire. Shocked, the vile bloodsucker staggered back and fell to the ground, convulsing in his death throes. *Good riddance*, thought Lucette. Like her mother always said, the only good vampire is a dead vampire.

Although rare in Xandra before her birth, vampire attacks were now common. Still, her father refused to declare war on Sanguinia—which was another source of conflict between her parents. Her mother wanted Sanguinia crushed.

Outside, another slayer leaped through the air to plant his heavy boot in the chest of a vampire, and Lucette turned from the window to mimic the kick. She fantasized about how amazing it would be to be a slayer, to kill the evil beasts, but then she shook her head to bring herself back to reality. Her parents would never allow it—even her mother, who wanted every last vampire dead.

She searched the courtyard and saw that the remaining vampire and the slayer pursuing him had climbed to the top of the opposite roof. The vampire lifted the slayer and tossed him from the side of the building.

Lucette gasped, but as the slayer fell, he shot a grappling hook from a crossbow and it snagged a window ledge. He swung back and slammed into the stone wall, then dropped gracefully to the courtyard.

Back on the roof, more slayers arrived from inside the building and cornered the remaining vampire, who sprang forward. The group of slayers parted to reveal another slayer crouched down in the middle, holding out a stake. He braced himself as the leaping vampire impaled himself on the stake and writhed in agony.

Slayers never failed to impress Lucette with their skill and courage. They were so cool and powerful. Mimicking their motions, she leaped up and kicked to strike an imaginary vampire. Empowered, she twisted to kick behind her, and then dropped to the carpet, rolled to the side, and jumped up to deliver a series of chops and punches. Attempting to replicate another move, she jumped and twisted, but her foot accidentally connected with the edge of her vanity table, and a gold candlestick fell, clattering and shattering the silence.

"Lucette!" Her mother sprang out of the bed and strode over, her long nightdress shining in the moonlight. "What was that noise? What are you doing out of bed?" The queen, nearly five inches shorter than her daughter, grabbed the young girl's shoulders.

The door to their room slammed open and in strode King Stefan, followed by six royal guardsmen. "Catia, what is going on in here?" he demanded.

"Nothing, Dad," Lucette answered, before her mother could. She hid her hands behind her back. "It's not Mom's fault. I just knocked something over."

"Catia," Stefan yelled, "how could you let this happen?"

Her mother pulled her long blonde braid to the side and reached for her robe. "Will you please ask the guards to leave my daughter's bedroom?"

Stefan nodded to the guards and they stepped back into the hall.

While her father's attention was focused on her mother and the guards, Lucette grabbed her gloves from atop the vanity table and slipped them on before her father could notice her bare hands.

"Dad." Lucette walked up to her father, took his hand, and looked up into his eyes, wishing she were still small enough to jump into his arms. "It's no big deal, really."

He pressed a kiss into her forehead, then turned back toward her mother. "If you can't handle the responsibility of keeping our daughter safe at night—" He paused and rubbed his stubbled chin.

"Stefan," said her mother, her voice calm but stern, "she's perfectly safe."

Her father dropped her hand and stepped toward her mother. Lucette's chest tightened. *Don't fight. Don't fight. Please don't fight.*

"Catia," her father said, "it's bad enough you don't enforce the safety rules when I'm not around—don't think I don't hear about it—but I can't believe you let her leap about the room at all hours of the night. There are dangers everywhere in the dark." He narrowed his eyes. "If you can't handle it, we'll hire someone to watch our daughter while she sleeps."

Lucette felt sick. Her father wanted to hire strangers to watch her sleep? This was over the top. "No, Dad! Please! Mom keeps me really safe at night. She'd never let anything happen."

"Your mother proved to me long ago that she can't be trusted."

"Stefan." Catia's cheeks burned red and Lucette fought back tears. "Your extreme measures are highly unnecessary. Until she's sixteen—"

The king raised his hand and Catia stopped.

It wasn't the first time Lucette had heard references to her turning sixteen, and she couldn't wait until she reached that magical age. It must be the age at which her parents would consider her old enough to take care of herself. Maybe when she turned sixteen she'd be able to do things like walk down a flight of stairs without holding an adult's hand, use a pencil, and cut her own food—things most four-year-olds were allowed to do. She knew she was a princess, but her parents, especially her father, treated her like glass.

He was so obsessed with protecting her, especially her hands, claiming she needed to develop good safety habits for the future. It all seemed crazy. Good safety habits for what? No teenager or adult she knew wore gloves or protected their hands so well.

Her mother patted the bed. "Lucette, get under the covers and go back to sleep. I need to talk to your father."

Lucette did as she was told, turned onto her side, and pulled the covers partially over her head. Closing her eyes, she pretended to fall back to sleep as her parents continued to argue outside the bedroom door.

A tear slid onto her pillow. She was always causing arguments between her parents. She tried not to, but it was like a curse with her—as if everything she did or said drove disagreements between them like stakes. Everyone else in the palace seemed to hold her responsible for the king and queen's bad relationship, too. They were all so cold to her—no one even looked her in the eye.

She had to be more careful, to pay more attention to what she said and did. Maybe if she were really good, her parents wouldn't fight.

A few months later, Lucette rolled over onto her back, atop the thick pile of animal skins on which she'd been instructed to stay. Utterly bored, she stared at the night sky.

It was bad enough that—after offering her a rare night outside the palace—her parents had brought her to this dull concert of the slowest, most tedious music she'd ever heard. To add insult to injury, they'd insisted it be a private concert, claiming Lucette could not be exposed to crowds. Some treat. Even while traveling to the concert, held in a huge grassy field surrounded by woods, she'd been bundled up in the back of a padded carriage. She was barely able to breathe in the heat of the warm summer night.

What did they imagine would happen if she were seen in public? Barely anyone in the kingdom even knew what she looked like, and even if her parents didn't want to take her to a public concert, would it have been so horrible to bring along some other members of the palace household, or some of their kids? Even Gloria and Heather, who barely talked to her, would be better than this. But no, it was just the three of them in a huge, grassy field with the orchestra fifty feet away on a clamshell-shaped stage.

Maybe if her parents had other children they wouldn't be so overprotective, but the few times Lucette had asked about that, it had opened more of a rift between them. And now that she had learned how babies were made—well, given how little time her parents spent together, especially at night—Lucette wasn't banking on a little sister or brother to take off the pressure of being an only child anytime soon.

She studied her parents, who'd risen from their chairs to talk—more likely to argue—then she turned toward the woods at the edge of the grassy clearing, imagining what it would be like to walk through a forest. In the stories she read, kids often played among the trees, and Gloria and Heather had shown her drawings of flowers and animals they'd seen there. Tiny lights flitted around in the darkness. Startled, she sprang to her feet. The lights flitted and dove, as if they were chasing each other. Fireflies! She'd read about them in her books. If only she could actually see one up close.

She looked back toward her parents. Her mother's slender arms were crossed tightly over her chest, and her father towered above his wife like an angry mountain.

Lucette's parents were absorbed in their argument, so sure of their obedient daughter that they probably wouldn't even look back at her until the music was over. And the boring music showed no signs of stopping.

A rush of adrenaline flooded through her. If she bunched up the fur and put one of the cashmere coverlets on top, they might assume she'd fallen asleep on the blanket if they glanced back to check.

She scanned the area. Some guards were chatting, and others were looking for approaching intruders. Keeping one eye on her parents, she built her decoy, and then stepped off the blankets onto the grass.

She took one step—two, three, four—then turned to look over her shoulder. Her parents hadn't noticed her, so she ran faster toward the woods, joyous at the feel of the dew splashing up onto her ankles and the fresh night air filling her lungs.

As she entered the forest, wonderful musty, mysterious scents swarmed around her. Moonlight filtered through the trees, and the fireflies seemed even brighter, but in spite of the warm night, a chill traced down her spine.

It was the first time in her life she'd ever been truly alone. It felt pretty great, but also scary. What if there were vampires? Big, horrible bloodthirsty vampires!

She blinked, hoping her eyes would adjust more quickly to the darkness. Then, seeing a group of fireflies whirling around a tree, she bounded toward them, but they were too fast. The fireflies wound down through some underbrush, so she cautiously walked forward, not wanting to scare them away. Placing her hand on the trunk of a tree, another rebellious idea flashed into her head. What would the surface of the bark feel like without gloves? After checking behind her to make sure her father hadn't followed, she slipped off one glove and placed the tips of her fingers onto the bark. Hard. Rough.

A twig snapped above her. Heart racing, she slipped her glove back on and looked up. An owl flew between two trees. Scolding herself for being frightened of a bird, she tried to shake the uneasiness inside her. If she were a slayer, she'd never feel fear.

She needed a weapon. Scrounging in the underbrush, she selected a fallen branch. It certainly wasn't as strong as a proper stake, and probably wasn't sharp enough to pierce a vampire's chest—if she even had the skills to do so. Still, she felt better armed.

"Are you lost?" a male voice asked. Lucette jumped back, almost tripping over a large fallen branch behind her.

She froze. "Who's there? Go away!" Her heart galloped. "If you hurt me, you'll be in big trouble!"

A pale, red-haired boy, not much older than she was from the look of him, stepped out from between two trees a few feet away.

She raised her stake—doing all she could to keep her hand from shaking.

He chuckled. "Don't worry, I'm not going to hurt you." He stepped into the light of a moonbeam. He was skinny and tall, at least four inches taller than she was, and his skin was so pale that it appeared to glow.

"My name's Alexander," he said. "But you can call me Alex. What's yours?"

"Lucette." Her voice came out lower than she'd expected, and wanting to hide her fear, she threw her shoulders back and raised her chin. "And you'd better not mess with me."

He raised his hands, palms out. "I surrender!" He grinned mockingly and pointed at her small branch. "What've you got there?"

"A stake."

"What for?"

"Slaying vampires. What else?"

"Really." He stepped forward slowly until he was close enough that she could touch him with the makeshift stake. Another step and she could touch him with her hand.

"Funny, you don't look like a murderer." He smirked.

"Don't make fun of me." She stepped back and furrowed her brow.

"So you're not a murderer?"

She thrust her chin out. "It's not murder to slay a vampire."

"Really? Why not?" He leaned against a tree.

"Because it's not murder to defend yourself against an evil, bloodsucking monster, that's why."

He cocked his head to the side. "What makes you think vampires are evil monsters?"

"Everyone knows that." According to her mother, anyway.

"Name one thing that makes vampires evil." One corner of his mouth turned up and he crossed one leg in front of the other as he leaned against the tree. His casual manner was both calming and annoying, his confidence fascinating. She felt oddly comfortable with him, as if something about him seemed familiar. Still, he was misguided about vamps.

"Vampires bite people's throats, suck their blood out, and kill them."

"Not true." He held up a finger. "First, it takes three bites to transfer enough venom to kill, not just one. But more to the point"—he dropped his hand—"most vampires never bite animals, never mind humans."

Lucette crossed her arms over her chest. "You don't know what you're talking about. I know all about vampires. I've seen them attacking slayers outside the—outside my house." She didn't want him to know she lived in the palace.

He twisted his shoe in some dead leaves and looked down. "So, you'd condemn an entire species by the actions of a few?" He looked up. "Drinking human blood is gross."

"No kidding." She loosened her grip on her branch, as all the conflicting information she'd heard about vampires swirled in her mind. "It's gross to us, but not to vampires. They live off blood, everyone knows that."

"True, but most don't suck on living things to get it." He twisted his lips in disgust, then tipped his head to the side. "Besides, do you eat meat?"

"Of course, but there's no comparison." Lucette rolled her eyes. It wasn't like she killed the animals herself—with her teeth.

"You're right." The boy crossed his arms over his chest. "There is no comparison. In fact, vampires are more compassionate than humans. Vampires live off animals, but they don't need to kill to get their nutrition. It's more like drinking milk."

"But after three bites—"

"I already told you," he said and stepped forward, "most vampires don't feed that way. It's so old-fashioned. In Sanguinia, blood comes from farms and it's bought at the market."

"How do you know?" She'd never considered that vampires might feast on anything but necks—with a preference for human ones.

"I just do." He shot her a reassuring smile.

The fact that this boy was winning the argument filled her with frustration. "Yeah, well, you don't know everything." Her mother had told her the truth about vampires, and once she got older and gained some freedom, she planned to be a slayer. "Vampires do lots of evil things. They can read minds and influence you and make you do things against your will."

"You believe that?" He looked at her with disdain. "Old wives' tales. Besides, a pretty girl can make me do things against my will. Does that make her evil?"

She dropped her arms from across her chest. This boy seemed nice enough, but didn't understand anything. "Yes, well, vampires are evil, hideous creatures, with no redeeming qualities. It's impossible for them to be good. It goes against their nature."

"Tell me," he said, and leaned forward until she could see the slight yellow glint in his green eyes. "Do I seem evil to you?"

He smiled and she saw his pointed teeth.

He had fangs!

Trembling, she backed into a tree. This tall, red-haired boy wasn't a boy at all. He was a vampire.

"Lucette," he said, "if I'm so evil, why haven't I attacked you yet?"

As his question came out, she found her courage and lunged, stake in hand. He brushed her twig aside and grabbed her arm.

She drew in a sharp breath and scolded herself for disobeying her parents and wandering into the woods. She'd left them arguing, without even trying to mediate, and now she'd die and they'd fight over that, too.

She could not let that happen. She screamed and stomped on his foot.

"Ouch!" He pushed her away. "Why did you do that?"

She fell back, but moving quickly, he caught her before she hit the ground. He moved so quickly, and demonstrated such strength.

"Don't worry," he said. "Like I said, I don't drink human blood. And even if I were starving, I wouldn't drink yours. I have no idea what you've been eating." He grinned, but she didn't find it much of a joke, and backed away.

"Lucette, believe me—most vampires believe it's just plain wrong to drink blood straight from the vein of any animal. It's immoral, not to mention wasteful, to risk killing a source of food. Sanguinian vampires only drink blood from certified ranches, where the animals have been properly fed, compassionately treated, and hygienically bled."

"I don't believe you!" She wrenched her arm back. "You're just trying to control my mind."

"I can't control your mind. Only our queen, the holder of the Stone of Supremacy, holds any magical powers, and even she can't control people's minds—much to her chagrin." He chuckled.

"Liar! I just saw your powers. You're so strong and fast."

"Of course. I live off of a very pure diet. I can't believe the garbage you humans put in your bodies. No wonder you're so weak."

The music stopped and Lucette turned to the clearing to see if anyone had discovered her absence. When she turned back, Alex had vanished.

Before she could even start back, her father came crashing through the forest. She dropped the twig to the ground and double-checked her gloves. Boy, was she in trouble. At least this time she'd be in trouble with *both* of her parents. Maybe punishing her would bring them closer together.

When they got home, Lucette slunk into her room and collapsed onto her bed. She heard the door shut as her mother entered behind her. Never had she seen her father so angry or her mother so shaken. And if that weren't bad enough, she was confused about everything. Not that she believed everything the vampire boy had said, but it was hard to discount him completely. He'd been so sincere, and kind of nice, even while she kept arguing with him. In fact, before she knew what he was, she'd been starting to like him a little bit. He *was* the first boy she'd ever talked to. If he had been a boy, that is.

"How are you feeling, Lucette?" Her mother sat down on the bed, leaned over her, and placed her hand on her forehead—cool and soft and soothing.

"I'm so sorry, Mom. It's just that I've never been in the forest before and the music was so boring and I'd never seen fireflies, and . . ." If she said she'd also seen a vampire, her mother would become as overprotective as her father. That information had to stay secret.

"We've kept you too sheltered," her mother said. "I keep telling your father—"

Lucette sat up and interrupted her mother with an embrace, longing for the days when she could curl up in her lap. She'd been taller than her mother since age ten, and her mother could probably curl up in *her* lap now. Worse, her mother yet again confirmed what Lucette had known since she could remember. Her parents' fights were always about her.

It would be better to change the subject to one her mother never tired of. "Are all vampires evil, Mom?"

Her mother stroked her hair. "Where did that come from?"

"I'm just wondering. I mean, Dad always says that they aren't all bad, but I know you don't agree, and every time I bring it up, Dad gets mad and I don't want . . ." She let her voice trail off instead of adding "to cause another fight."

Her mother cupped her cheek. "Since marrying your father, I've learned to tolerate most nonhuman creatures, but vampires are vile, evil monsters, and their queen is the worst of all." She dropped her hand and her expression hardened. "The only good vampire is a dead vampire."

Goose bumps rose on Lucette's arms and neck. Even though her mother had said those words before, she'd never seen such hatred in her mother's eyes and her insistence that all vampires deserved to die seemed extreme—especially after meeting Alex. But if her mother were right, it was chilling to think how close she'd been to a vampire tonight, how close she'd come to death.

She felt foolish for running off into the woods. Some days it felt as though she couldn't take one right step. She sighed and hugged her mother. "Some days I feel like I'm cursed."

Her mother stiffened and pushed her back to arm's length. "Who told you about the curse?"

Lucette sucked in a ragged breath. "What?" She scrambled off the bed. "Do you mean I really *am* cursed?" She'd only said it so her mother could say "Don't be silly, Lucette. Of course you're not cursed." Instead, it felt as if the world had tilted on its side, as if the room were closing in around her, as if the air were suddenly too thick to breathe.

"What do you mean?" She looked at her mother, hoping for answers.

Her mother slid off the bed, stepped up to Lucette, and hugged her tightly. "My darling daughter, it's time you knew the truth." She pulled back, but gripped Lucette's upper arms tightly. "And it's time you learned how to defend yourself, how to fight."

"Like a vampire slayer?" Her mother had to be kidding. Her parents were so overprotective it was crazy, and the idea that they'd let her learn to be a slayer—it was too much to hope for.

But her mother's expression remained serious. "Your father thinks he can protect you. He thinks it's his job to keep his wife and daughter safe, but I think it's important we also learn to protect ourselves."

"I'd give anything to be a vampire slayer." Lucette felt excitement bubble up inside her. Had her mother been watching the other night when she'd been practicing her slayer moves? Reading her mind? She looked into her mother's eyes for clues.

"Lucette," her mother said evenly and calmly. "It is crucial that you train as a vampire slayer."

Crucial? Confusion set in. This afternoon she would have jumped for joy at the opportunity. Now she wasn't so sure. But if training to be a slayer meant shedding the protective blanket her father had smothered her under, she was on board.

"Are you serious, Mom?" Lucette wasn't convinced she could actually kill a vampire, but the training sounded exciting, and she wasn't about to question her mother's motives and risk her changing her mind. This was sure to spark another parental fight, though. Torn between her dreams and keeping the peace, her stomach hurt.

Her mother let out a heavy sigh. "Lucette, your father doesn't want to scare you, but I think you're old enough to know what happened when you were a baby."

Lucette opened her eyes wide.

"Sit down," her mother said. "It's time you learned about your curse."

The next morning, Lucette approached the room to which her parents had summoned her and kept her gaze focused on the marble floor with its alternating pattern of silver and blue tiles. She'd barely slept last night, and learning about the curse had left her feeling numb and in a state of disbelief. She couldn't imagine why a vampire queen, whom she'd never even met, would hate her enough to curse her.

A guard opened the door, and she bit down on her lip in irritation. She wasn't allowed to touch any doorknobs herself, even though all the doorknobs in the palace were perfectly smooth. It seemed unlikely that one would ever cut her—especially since she'd worn leather gloves every day for her entire life. But at least now she understood her father's obsession with finger safety—sort of.

According to her mother, her father thought she needed to develop good safety habits before turning sixteen—hence the gloves and his rules—whereas her mother thought she should have a chance to live a normal life until that fateful birthday. They also disagreed on the subject of her learning how to defend herself. Her father thought the idea of her training to slay was ridiculous and morbid, and his focus was completely on finger-prick prevention. Her mother, however, thought the curse was inevitable and that it was better to face it head-on. At least some of their fights made more sense now, even if it confirmed Lucette's fears that she'd caused them.

As she walked up to her parents, the air in the room seemed icy, and she imagined what it would look like if one of them reached out to take the other's hand. Better yet, what if both of them reached out at the same time, then turned to smile at each other as their hands joined? The image felt as real as a memory, yet Lucette knew she was projecting the actions of other couples she'd seen around the palace onto her parents. She'd never seen her parents hold hands. She herself had never held anyone's hand—without a glove.

Lucette stepped up to her parents and clasped their hands; at least now they were connected through her. She looked at each, timidly wondering what her punishment would be. "I'm so sorry about going into the woods. It was foolish and crazy, and I'll never do anything like that again. I promise I can be more careful."

"I hope you learned your lesson." Her father's face was stern. "But we called you here to discuss something else."

She felt the tension build in the room. "Is this about the curse?"

Her father spun toward her mother. "You *told* her?"

"It was time she knew." Her mother shrugged. "She's not a little girl anymore."

"How could you!" the king bellowed. "She's just a child! Look how you've scared her."

Lucette scrambled to find some way to intervene. Her big mouth had done it again, and she'd made everything worse.

"We can't keep her sealed in a bubble, Stefan." Her mother's cheeks flushed. "It's crazy. If you're doing all these things now, what do you plan for after she's turned sixteen?"

"So you want to just give up and let the curse fall?"

"Of course not! I simply believe she deserves to have a tiny bit of freedom—especially until she's sixteen. After that, she may end up isolated and alone in the night without having any skills or preparation."

"That will never happen if she follows her safety rules."

Lucette's knees threatened to crumple as the full weight of her curse sank in.

Alone. In the night. With vampires. And they wouldn't all be as nice as Alex.

Her mother shouted, "You treat your own daughter like a prisoner!"

Her father raised his voice. "The precautions and rules I've set up have helped her develop good habits to prevent the curse! You think I *like* restricting our daughter?"

"Stefan, let's discuss this later." Tight-lipped, she glanced at Lucette, then back at her husband. "You promised we would offer her the choice."

Lucette looked up at the word *choice*. At this time yesterday, she'd felt so mistreated because she had to wear gloves, be escorted everywhere, and was coddled like a baby. In less than twenty-four hours, she'd met a vampire, learned she carried a horrible curse, and caused yet another big fight between her parents. After all that, they were expecting her to make some kind of choice?

A solution popped into her head. "Mom, Dad. If I'm going to bring a curse down on the kingdom, why don't we just leave Xandra? Go somewhere else?"

Her father shook his head. "I can't leave. I'm the king."

"But—" She stopped herself. The last thing she wanted to suggest was that their family split up.

"I thought of that too, Lucette," her mother said. "If it would work, I'd have taken you from Xandra the day after your naming ceremony, but it won't. I asked the fairies. If you leave the kingdom, everyone else in Xandra will fall asleep forever."

Lucette gasped and felt tears spark the backs of her eyes. This couldn't get any worse.

Lucette's father turned toward her, his expression showing obvious pain. "Let's not dwell on things that can't be. Let's focus on the present." He tugged down on his velvet jacket. "Your mother thinks we should allow you to leave the palace on weekdays, but I think it's a bad idea. Even though I've banned most sharp objects and regulated their use for essential services, there might be a few sharp objects that could prick you."

"I think you should attend charm school," her mother stated quickly.

"Charm school?" Lucette repeated slowly. Last night her mother had promised she'd find a way to let her attend slayer school. Was this part of that plan? Linking her daily trips outside the palace to a charm school seemed clever, if devious. Her mother had chosen a lie the king might actually support.

"I do agree that you'd benefit from such training." Her father stepped toward her and cupped her chin tenderly. "It takes more than great beauty to charm young men, but"—he shook his head in disappointment—"I had expected your mother would teach you such things."

Her mother pursed her lips, as if holding back arguments, and Lucette was grateful.

"If you do need charm lessons"—he squeezed her gloved hand—"I'd prefer we bring a tutor into the palace. Certainly your scare last night showed you that you're much safer at home."

"The charm school is very safe." Her mother's voice was sharp, but she didn't argue any further.

Her father sighed. "As long as you promise to follow your safety rules, I'll allow you to attend—but only if it's what you want."

The door to the room opened and a guard stepped in. "Your Highness, the king and royal wizard from Judra are here for your meeting."

"Lucette," her father said, "you're a sensible girl. In spite of your escapade last night, I'm sure you'll make the right choice . . . the *sensible* choice." He kissed her cheek. Then, without looking back at his queen, the king left the room.

As soon as he was gone, her mother grabbed her hand. "Lucette, of course you'll choose charm school over a private tutor. Your father will never know that I'm having you taken to the Vampire Slayer Academy instead."

"But, Mom." Lucette was beyond excited, yet nervous. "Someone will tell him and when he finds out, he'll be so angry."

The queen shook her head. "I'll register you under a secret name so no one will know it's you."

Lucette lowered her eyes. Training as a slayer was her greatest dream, what she'd always wanted, but a lie between her parents meant another reason for them to fight. Excitement and trepidation mixed inside her. She looked back up at her mother. "Keeping such a big secret will be impossible."

Her mother shook her head. "The palace staff members who came with me when I married your father are loyal, and they'll take you each day. You'll train as a slayer and your father will never know."

"Do you really think we should lie to him?" Nerves scrambled inside Lucette.

Her mother put her hands on her hips. "I don't like it, either, but do you think he'll agree willingly? He won't even let you hold a pencil. Do you think he'd let you touch a sharpened stake?" Her expression softened and she reached forward to touch Lucette's arm. "Darling, I wish there were another way, but learning to defend yourself is important. Of course, I hope the curse will never come to fruition, and after you turn sixteen, you should do everything you can to prevent it. But until then, I want you to learn some basic survival skills in case the worst happens."

Anxiety rushed through Lucette's body, increasing her heart rate and making her queasy. She feared the consequences if her father ever found out about this deception.

If you were Lucette, what would you do?

OPTION A: Lucette should go along with her mother's lie. She's always longed to train as a slayer, and as terrifying as she finds her curse, someday she might be the only one awake at night to defend herself and protect her family. Isn't it her duty to learn? The Vampire Slayer Academy is the best place to study. If you think Lucette should choose option A, go to section 2: The Academy (page 43).

OPTION B: Lucette should refuse to lie to her father. With time, he might become reasonable and agree she needs slayer training. Avoiding this lie, she has a better chance of keeping the peace, and if she causes another fight between her parents, she'll never forgive herself. If her father finds out about the lie, he might never forgive Lucette and her mother. If you think Lucette should choose option B, go to section 3: Big Secrets (page 77).

Section 2

The Academy

2

Lucette fumed. She had only been at the school for a week, but so far her classes, beyond the regular school stuff such as math and history, had been more like charm school than slayer school. Grooming? Flirting? What was the point? The only "point" she cared about was the one she could drive through a vampire's heart.

"Now, class," Miss Eleanor began. A statuesque woman with light blonde hair and way too much makeup, the teacher stuck out a hip and set her hand on it. "Flirting is crucial to our cause and it's the best tool to lure vampires into our traps. The creatures are very amorous and have little self-control, making your beauty a lethal weapon."

Lucette clenched her jaw and her fists.

Miss Eleanor swept a hand out in a broad gesture. "Girls, it's your duty as a slayer to use your feminine wiles against these horrible animals."

Lucette pounded a fist into her thigh, then lifted it and accidentally hit the underside of her desk. The sharp sound reverberated throughout the room.

"Lucy," Miss Eleanor said sternly, "if you insist on disrupting class, I'm going to have to ask you to leave the room." She wrinkled her heavily powdered nose.

"Feminine wiles?" Lucette murmured to herself. "Ridiculous."

"If you'd like to ask a question, please stand," Miss Eleanor said, and the entire class turned back to stare at Lucette.

She shot to her feet. "I didn't register in the academy to use feminine wiles." The phrase itself was stupid. "I came here to learn to be a slayer—to kill vampires. When do we get our stakes?"

The other girls, all much shorter, curvier, and prettier, burst into laughter, covering their mouths with their hands, as though doing so negated their rudeness.

A girl with curly blonde hair said, "She'd have more luck attacking vampires than luring them." She leaned toward her brunette friend across the aisle and whispered, "Flat as a board!" The two giggled. They'd established their roles as teacher's pets when they easily mastered mascara application in grooming class.

"And those eyebrows!" the brunette said, her ringlets bouncing. "She's like a wild animal!"

"Now, girls," Miss Eleanor said to her pets, "Lucy may not be as mature as you, but she could be quite striking. That bone structure—"

Lucette pounded her fist on the desktop. "Who cares how I look?" She had realized years ago that she was no beauty, in spite of how her parents insisted she'd grow into her strong features someday. "I came here to learn how to fight! How to slay! How to defend myself." She couldn't tell her teacher why it was so important, but she wanted to—desperately.

"*Lucy*." Her teacher's voice was sharp. "We leave the slaying to the boys. It's not our job. Not only is it highly undignified and unfeminine, but ladies lack the strength and agility to slay vampires—not to mention the courage of spirit." She shook her head as if Lucette were a child learning the most basic lesson. "Vampires can sense emotions. They feed off your fear."

"Boys don't get scared?"

Miss Eleanor sighed. "Boys learn to mask their fear."

"And girls don't get scared when they're acting all sexy to lure vampires into traps?" Eventually her teacher would admit to the holes in her logic.

"Lust is a powerful force, Lucy. It clouds a vampire's judgment. They don't have higher reasoning powers to help them overcome their animal instincts, as we humans do."

"How do you know? Have you ever met a vampire?" Lucette sensed it might not be smart to admit that she had met one—not right now, anyway. "And why do we need to flirt to draw the vampires into traps? I mean, if vampires are so thirsty for human blood, isn't the fact we've got it running through our veins enough to lure them?"

Miss Eleanor's cheeks reddened and she smoothed her skirt with her hands. "Lucy, if you're not here to learn, you can leave my class right now. I will not tolerate this insubordination. You girls are training to play vital roles in the slayer army, and if you want to stay, you must learn to follow orders."

A member of the slayer army? Ha! Lucette narrowed her eyes. This school wasn't training the girls to be slayers—it was training them to be bait.

Her mother was going to hear about this.

The next Friday night, Lucette glared at her father as she sat opposite him in his office waiting for the scolding she knew was coming. How could he have expected her to be nice to those boys?

She shifted her glare down to her dress—the lace, the frills, and the way-too-low neckline—and crossed her arms over her chest, disgusted by the hideous pink nightmare with its itchy crinoline. Girls with small breasts and no hips shouldn't wear dresses cut like this. She felt humiliated. Tonight had been worse than her classes at the academy. And those had gotten harder to bear since she'd learned her mother wouldn't interfere with the school's curriculum, claiming it would threaten Lucette's secret identity.

"Lucette," her father said, "stop fidgeting. When you sit still, you look lovely in that dress."

"I do not." She slumped back. "I look freaky enough in my normal clothes, but this dress is frilly—and pink! I hate pink!" She grabbed a handful of the offending fabric and tugged.

"Well, I think it quite becomes you," he said. "And from what I saw and heard, all the boys you met tonight agreed with me." He set his face into what looked like a forced smile. "Every last one of them has asked me for permission to court you."

She clenched her fists and fought the urge to shout, still barely believing her father had paraded her in front of all those boys as if she were some prize to be won. "Dad, I'm only thirteen."

Her father leaned forward from his chair. "Don't you like boys?"

"No. No, I don't. They're smelly and pimply and boring." And the ones at her school could train to be real slayers, while she couldn't. It wasn't fair and she planned to take out her frustration on every single member of the male gender.

"Lucette, you're becoming a young lady." Her father's strong dark eyebrows pushed together and his forehead wrinkled. "Most girls your age would be happy to have their father's permission to date boys."

"Well, I'm not most girls, am I?" No, most girls her age didn't have huge curses hanging over their heads. Most girls her age actually looked like girls. Most girls her age weren't enrolled at the Slayer Academy.

"What's the problem, Lucette?" Her father's concern had turned to irritation. "Why are you so upset that I introduced you to a few nice boys?"

"You can't force me to date against my will." Especially since these so-called dates would involve chaperones and guards, and the boys would probably be frisked for sharp objects and scrutinized for splinters before they'd be allowed near her. Her father would probably insist the boys wear gloves, too, in case one broke a nail or had a callus. It was beyond humiliating.

Her father's expression turned serious. "Lucette, it's vital you find true love."

"Why? So I can give you an heir to your throne?" Really, she was only thirteen!

He rose from his chair as if he planned to discipline her, but then his face softened. "Didn't your mother tell you that true love is the only way the vampire queen's curse can be lifted?"

That was why her father wanted her to date boys? To fall in love? Like that would happen. She let out a disdainful laugh.

"Take this seriously, Lucette." Her father cleared his throat. "The fairies made three alterations to the original curse. One to keep you safe until you turn sixteen, one to prevent the vampire queen from entering Xandra, and another to lift the curse when you prove you've found true love."

"But I'm thirteen!" Lucette's mind felt muddy. She wasn't exactly a little girl anymore, and wanted her father to treat her like a grown-up most of the time, but not about this. She wasn't ready for love.

Her father tapped his fingers on his huge marble-topped desk. "Maybe you're not old enough to attend charm school then, either."

"What?" Lucette's heart rate tripled. "That's not fair." Even if training to be a female slayer wasn't what she hoped for, at least there she had a chance to get close to the weapons.

He frowned. "The fairies paid a high price for altering your curse. You can't take them for granted."

She nodded, and a little bit of the muddiness cleared. "What price?"

He sat down and gripped the carved arms of his chair, as if he might crush them. "The vampire queen was very angry that the fairies helped you." He paused, looked at her, then continued. "So she punished them—brutally."

Lucette felt a lump form in her throat, and a sense of guilt overcame her as she thought of the price others had paid to help her. "Punished them how?"

He shook his head. "Don't worry about that. It's better if you focus on preventing the curse. Finger safety and finding true love are the keys."

Lucette sat silent for a moment. She didn't think her father was wrong; it was smart to prevent the curse. But she also thought her mother was right, that she should be prepared in case the curse did fall. Her father was in denial if he thought he could protect her from every danger, or if he thought she'd ever find love. She wished she were interested in boys, but she wasn't. Not like that.

"Did you say the fairies' magic says I have to *prove* I've found love?" she asked, and he nodded.

"How do you prove that?"

He ran his fingers over his chin, and Lucette wondered if he knew the answer, but then he cleared his throat. "If your love is true, proving it will be easy."

"Did you and Mom have"—she took a deep breath to calm her nerves—"true love?"

Her father looked as if he'd been struck by lightning, then his eyes turned glassy. "Lucette, your mother is the most beautiful and quick-witted woman I've ever met. And the way she used to look at me . . ." He closed his eyes for a moment. "I love your mother. I do. Very much. But perhaps she was too young when we wed. Perhaps she wishes she'd had more time on her own first." He looked away, and Lucette could feel waves of sadness drifting from him.

She rounded his desk and sat on his lap, wrapping her arms around his neck and burying her face in his velvet jacket. "Don't be sad, Daddy."

It was clear he loved her mother, or at least he had before the curse ruined everything, before *she'd* ruined everything. Lucette had to make up for that. From now on, she'd try harder to please her parents and make them happy.

The next week, Lucette leaned over the balcony railing above the school gymnasium to see the action below. Her hands itched to hold one of those big sticks the boys were thrusting and swinging as they leaped around the gym. Even though this was an advanced class, some of them were complete klutzes.

Others weren't.

A tall blond boy, about sixteen from the looks of him, was completing an obstacle course and Lucette couldn't keep her eyes off him. He climbed nearly twenty-five feet up a rope, the muscles in his bare back and shoulders flexing and straining as he moved impossibly fast. Reaching the top, he swung the rope to gain momentum and height, and then released it as he propelled himself toward an even higher platform. As he landed, Lucette sucked in a quick breath, watching how the strong muscles in his legs flexed. He sprang again, this time executing a flip in the air, and landed on another platform. A straw-filled dummy shot skyward. He picked up a stake and leaped to stab it midair.

The stake went straight through the dummy's chest and the boy landed on the gymnasium floor.

Lucette lifted her hands to clap, but noticed that no one else did. The other girls had all turned their heads or covered their eyes, as if real blood had been spilled instead of just a little straw. Wimps.

Miss Eleanor stepped up beside her. "You see now, don't you?"

Lucette studied a group of boys about to start a sparring exercise and lifted her arm to mimic their stance. "See what?"

"That slaying is no job for girls," Miss Eleanor said, a smug look on her face.

Lucette dropped her arms. "No, I don't see that at all. Look at him." She pointed at a skinny boy struggling to push a huge block of stone across the room. "I'll bet I'm stronger than he is."

"They all have their specialties, Lucy. That boy is the fastest in this group at rope climbing. He can scale a three-story building in thirty-two seconds."

"So could I, I'll bet. If someone would just give me the chance."

Miss Eleanor pushed back from the railing. "Bringing you girls up here was a mistake." She shook her head. "I hoped that by showing you the brutality of the boys in action, you'd come to your senses."

She *had* come to her senses. Nearly every night vampires roamed Xandra looking for necks to bite, and Lucette now felt sure that the vampire boy she met in the woods had been the exception, not the rule. Vampires were vicious, and in only three years she might find herself facing them alone. She wished her father would declare war like her mother wanted, but while he'd reinstated the slayer army for defensive purposes, he still refused to declare war on Sanguinia. He was determined to find a diplomatic solution.

She shuddered. The possibility that her father might find a solution someday didn't make it any less horrible for the nightly vampire victims. And if the curse came true, she'd be left to defend the entire kingdom on her own.

Her hand rose to cover her neck. She was doomed unless she learned how to slay. Arguing with Miss Eleanor would be nothing compared to fighting a vampire. She would make the teachers at the school see. She'd make them believe she could do it. If only she could tell everyone she was the princess, then they'd have to do what she wanted.

She stepped back from the balcony and turned to the stairs. "I'm going down to join the boys."

"Lucy! Stop right now!" Miss Eleanor called after her as she ran to the flight of stairs leading to the gym.

Dizziness seized Lucette at the top of the stairs. She hadn't walked down a flight of stairs alone in her entire life, but after drawing a deep breath to steady herself, she took hold of the banister and raced down.

"Lucy!" Slowed by her high heels, Miss Eleanor reached the top of the stairs just as Lucette reached the bottom. "Girls aren't allowed on the gymnasium floor! There are weapons! You'll get hurt!"

Hearing the thuds and smashes of the weapons and bodies slamming into each other, fear and excitement coursed through her. Training with these boys, she might get an injury way worse than a finger prick.

Nonetheless, she stepped onto the floor. Two tall boys were sparring right in front of her, so close she could smell their sweat. She stepped to the side and saw a rack of stakes about twenty feet down the wall she was standing against. What she wouldn't give to hold one in her hand, to feel its weight, to leap and strike one of the dummies. She headed toward the stakes.

"Watch out!" Someone yelled, and she was tackled from the side.

An arrow swooshed over her head and thunked into the wall. Lucette looked up. Just above her head was a bull's-eye, the arrow still vibrating at its center.

"What were you thinking, walking in front of a target?" An angry voice startled her, and she realized it was the tall blond boy she'd been watching earlier. He had her pinned down, and she could see his eyes were bright blue, flashing with life, and very, very angry.

"I didn't know," she said. "I'm sorry."

Miss Eleanor's voice rang out, "Mr. Harris, one of my young ladies is on the floor and one of your young men has attacked her! Stop your boys right now!"

A horn sounded, and the mock battles stopped.

"Tristan, help her up!" someone yelled from the other side of the room.

The boy named Tristan shook his head in disbelief and his eyes narrowed as he rose to his feet. Lucette still sat, feeling hot and scared and excited. Her heart was beating so quickly she wondered if it might pound its way out of her chest.

Miss Eleanor's heels clacked across the gymnasium floor. "Lucy, you are on warning! Behave or I'll have you expelled. You're a young lady—even if you don't much look like one—and I'll have you act accordingly."

Lucette's cheeks burned. Having her appearance derided in front of half the boys in the school—not to mention her blond lifesaver—both enraged and embarrassed her.

She would not be treated like this. She would not be held back by people like Miss Eleanor. Somehow, she would learn how to fight.

That night, Lucette stared into her bathroom mirror at a face that looked back at her with angry red cheeks, and lifted another clump of her long, wavy black hair to the side. Her father loved her hair, and she considered it her best feature, too—her only feminine feature, even though she usually kept it bound up in a braid. But what good was a lot of nice hair on top of a toothpick body, or around a bony face?

Grabbing the knife she'd smuggled out of the gymnasium, she sawed her hair, and a three-foot-long section fell onto the marble floor. She'd show her father she wasn't some dainty doll for him to put on display for boys. She'd show Miss Eleanor what she thought of her grooming lessons. With short hair, she'd look even more like a boy than she already did. Maybe then the school would see her slayer potential. Maybe she'd reenroll in the Slayer Academy under a new secret identity—Luke.

Somehow, she'd make everyone see that she needed to train, even though no one could know why it was so important.

She cut off another chunk of her hair, close to her scalp, and furrowed her brows. Her eyebrows might be thick and ugly, but no way was she letting Miss Eleanor's tweezers within ten feet of her face. The other girls all looked permanently startled with their overplucked arches.

"Lucette, what in the world are you doing?"

She spun away from the mirror to see her mother standing in the doorway, her face stricken with concern. But Lucette refused to cave in to her mother's obvious hurt. She turned back to the mirror and sawed off another chunk of hair. Her father hated her for not cooperating on his matchmaking project. Miss Eleanor hated her for not playing nice at school. That tall, handsome boy Tristan hated her for being careless in the gym. Now her mother could hate her, too. She didn't care.

"Go away, Mom! Leave me alone." She shut the door to the bathroom and continued to hack away at her hair.

Two weeks later, things still hadn't turned out as she planned. In spite of her new haircut, the teachers had not let her train with the boys, and Miss Eleanor forced her to wear an itchy wig at school. Worse, her haircut had broken her father's heart. He could barely look at her now, yet still insisted she meet boys every Friday night.

But Lucette wasn't one to let rules interfere with what she wanted. She peered through the posts of the balcony railing and studied

Tristan. He trained here every day at three o'clock, once classes were over, and she never missed it. From up in the balcony where he couldn't see her, she copied his actions, learning as much of his training routine as possible.

After watching his last sequence, she leaped, spun, and kicked into the air. Without a real stake or the straw dummy to strike, it was difficult to tell if she had used enough force or if her form was correct, but it felt good. She felt strong, having developed so many new muscles since beginning this shadow-training regimen.

Tristan threw a spear down the length of the gym to impale a straw dummy. With nothing to throw, Lucette wound up and launched an imaginary spear, visualizing it sailing through the night air to pierce a vampire's heart.

"Why don't you come down and try with a real spear?" Tristan called, and Lucette froze. He had seen her.

"Come on," he said. "I can hear you up there and I see your shadow. Your form on your roundhouse kick is getting better. Pretty good, considering all you're attacking is air."

She stepped up to the railing and, after drawing a deep breath, leaned over to see if he was serious. If he were mocking her, she'd try out one of those real spears—on him.

He smiled and ran a hand through his short blond hair. "Come on down. I don't bite." He flashed a wide smile.

"No," she said, "but you do tackle."

He chuckled. "Hey, I saved your life. The least you could be is grateful."

"Yeah, well, if they'd let me train as a slayer, then maybe one day I could pay you back and save *your* life."

He laughed again and crossed his arms over his chest. "Not if you stay up there."

Excited, she headed for the stairs. If he was serious about helping her train, no way was she going to turn that down.

"Hey," he called up before she reached the first step. "Do you want to be a slayer, or not?"

She walked back to the railing and looked down at him. "Why else would I be up here every afternoon, copying you?"

"Great." He grinned. "Then why are you headed for the stairs?"

"Um, you said I could come down to train. Do you want me to come down or not?" she asked. Tristan was strange and infuriating, even if he did make her feel kind of fluttery inside.

He folded his bare arms over his broad chest. "A real slayer wouldn't use the stairs."

She looked down to the gymnasium floor and shook her head. "It's at least a twenty-five-foot drop! I can't jump that!"

"Take a look around you," he said, his voice calm and deep. "What can you use to help?"

There was a rope hanging a few feet away from the balcony. It should be a relatively easy jump, but she'd never tried anything like that before. She had only recently been allowed to walk down a flight of stairs unaccompanied, and had never tried anything where failing had real consequences. She wondered what would happen if she died before she turned sixteen. Would the kingdom be saved—or cursed forever?

"Just concentrate," he said, breaking her out of her morbid thoughts. "Focus on the rope, see yourself grabbing it, and don't think about the floor. It'll take care of itself."

"That's what I'm worried about."

"Slayers don't worry. They train, they develop skills, they practice, and then they act."

Trembling, she nodded. He was right. If she wanted this, it was time to prove it. But to leap for the rope, she'd have to stand on the railing. She briefly considered whether she could sit on it, but she wouldn't get enough momentum for launching from that position.

She looked down. Tristan looked up at her with calm encouragement on his face. He wasn't prodding or daring, he wasn't teasing or goading—he simply nodded encouragement. Confidence flowed into her. She had good balance. She was a good climber. She could jump. She could climb ropes. She'd tried all these things over the past two weeks of sneaking into the empty gym. Other than falling, there wasn't one part of this challenge she hadn't done before. The problem was, she'd never done all those things together.

Pulling courage from deep inside her, she pushed to rest her hips on the railing, then lifted one foot up. After testing the railing with her bare foot and centering herself, she leaned to the side and brought the other foot up.

She wouldn't win any prizes for grace—balanced in such an awkward side lunge on the railing with her hands holding onto the wood between her legs—but grace wasn't what this was about. This was about proving to herself she could do it. And if she didn't believe she could do it, how could she possibly convince the school's administration?

She drew her second foot closer, shifting her weight until she was securely in a crouch. Then she raised her hands in front of her, and balancing, she slowly straightened her legs until she was standing on the railing.

"Lucy," a voice came from behind her, "what are you doing?" Miss Eleanor's high heels clacked on the wooden balcony floor, approaching quickly.

"It's fine!" Tristan yelled up. "She's coming down to train."

"Lucy, if you go down there . . ." Miss Eleanor's voice trailed off, as if she'd run out of threats. "If you go down there, I wipe my hands clean of you. I won't send anyone down to rescue you." She really had run out of threats. That last one sounded like more of a promise.

It was now or never. Lucette blocked out everything except the rope, and then leaped. Her hands gripped the rough rope, but she slipped, wishing for once she was wearing her gloves. She wrapped her legs and feet around the swinging rope to stop her rapid, hand-burning slide, and then, with her heart racing and her feet squeezing together to control her speed, she lowered herself, hand over hand, until she was close enough to the floor to jump down.

She landed and turned to Tristan.

He nodded, looking impressed. "Not bad. Not bad at all."

Her entire body felt flush and her mind raced.

Maybe finding true love wasn't so impossible, after all. Maybe if she kept training with Tristan, they'd fall in love. Maybe Miss Eleanor's flirting and seduction classes wouldn't go to waste. Maybe some afternoon soon, if Tristan didn't kiss her, she'd kiss him.

Cheeks still pink, she smiled as seductively as she knew how.

He reached out and rubbed his hand over her chopped-off hair. "Nice haircut, by the way. Now you fit in with the boys."

She flinched and backed up a few feet, crossing her arms over her flat chest. "Are we going to train or not?" No way would she show him how much his comment had hurt.

Queen Natasha stood in front of the elected Sanguinian military council. *What a bunch of weaklings,* she thought. Using the Stone of Supremacy, she could crush them all, and she felt a smile form as she imagined their throats closing, their heads exploding.

But more delicious was the fantasy of these same strong and powerful vampires bowing down before her, exclaiming their admiration, demonstrating their devotion. There was no greater thrill than exercising cruel power over those who thought they were safe. Killing King Vladimir had taught her that. Seeing the love and devotion in her late husband's eyes right before she'd driven a stake through his heart had been the ultimate rush. And she wanted more. Soon every vampire in Sanguinia would worship her. Then, and only then, would she be ready to act. Ready to invade Xandra, capture its riches, and crush its royal family's heads between her hands.

"Ha!" She realized she'd exclaimed aloud only when the faces of the generals turned toward her.

"You are amused, Your Highness?" General Adanthas, a broad-shouldered vampire with a head full of thick brown hair, addressed her.

"Amused at your naïveté," she replied.

"Naïveté?" The general rose.

She leaned onto the table, her long sharp nails scratching the stone surface. "Would you rather I questioned your loyalty to Sanguinia?"

"Madam," the general said, "with all due respect, how dare you question my loyalty? I was serving this kingdom—under both your husband and his father—when you were still human."

"But now you side with these very humans of Xandra and their murderous slayers?" She shook a finger in his direction and displayed her most indignant expression. "For shame." Natasha scanned the rest of the generals and guessed, based on their expressions, that only two of the thirteen sided with her. Not enough.

"Your Highness," General Adanthas said, "the slayers are merely defending the humans against vampires, citizens of your kingdom, who threaten the long-held peace between our nations by drinking from their necks."

A few grunts of agreement rose from around the table and anger rose in Natasha's throat, but she choked it back. Acting now, killing Adanthas, would provide only momentary satisfaction. She had her eyes on a longer-term prize.

"Once again, General Adanthas"—she tried to look sad and disappointed—"I find you siding with the Xandrans against your own kind. These vampires merely take a few sips of blood, something we all require to sustain life, and King Stefan's answer is murderous slayers?" She shook her head. "You forget, I grew up in Xandra. I know firsthand the prejudice against vampires. Our citizens will not be safe until we invade and crush—" She stopped herself and drew a deep breath, then said in a calm voice, "Only under our rule will the humans understand vampire nature, and how peacefully we can coexist."

Three of the generals nodded in approval as she sat. Yes, the humans would be peaceful once she ruled Xandra, because they'd be tamed as blood slaves, farmed for sustenance, or hunted for sport.

But the potential for human bloodshed would be greater if *all* the vampires of Sanguinia were on her side. Persuasion took time.

She'd plucked the wings of sixteen fairies—one for each year they'd delayed her curse—but she now wondered if they'd done her a favor.

With more time, she'd have more vampires behind her before the princess was plunged into darkness, and more willing volunteers to terrorize the child and teach her parents a lesson.

Oh, how Stefan and Catia would pay for what they'd done. As soon as the royal family of Xandra was dead, the Sanguinian armies would march across the border and she'd have what she'd always wanted—the throne of Xandra.

Lucette leaped from the high platform and thrust her stake into the vampire—well, a straw dummy vampire—then, after hitting her mark, she landed on the gymnasium floor and rolled.

"Forget something?" Tristan stared down at her. She'd been training with him five days a week for almost eighteen months now, and he still took her breath away every time she laid eyes on him.

She rose to her feet. "What?" She'd drawn her arm back fully to maximize her forward thrust. She'd hit the vamp's heart. She'd rolled through her landing. She'd done everything he'd taught her.

He grabbed her in a tight hold from behind and pressed his teeth to her neck. Every nerve in her body tingled. Trapped in Tristan's arms, her knees grew weak. Not minding that he'd demonstrated the potential implications of her mistake, she stretched her neck and sighed.

He dropped her and she fell a few feet before he grabbed her arm to let her hit the floor softly. "You left your stake in the dummy. What if there'd been a second attacker?" His scolding voice reminded her that he was her coach, not her boyfriend. Of course, in her nightly dreams, things were different.

Cheeks burning, she sprang to her feet. "But I hit the right spot, didn't I? Straight through the heart?"

He nodded, and what looked like pride flashed on his face. Just six months from her fifteenth birthday, she still hadn't gathered the courage to tell Tristan how she felt. She ran her fingers through the loose, dark curls that had regrown since she'd chopped them off, and wondered if he thought she was pretty.

"You did hit the right spot," Tristan said. "And hard enough, too. But think about it, Lucy. What did you do wrong?" He backed up a few feet, and she moved forward, not wanting to lose the sensations she felt when he was close.

Thinking about Tristan more than his lessons, a tiny thrill raced through her. Then, remembering some of Miss Eleanor's silly flirting lessons, she traced her finger through one of her curls, tipped her head to the side, and cast her eyes slightly down. She might have purposefully failed her flirting exam in protest, but it didn't mean she hadn't been paying attention in class.

Looking uncomfortable, Tristan stepped back again and said, "Your hair."

He'd noticed. She took another step toward him. "What about my hair?" Would he compliment its sheen? Its soft texture? Its springy curls?

Surely, what she was feeling couldn't be one-sided. The boys her father forced her to meet every week had started looking at her differently the past few months. She was getting prettier, more feminine—finally. Surely Tristan's taste in girls couldn't be all that different from that of all those other boys who seemed to like what they saw. Tristan liked her. He must. After all, he had just been hugging her and pressing his lips into her neck.

He looked at her intently, but then quickly averted his gaze. "You should cut it again." His voice was gruff. "Or at least tie it back. Now that your hair's grown past your chin, it's becoming a liability." He lunged forward, grabbed a handful of her hair, and pulled back. Not so hard that it hurt, but hard enough that she had to bend. "Don't give the vampires anything to grab on to. You need to get them before they get you."

He let go of her hair and she staggered back. Her cheeks burned, and her breaths quickened as if she'd run laps, but she refused to take this as a rejection. Maybe he'd just used the insult as an excuse to touch her hair? To get close to her again? She would not give up. She smiled softly and touched her hair the way she'd learned to in class, marveling at how natural the gesture felt in front of Tristan. She wondered if this proved she was in love.

"Would you like my hair better if I cut it really short, like yours?" Her voice came out lower and more breathy than normal.

"If it keeps you safer against a vamp, sure."

A rush of happiness flowed through her. He wanted to protect her. How sweet. She stepped forward slowly, wondering what the skin on his chest would feel like under her palm.

Without thinking, she reached forward and pressed her hand against his chest muscles just below his shoulder.

He yanked back. "What are you doing?"

She felt embarrassed, yet bold. This was her time. This was her chance. If she proved her love, she'd save everyone. "Tristan." Even her voice was not her own. "Are you going to the ball?"

Tristan took a step back and looked at her quizzically. "Sure. Probably."

She sucked in a ragged breath, closed her eyes, and blurted out, "Will you take me?" Her throat closed.

"Take *you*?" He stared at her, almost as if he didn't understand her question.

"Yes." She bit her lip and gathered her courage.

"You're not graduating," he said.

Her heart thumped, and her mouth went dry. "I thought I could go with you, as—as your date."

He staggered back a few steps, his eyes opening wide. Then a smile flashed on his face, flooding her chest with a second of hope before she recognized the type of smile—a patronizing smile. The kind of smile her father used when he treated her like a child.

"Lucy," Tristan said as he lifted a hand toward her, then dropped it and put it behind his back. "I'm seventeen, almost eighteen."

"So?" She stepped forward, suddenly more sure of herself. Her father was nearly fifteen years older than her mother. The three years that separated her from Tristan were nothing.

He frowned. "You're fourteen."

"I'm almost fifteen," she boasted. "And who cares? True love is all I care about, and you're the first boy I've ever—" She stopped herself, not knowing how to complete her sentence, not knowing how to describe the emotions bubbling inside her. And she hated the idea that he might not feel the same way.

"Lucy"—Tristan's patronizing smile turned to something more like pity—"I don't even live in Xandra. I came here from Judra to train, in case the vampires attack our kingdom, too."

"I know, but you could stay here." Her voice sounded thin and tiny, but she had to make him understand. She wished she could tell him who she really was, and how he could help lift her curse—maybe even prevent it—but she couldn't. She closed her eyes and said, "If I don't find true love, I'll die."

"You'll die?" He took a deep breath and the pity came back to his expression. "Isn't that a tad dramatic, Lucy? Everyone wants to find true love, but not finding it isn't going to kill you."

She felt on the verge of telling him everything—about the curse, about finding true love—everything. He was hiding his feelings, denying them, and if only he knew the truth . . .

"Will you take me to the dance or not?" she blurted.

"Lucy, you're just a kid." He shook his head, clearly trying not to laugh.

Her chest caved, and she fought to draw air. "I am not a kid! I'm almost fifteen! I've been going on dates since I was thirteen. I am *not* a kid!" Her words came out in short, loud bursts and she fought tears. She would not cry.

He reached forward as if he was going to touch her, but he didn't. "Lucy, I only wanted to help you train, because I knew how frustrated you were and could see you had talent and potential. I didn't mean—" He shook his head and backed away. "I'm really sorry." His cheeks grew red, and he turned and walked away.

As soon as Tristan left the gymnasium, Lucette ran into the far corner and curled up into a tight ball, trying to crush the pain inside her. Even being left alone in the darkness to fight vampires would be easier than this.

The next year, three days before her sixteenth birthday, Lucette tied her hair back, wrapping it in a tight bun. She might not have earned a place among the boys who were graduating today to become real slayers, but she'd accomplished what she came to the academy to do. With Tristan's help, she'd learned to fight and to defend herself.

And now she felt somewhat prepared, should the worst happen.

After Tristan left, it had been difficult to convince any of the other boys to challenge her—especially after her body developed—but following Tristan's example, a few had trained with her after classes. She'd continued to improve and now was as good and strong as at least half of the boys graduating today. But most didn't know it.

She looked into the mirror at her body, dressed in the clingy black uniform worn by the female students at the academy. Her breasts had taken their time getting here, but now that they had arrived, they filled out the low-cut uniform well. She still felt embarrassed, but at least this would be the last time she had to wear the hideous outfit. She had no intention of actually serving as part of the slayer army, and had stayed in school only for the easy access to the weapons and gymnasium. It had been nearly three years, and her father hadn't found out. At least after today, she and her mother could stop lying to him about "charm school."

Twisting to the side, she studied herself. Her body was still long and lean, and she was still taller and broader in the shoulders than any of the other girls. Now that she'd developed breasts and a waist, however, she kind of wanted her old body back. What was the point of looking like a girl, if Tristan—the only boy she had ever liked—was so far away in Judra?

Setting her graduation cap on her head, Lucette moved from the mirror to join the rest of the girls in her class, all of whom seemed very proud of their uniforms and wore enough makeup to put Miss Eleanor to shame.

As if on cue, Miss Eleanor chose that moment to breeze into the room, dressed in black herself—in fact, in the same dress worn by the girls. On their teacher, however, the neckline was cut even lower.

"You look lovely, girls. Just lovely. I'm so proud." She walked down the line. "Even you, Lucy. Just look at you in your uniform." She grabbed the sides of Lucette's dress and tugged the neckline down lower. As soon as her teacher turned away, Lucette tugged it back up. Really, there was no need to show that much cleavage.

"I have very exciting news, girls," Miss Eleanor said.

Lucette realized she'd wrinkled her nose, so she tried to relax it.

"A very special guest will be presenting you with your diplomas."

"Who?" asked one of the other girls, and Lucette almost wished that she cared. The others chattered excitedly, and some wondered whether it might be the slayer commander himself, or one of the handsome actors from the palace theater company, or the lute player from the musical ensemble that had entertained them all at the graduation dance last night. Lucette had attended at her mother's insistence, but she had hung out in the back room, practicing her backflips and lunging stabs all night. It had been difficult to explain the torn dress to her mother, who'd made all the wrong assumptions.

"I don't want to spoil the secret," Miss Eleanor said, clasping her hands together.

Lucette yawned.

The music started, and the girls watched as the line of boys dressed in slayer uniforms—tight black fabric from head to toe, masks with hoods that attached firmly to their shirts, and virtually impenetrable neck protectors—marched into the room. Why didn't the girls get masks, not to mention neck protectors?

A mask would help her right now. There was an uncomfortably high risk that someone from the royal court would be in today's audience, and if anyone saw her, her father might find out. She didn't fear for herself—he always forgave her, even when she cut off her hair. But her mother was another matter. The charm school lie weighed around her mother's neck like a stone.

If her mother weren't so proud that Lucette had made her way through nearly three years of school, Lucette would not even have attended the ceremony today, but her mother planned to be in the crowd in disguise. And after all the queen had done to ensure that her daughter obtained vampire-fighting skills, walking across a stage to pick up a certificate was the least Lucette could do to make her mother happy.

The girls were supposed to slink across the stage and strike a provocative pose before receiving their diplomas, but when her turn came Lucette stepped onto the stage and stopped, momentarily blinded by the bright lights. *This is crazy*, she thought, and in one final act of defiance, she kicked off her uncomfortable high-heeled shoes and strode across the stage, executing a high sidekick, and then a series of walking punches before finishing with a series of cartwheels—no simple feat in the clingy dress. Finished, she landed next to the mystery presenter.

The crowd fell silent, and then people began to murmur, seemingly shocked by her behavior. She hoped her antics at least had distracted anyone who might've recognized her. Even if they were shocked, it was better than suffering the humiliation of wearing that dress in front of the crowd.

After making a short, sharp bow to the masses, she turned . . . and looked into the glaring face of her father.

A few hours later, Lucette pressed her ear against a thick, wooden door. Behind that door, her parents were talking—more like yelling. At least they were in the same room, which was an improvement these days.

"Princess," one of the guards said as he stepped toward her, "I'm supposed to make sure you don't touch the door."

Lucette gritted her teeth. As if a splinter could even get through the ever-present gloves that she was still forced to wear around the castle. She stepped back, pretending the guard had won, then leaped and kicked. Her foot passed inches from the guard's shocked face. "Leave me alone!" she snapped.

He backed away, and feeling slightly guilty, she pressed her ear to the door again.

"This is the last straw, Catia!" Her father sounded furious. "I know we disagree about how to best protect our daughter, but how could you have let this happen?"

"Don't you see, Stefan? The curse is inevitable—that's how curses work. If you'd had your way, she would have ended up alone in the dark, night after night, tormented by those monsters with no way to defend herself. At least now she can fight."

"The curse won't happen!" Stefan yelled. "I won't allow it! From now on, I make all the decisions about Lucette's care."

"No, you won't." Her mother's voice rose. "She's my daughter, too!"

"But I can keep her safe. I'll request a meeting with Natasha. I'll talk her into lifting the curse. Maybe enough time has passed since I last asked. Maybe she'll see she's punished us enough."

"Natasha won't speak to you." Her mother's voice was hard and cruel.

"How do you know if I don't try? Unlike you, I will not take it as fate that our daughter is doomed. What kind of mother are you?"

Listening to their harsh words, Lucette's heart ached for both of her parents. They only wanted what was best for her, but had opposite ideas of what "best" meant. And the fact that she agreed with her mother's approach more often hadn't helped smooth her parents' relationship. Maybe if she'd sided with her father more often, she could've kept the peace.

But as long as her parents kept talking, they had a chance of reaching a compromise. She pressed her ear harder against the door. Their voices had grown quiet and she could no longer make out their words. Lowered voices were a good sign, weren't they? Had they made up?

Hope stirred inside her. Her father had to see that her mother had only been trying to help protect her, that she hadn't meant to deceive him. Back at the ceremony, Lucette had explained to her father how it had all been her idea, her fault, not her mother's, but she wasn't sure if her lie had been convincing enough. She'd ruined everything by going to that graduation ceremony and making a fool of herself. Perhaps if she'd done as she was supposed to and slunk across the stage, her father wouldn't have gotten so angry. Perhaps he'd have been happy to see her looking feminine and pretty. The thought that she'd found yet another way to make things worse between her parents made her stomach twist.

She heard footsteps inside the room, so she backed up and checked her gloves.

The door opened and her father stepped out. He looked defeated and tired. "Lucette, will you join us, please? Your mother and I have something to ask you."

She followed him inside, hoping her father's calm demeanor meant they'd reached a compromise. Lucette sensed a real shift in the room, as though a big decision had been made, and her mother stepped up to stand beside her father. They weren't holding hands, but they were standing closer together than Lucette had seen in years. Even better, neither of them was glaring at the other. There was no yelling, no fighting.

"Lucette," her father said, "I know I've made some mistakes"—he looked over to her mother—"we both have. But we've agreed to leave this decision up to you."

A huge grin spread on her face. Her father realized that now that she was almost sixteen, she deserved to be treated like a grown-up. It was about time she gained some freedom. She was old enough to make decisions, and without their constant sparring for control over her life, she could figure out a way to make peace between her parents. Her heart felt lighter.

Her father cleared his throat. "Lucette," he started, "we have something important to tell you." He paused for a moment. "We're getting a divorce."

Lucette staggered back as if she'd been punched in the stomach.

"What?" Her ears rang and all the blood in her body raced to her head, making her dizzy. She had to remind herself to breathe.

"Darling," her mother said, stepping forward, "I'm moving back to my father's estate in the country. No vampire has gone near there for centuries. You'll be safe there with me."

Her father stepped in front of her mother. "You'll be safer *here* in the palace, with guards and slayers who will make sure nothing ever happens to you."

Her mother pushed forward again. "Lucette, we've agreed that you're old enough to choose."

If you were Lucette, what would you do?

OPTION A: Lucette should stay with her father. Her father was so hurt by the lies she and her mother told him. She's betrayed him so much, and living with him now would help make up for that. He's more likely to keep her safe and ensure the curse never falls. Lucette can reach a compromise with him that gives her some freedom while still keeping her fingers prick-free. Plus, maybe if she decides to stay with him, her mother won't actually leave. If you think Lucette should choose option A, go to section 4: Glass Houses (page 113).

OPTION B: Lucette should stay with her mother. Her mother has always supported her. If it weren't for her, Lucette wouldn't be trained as a slayer. Her mother might allow Lucette more freedom, but she doesn't want the curse to happen any more than her father. Her mother will do everything she can to keep Lucette safe, too. If you think Lucette should choose option B, go to section 5: Country Living (page 147).

Section 3

Big Secrets

3

Lucette felt sure she'd made the right decision. Lying to her father about the Slayer Academy would have been wrong. And as proof that he admired her choice, he'd finally stopped treating her like a little girl. She was thirteen and coming into her own, and her father knew it.

First, he'd let her decide about the school—even if he didn't know what her mother had planned—and even more telling, tonight he'd invited her to a real grown-up event. She felt sure that, with enough persuasion, he'd change his mind and realize that she was old enough to train as a slayer. Otherwise, if the curse happened, she'd end up defenseless, all alone in the dark.

Jenny, her dressing maid, slipped a dress over her head and laced up the back. Lucette turned and scowled into the mirror. Pink with tiny white roses, the dress seemed better suited to the delicate girls she'd seen from the shielded viewing galleries during her parents' parties. The dress looked ridiculous on her, like putting lace on a wooden spike. "Are you sure this is the dress my father wanted me to wear?"

"Yes, and it's very pretty." Jenny wrapped the bright pink sash around on Lucette's waist and tied a bow. While her invitation to this party made her feel grown-up and important, this dress made Lucette feel like an idiot.

Lucette swiveled and then winced when she saw the size of the bow that flopped down over her hips, its tails hanging over her flat backside. She ran her hands down the bodice of the dress, which was scooped down in front and was no doubt meant to show off assets she lacked.

"Don't worry," Jenny said, pulling the ties in back tighter so the bust line didn't sag so much. "We'll add some crinolines under the skirt to give you some shape. And any day now you'll fill out that bust and you'll be fighting off the boys."

"I don't want to fight off boys." Lucette struggled not to pout. She wasn't a baby and reminded herself not to act like one.

"Oh, so you want them to catch you?" Jenny winked.

Lucette furrowed her brow. "That's not what I meant." She bit down on her tongue to keep from saying that she didn't like boys, that she found them noisy and rude and smelly and distasteful.

"You'll change your mind soon enough," Jenny said. "Now sit down so I can fix your hair."

Half an hour later, with her hair piled up like a complicated puzzle, Lucette walked along the corridor she'd been scolded for running down as a child. A guard held her hand as she struggled to stay upright on the high heels Jenny had insisted she wear. She couldn't comprehend why grown-ups wore these things. She much preferred to be in shoes designed for running and leaping.

But if putting on this dumb dress and shoes would please her father, she could suffer through wearing them for a few hours. Making him happy would help butter him up, and she needed all the parental coaxing she could muster to convince her father to let her learn some slayer skills. Part of her believed her father's claim that he could fix everything and find a way to make the vampire queen lift the curse—or prevent it altogether. But if there was even a chance she might end up alone in the night someday, she needed training. Surely she could make her father understand.

She also hoped that once he saw her tonight, the truth about this dress would be obvious. She wasn't the type of girl suited to being dressed up in anything frilly. She was too tall, too skinny, too pale, her features too severe and boyish. Even worse, with the makeup that Jenny had rubbed onto her cheeks and lips, Lucette felt she looked like a clown.

The guards opened the back doors to the reception room and bright light poured out toward her. She blinked and raised her hand to her eyes to adjust to the light.

"The Princess Lucette," a deep male voice said, and someone nudged her forward. She teetered on the ridiculous shoes, her eyes focused down to see where she was going, and prayed she wouldn't fall flat on her face. A collective gasp rose in the room, followed by polite applause. A huge crowd was gathered in the reception hall, and at the front of the crowd were dozens of boys. What the heck was going on?

"For goodness sake, straighten up," her father said as he stepped next to her. Her mother stepped up to her other side.

"I can barely walk in these shoes," she said to her mother, who looked delicate and elegant in a pale blue gown. "They pinch."

"I told you it was too soon for this," her mother snapped at her father. Lucette bit her lip and felt guilt drench through her. Even while trying to prevent it from happening, she'd caused yet more harsh words between her parents.

Her father tucked her gloved hand through the crook of his arm, the way he did with her mother at big events, and pulled her forward to the raised platform that was covered with vases full of daisies. She sneezed, and a collective twitter rose from the crowd, but just as quickly died down. A fire rose inside her. They were laughing at her, and she could only imagine how red her cheeks looked now through the makeup. She raised a hand to wipe off some of the rouge.

"Stop that." Her mother grabbed her hand and held onto it. "You'll ruin your gloves."

Lucette fought the impulse to turn and run. As if running in those shoes—or with the crinolines under her heavy skirt—were even possible. She felt as if the bulky clothes had doubled her weight.

"What's going on?" she asked her mother.

Before her mother could respond, her father raised his hands to silence the crowd. "Thank you for coming this evening," he said, his deep voice failing to reassure Lucette the way it normally did. "It gives me great pleasure to stand before you all today and introduce my daughter, the Princess Lucette."

Polite applause ensued, along with less polite hoots from some of the boys. Squirming under the itchy crinoline, Lucette turned to her mother to ask for a better explanation, but her mother raised a finger to her lips.

Her father gestured to his left. "Young men wishing to express their desire to court my daughter, please form a line over here."

Noise filled the room as a hundred boys stampeded into line. They pushed and shoved for a few minutes before settling down to stand at attention.

"What does he mean, 'court me'?" Lucette asked her mother.

"I told him you're still too young." Her mother shook her head. "You've got three years before you're sixteen. There's still time."

"Still time for what?" Her stomach clenched. Surely her mother didn't mean she should *marry* before turning sixteen. Lucette didn't even want to *date*.

Her father put his hand on her shoulder. "Come, Lucette. One of these boys is bound to be your true love."

"What?" She tensed and stared at her father. This had to be a joke.

He leaned down toward her and his strong, dark brows drew together. "It's time you started meeting eligible young men, Lucette. It's important you find true love, and there's no time like the present."

"But—"

Her father raised his hand to silence her protests and then stepped over to the line of teenaged boys.

"Mom, do I have to do this?" Lucette asked. "I don't want to. And I feel so stupid in this dress." Terror grabbed hold of her. Would these boys want to kiss her? Yuck.

She tried to back up, but her mother slipped an arm around her waist. "I know this is ridiculous." Her voice was tense. "Just say hello and let them kiss your glove. I couldn't stop your father from doing this, but I'll help you get through it, I promise."

Her parents were already divided on this, so if she made a fuss and ran, it would give them something else to fight about. Lucette drew a long breath and resolved to grin and bear it. Staring down at the line of boys—most of them shorter than her, which made her even more self-conscious—Lucette twisted her toe on the floor and hunched her shoulders. Her knees trembled as she studied the line of suitors.

Her father beamed as he greeted each of the boys standing in the line, shaking their hands and asking polite questions. He turned a few away, but she wished he'd be more discerning. From the looks of these boys, it seemed as if her father would deem anyone suitable as long as he had a pulse.

Her father led a pudgy, pimply boy up the two stairs to the platform. On display at the top, Lucette squirmed in humiliation.

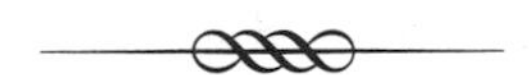

Two hours later, Lucette stomped out of the reception, keeping her head down to hide the scowl on her face. Her mother had stayed behind to talk to her father.

Great. Another fight.

Even if it was her fault, so be it. She was done trying to keep the peace in this family. Done with being a pawn in their games. Letting those boys ogle her had been beyond horrible, and both of her parents were responsible for tonight's humiliations. It would never happen again. Not if she could find a way to stop it.

After a guard led her back to her bedroom and Jenny helped her out of her hideous dress, Lucette stared at the offending garment, wanting to stomp on it, or better yet, shred it.

Her scissors! She'd smuggled a pair out of the library a few months ago. She pulled a book off her shelf and opened it to reveal the scissors hidden in a cavity. After removing the scissors, she grabbed the dress off her rack and narrowed her eyes. She'd make sure she never had to wear this ugly thing again.

Sitting cross-legged on the carpet in front of a huge mirror, she pulled the dress onto her lap, but as she was about to make the first cut, she glanced up at her reflection and then wiped the back of her gloved hand across her still-rouged cheek. What was the point of destroying the gown? It would just be replaced, perhaps with another one even more hideous.

Rebellious thoughts flooding through her, she pulled a chunk of her long, thick hair from the fussy updo Jenny had fashioned and held it to the side. Then using the dull scissors, she chopped and sawed close to her scalp.

Holding the nearly three-foot-long tail of hair in her hand, her insides stirred with excitement. She'd really done it. This would show her father and make him sorry for all he'd put her through. She chopped off another section, then another, until almost half of her long hair was gone, leaving ragged chunks about an inch from her head.

The door to her bedroom opened. "Lucette!" her mother cried. "What have you done?"

She tucked the contraband scissors under her leg. Her mother ran over, grabbed her by the shoulders, and tried to pull her up. But Lucette was both taller and stronger than her mother, so the queen's attempts were futile. Lucette curled her body over, sobbing, ashamed.

Her mother sat down beside her and rubbed her back. "Why, darling, why?"

"I wanted to prove to Dad that I'm not pretty enough to date boys. They only pretended to like me tonight because I'm a princess. It was horrible. I wanted to make sure he didn't make me do that again."

"Oh, Lucette." Her mother ran her hand over the scarred remains of her hair. "You *are* beautiful, you'll see that someday, and there's a reason your father wants you to find love."

"Why? So I can make sure there's an heir to the throne?"

"No, Lucette. So the curse will lift. You need to prove you found true love."

Lucette snapped her head up. "You were serious about that?" She shook her head, vaguely remembering her mother telling her something about the curse lifting if she proved she'd found love, but she'd been more focused on the part about being alone in the night with vampires.

Her mother pulled her face to hers and kissed Lucette's tear-stained cheek. "I wanted to wait until you were older and showed interest in boys before talking more about this."

Lucette looked up to her mother, who wiped the tears off her cheeks, her soft fingers such a comfort. Hope flooded inside Lucette. "How do I find love and how do I prove it?"

Her mother picked up a chunk of Lucette's hair from the floor and pursed her lips as she set it aside. "I'm not sure, darling. There's no formula for love. But you'll know when it happens."

Lucette watched with wonder as the fairy queen flew across the room and hovered in front of them. The fairy, with her translucent wings and sparkling pastel dress, embraced Lucette's mother.

"Welcome," her mother said. "Thank you for coming so quickly. This is my daughter, Lucette."

Lucette tried to hide her awe as the fairy queen turned toward her and offered her delicate, long-fingered hand.

"Ah, Lucette," said the fairy queen. "I see my visions were right. You are turning into a great beauty."

Lucette dropped her head in embarrassment. Why did all these grown-ups keep calling her beautiful when she so clearly wasn't? Especially now that her hair was so short. To keep it even, the royal barber had to cut it all very close to her scalp.

"What can I do for you?" the fairy queen asked as she settled back down to the floor.

Lucette's mother cleared her throat and leaned forward. "It's about the curse."

The fairy queen flew back several feet, then drifted forward again, slowly. "I already told Stefan, I cannot interfere any further."

"You spoke to my husband?"

"Not since I enchanted those sheets of glass," the fairy queen replied.

"Oh yes, of course," her mother said, but it was clear to Lucette that her mother didn't know about any enchanted glass. "But we don't need anything from you. My daughter merely has a question."

The fairy queen crossed her slender arms over her chest. "When Queen Natasha found out I'd altered the curse, she tortured my attendants as punishment. My people paid a high price to allow your daughter to remain protected until sixteen."

"We appreciate it deeply," Queen Catia replied, bowing toward the fairy queen. "But our question relates to the other modification you made, the part about true love."

Looking somewhat relieved, the fairy queen nodded. "Go on."

Lucette's breaths quickened and her throat pinched at the thought that fairies had been tortured because of her. She'd thought the worst side effect of her cursed life was its impact on her parents' marriage, but knowing others had been physically hurt in order to help her was devastating. She tried to speak, but nothing came out.

"My dear"—the fairy queen ran her soft hand down Lucette's arm, making it tingle and tickle—"don't fret so. Everything done in the past was done with free will. There is no reason for you to feel guilt."

Lucette gasped. "Can you read my mind?"

She shook her head. "No, your expression spoke for you."

"Oh." Shocked that she'd revealed so much, Lucette tried to keep her face more neutral.

"What is your question?"

"True love. Um . . . how do I prove I've found it?" She shifted her weight onto her other leg. "I mean, I don't even have any idea how to find it, or if I ever will. But let's say I do find it someday when I'm older. How do I prove it?"

The fairy queen reached up and traced her fingers across Lucette's forehead, leaving a trail of tingling coolness behind. "So many worries for such a young girl." She shook her head. "Such a shame."

Lucette dug her teeth into her lip. If she was worried, it wasn't without reason. Realizing she was impatiently tapping her foot, she stilled it.

"My sweet girl," the fairy queen said, "finding or proving true love isn't a lesson one can teach. Keep your heart open and you'll find it. Then, if your love is pure, the proof will be natural and honest and instinctual. Don't worry one more minute about how to prove it. When the opportunity comes, you'll know what to do."

"I'll know what to do?" That was it? *That* was the fairy queen's advice? "How can you be so sure?"

The fairy queen cupped Lucette's face in her hands. "Have faith, Lucette. When the time comes, you'll know."

Standing alone in the dark, cold gymnasium of the Slayer Academy, where her mother had left her and told her to wait, Lucette could barely contain her excitement. She looked around the mysterious room, but it was too dark to make out more than shapes. After the disappointing meeting with the fairy queen, she and her mother had finally agreed: going behind her father's back was the only way she was going to learn how to defend herself against vampires. Putting all of her faith in finding true love was too risky, as was preventing a finger prick.

Yet her father remained adamant the curse would never fall, and that he could stop it. He believed that there was no need for her to learn to slay, since no daughter of his would ever put herself in such danger. Her father was in denial, unable to face up to what might happen, unable to even think of a world where his daughter had to face vampires alone.

So, her mother had secretly hired a Slayer Academy student—a boy from outside the kingdom who didn't know of the curse—as Lucette's private tutor. The plan was to train late at night, when her father was in bed, and at other times if they got the chance. To smuggle her out of the palace this evening, Lucette's mother had relied on a group of servants and guards she'd brought to the palace from her own father's country estate when she'd married. One of those servants was now waiting outside the gymnasium in a carriage to take Lucette home once she'd finished her training. But standing here alone in the dark, she wondered if she'd ever actually get any training. Had her mother's servants made a mistake with the arrangements?

Just then, the gas lights around the gymnasium flickered and brightened, and a blond boy strode into the room. He was tall, broad-shouldered, and muscular. When he passed under one of the lamps, it lit his short-cropped hair like gold.

Lucette's insides flipped. The only male she'd ever seen who combined power and good looks in such a decidedly masculine way was her father, but this was different. When she looked at her father, she felt protected and loved, but when she looked at this boy, her stomach twisted and her skin felt as if it had been set on fire.

"Hi," he said when he got closer. "I'm Tristan. You must be Lucy."

She nodded, her mouth suddenly too dry to form words. Instead, she tugged on the wrists of her gloves to make sure they were on securely.

"I hear you want to learn how to defend yourself against vampires." He crossed his arms and studied her.

She nodded again, feeling awkward under his scrutiny.

"You're kind of quiet, aren't you?" His voice was deep and strong, even with the mocking tone of that last line.

She shrugged. She didn't normally consider herself quiet, but she felt sure if she opened her mouth right now, all that would come out would be a croak.

"That's okay. Words won't protect you against a vampire, anyway. You'll need cunning, quick reflexes, and courage. You'll never beat a vampire's strength or speed, so it's essential that you outthink it, outmaneuver it, and attack first before it can attack you."

She nodded.

"You don't look strong enough for combat training." He headed over to a bar suspended between two tall poles, then jumped up to grab it and pulled his body up until his chin was raised above the bar.

He repeated this more than a dozen times, and her breath caught in her chest as she watched his bulging arm muscles flex and stretch. The speed at which he pulled himself up was impressive.

He let go and landed softly back on the polished gymnasium floor. "Think you can do that?"

"I can try."

"She speaks!" He grinned, and the warmth of his expression shot straight into her heart.

Suddenly, she realized her mother had been right. Her father, too. At long last, she'd noticed a boy, and—wow, what a feeling. It made her nervous and excited and shy, yet bold all at once. She wanted to know him, and wanted to make him like her. If her father introduced her to this boy, she wouldn't hate those receptions so much.

"Well?" He shook his head, an amused look on his handsome face.

"Excuse me?" Had she missed a question? Lost in these unanticipated and perplexing thoughts, she couldn't be sure.

"Chin-ups," he said. "Ready to try?"

She looked up to the bar. It had to be nearly twelve feet off the ground. She was tall, but not that tall. "How do I get up there?"

"Jump." He crossed his arms over his chest. "Unless you don't think you can do it . . . I mean, I heard you wanted to learn how to fight like a slayer, but if you don't think you can cut it—"

She interrupted. "I can do it." She moved under the bar, bent her legs, and jumped with all her might. Her fingers grazed the bar, but she couldn't grab it.

"First of all," he said, pointing to her hands, "those have got to go. You can't grip the bar with gloves on, and you certainly can't grip a stake. Why are you wearing them, anyway?"

Feeling silly for leaving them on, Lucette's cheeks flushed. She ripped them off, flung them aside, and wiped her sweaty hands on her pants.

"Try again," Tristan said, and she moved back under the bar. From the ground it looked impossibly high. "Use your whole body," he added. "Use the force of your arms and legs together. Push through your ankles, your toes. Most importantly, believe you can do it."

"It's so high!"

He shrugged and grinned. "Try."

She crouched under the bar, took a deep breath, and jumped, keeping her eyes on the bar. Her hands wrapped around it and a smile spread on her face.

"Now pull up," he said.

He'd made it look easy, and Lucette figured that chin-ups should be even easier for her, since she was lighter. She flexed her arms and pulled up until her chin passed the bar.

"Good," Tristan said from below her. "Now again."

She straightened her arms to drop down and one hand slipped off the bar. Swinging back, she reached up and grasped the bar again.

"Next time, let yourself down more slowly," he said. "Now pull up again."

She tried, but this time her arms shook and burned from the effort, and her chin barely crossed the top of the bar. She lowered herself slowly.

"Again," he said. "I want to see you do at least ten."

"Ten?" He had to be kidding.

"Do you want this or not? Put some back into it. And use your shoulders and chest, not just your arms."

She narrowed her eyes and flexed her back as she bent her arms to pull herself up. Struggling near the top, she felt his hands on her hips, helping her through the final inch.

"Good," he said, his voice encouraging. "Seven more. You can do it."

She couldn't dwell on the thrill of his touch, as she needed every ounce of mental and physical energy to finish the chin-ups. When she was done, all she felt was a mix of elation and exhaustion.

This slayer training was going to be harder than she thought, but she'd be glad to suffer through it with Tristan as her teacher.

Natasha, queen of the vampires, studied her son with a critical eye. Even though the boy didn't remember meeting his father—she'd killed the king just weeks after the boy's birth nearly fourteen years earlier—he held so many of the closed-minded and now-dead king's views. But where the boy might take after his father in disposition, he took after her in appearance. He was growing into a handsome young man, indeed.

She smiled. Attitude and disposition could be molded, but looks were inborn and everlasting. Especially for vampires who stopped showing outward signs of aging in their twenties, thus fueling the false rumors of their immortality. The boy might be misguided, but he was still young. There was time yet to sway his opinions before he became a full-grown vampire.

"Don't be such a picky eater," she said, pushing the carafe of human blood toward him. "Try it. You might like it. Blood never tastes as good from a jar as it does fresh from the vein, but even consumed this way, human blood is delicious and energizing. One sip and you'll see what I mean."

"You've fed directly from a human vein?" Her son tried to hide his shock and revulsion while she hid her disappointment and irritation. Her first act as reigning monarch, after killing her husband, had been to repeal the law against human blood consumption. But a law change couldn't alter centuries of custom and most of her subjects still abstained. Even her son. But she could change that.

"Yes, I have fed from a vein." She stood defiant. "Once or twice."

"That's disgusting," he said. "Plus, humans are so weak. It seems unsporting to treat them as prey."

"You're too soft-hearted." She pressed her nails into her palms to keep from slapping him. His tutors had turned the boy into a weakling, but if she were going to gain the adoration and support of all the vampires in Sanguinia, she had to start with her son.

She nudged the carafe toward him again. "You don't need to *kill* a human to taste its blood." Although without that thrill, what was the point?

"May I ask you a question, Mother?"

She nodded.

"I overheard your conversation, earlier. If there are vampires drinking blood from unwilling humans in Xandra, aren't the generals right? Won't it provoke war if we don't do more to stop them?"

Rage rose inside her at the thought, threatening to burst out in a deadly strike, but she held back; she'd find someone to crush later. In a controlled voice, she answered her son. "If King Stefan declares war, it will prove what I already know to be true. Humans are brutal creatures with no morals or any sense of right and wrong. If they invade

Sanguinia based on a few harmless neck bites, then they deserve to be drained." If Stefan declared war, the vampire population would surely rally behind her, but her thirteen-year-old son wasn't old enough to understand politics.

The boy leaned back in his chair and stretched his arms over his head. His relaxed gesture eased her fears that he might go to the generals behind her back, even though she'd caught him talking to that idiot Adanthas more than once. Many of her subjects did not yet trust her, since she'd been born human.

"Where did you get this blood?" He nodded toward the carafe. "It wasn't brought back from Xandra, was it?"

She raised a hand to her chest as if his words shocked her. "Of course not." She made sure to add a worried expression to her face to play up the charade. "It was a willing donation." It wouldn't do to raise his suspicions.

In truth, the blood *had* been brought back from Xandra, harvested by one of her minions from some weak human. Natasha was gaining support, and soon every citizen in Sanguinia would bow down at her feet. Then she'd order an invasion and Xandra would be crushed.

Those infernal fairies had paid dearly in ripped-off wings for barring her from entering Xandra and making her wait sixteen years to torture Catia and Stefan's daughter.

But even though she couldn't cross the border herself, it was delicious to know that each night bloodthirsty vampires terrorized Stefan and Catia's precious kingdom and the throne that was rightfully hers. And in less than three years, her minions would be terrorizing something even more precious to the odious couple than their subjects—their daughter.

Then Catia and Stefan would suffer as they so richly deserved. If Stefan declared war in the meantime, so be it. Yet another way to see him crushed.

In time she'd rule Xandra, with its riches and strategic location. Soon after, she'd conquer the entire known world.

"Why don't I get to take my own stakes?" Lucette asked Tristan as they stood near the door of the gymnasium, ready to go out into the night. Almost nine months had gone by since they started training, and she was ready to kill her first vampire. She hoped.

He shook his head. "Not a chance." He pulled his black slayer hood over his short blond hair and zipped on his neck protector.

"But I've been training for nearly a year." She reached for a quiver of stakes, but he grabbed onto her arm and shook his head.

"We aren't going to get close to the action," he said. "This outing is just about observation." He leaned back against the wall, his long, lean body looking especially strong in his slayer uniform. "I shouldn't even be sneaking you out. If anyone from the academy finds out I brought a girl along to the first-year slayers' field trip"—he paused—"I'm not sure what they'd do. I'd probably get expelled."

"I thought we were going with *your* class," she said. Tristan was in his third year, and ever since he'd told her about his class outings to get real-life combat experience with the slayer army, she'd been pestering him to take her along. How else was she supposed to get experience?

Tristan slipped a hood over her head. Although she knew the hood and mask were because she was going out into the dangerous night, she couldn't help feel as if they served another purpose: him wanting to cover her face so he wouldn't have to look at her.

She chewed on her lip as he zipped her in. Then he strapped on her neck protector and checked the rest of her slayer uniform. It wasn't as if Tristan ever said anything to purposefully make her feel bad or ugly, it's just that he never seemed to notice she was a girl. In contrast, she sure noticed that he was a boy. Nearly seventeen, he was practically a man.

"That works." He took her by the shoulders and spun her around. "No one will guess you're not one of the boys."

She crossed her arms over her chest. Her lack of girlish attributes might make it easier for her to hide in among the class of boys tonight, but her fourteenth birthday was coming soon and . . . She shook her head. Even if Tristan might say yes, it would be too risky to invite him to her birthday party. How could she explain meeting him to her father? And asking her mother to concoct yet another lie was out of the question. Plus, she couldn't even tell Tristan who she really was. Taking him to meet her parents at the palace would blow her cover.

Tristan adjusted his weapons. "Ready?"

"No." She took a step back from him.

He closed the distance she'd created and ran his strong hands from her shoulders down to her wrists and then her hands. The gesture was so protective, she nearly dove into his chest for a hug.

"Are you frightened?" he asked, his gloved hands still over hers. "We don't need to do this."

She pulled away from him. "I am *not* frightened. But I should have weapons. What if I'm attacked? What if you are? How will I save you?"

He swung one arm and punched her lightly in the shoulder, but hard enough that she tipped to the side. "My brave little slayer girl."

Although she couldn't see his expression under his mask, she felt sure he was mocking her, and she gritted her teeth. What would it take for him to take her seriously—as a slayer or as a girl?

"Don't worry, little Lucy." He assured her. "I won't let anything happen to you."

Lucette tucked her short curls behind her ears. In the two years since she'd chopped off her long hair, it had grown down to her chin. At least it wasn't quite so boyish anymore, but even though she was now fifteen, her body still hadn't cooperated. Well beyond late-bloomer status now, Lucette figured it was time to face the fact that a curvy figure was not in her future.

She kept her eyes on Tristan as he demonstrated a wrestling hold on a younger boy, Hans, who'd been working with them and had been sworn to secrecy about the mysterious girl "Lucy" who trained in the gym late at night. Lucette had been training with Tristan at least five times a week, and although he didn't give out praise easily, she could tell he was proud of her progress.

She focused her attention on the demonstration she'd soon be expected to emulate. Tristan was playing the part of a slayer, and Hans was playing the vampire. Tristan lunged for Hans, feigning a frontal attack, but at the last moment, Tristan ducked down under Hans's arm and grabbed it.

Using one leg, he swept Hans off his feet. Once he had Hans on the ground, he twisted the boy's arm to force him onto his chest, then pinned him by kneeling on one arm and pressing the other into his back.

"Do you understand?" Tristan asked her, as he let Hans up. The younger boy rubbed his arm.

Lucette nodded. Her heart was thumping hard and fast. Not only was she unsure she could pull off this maneuver—especially on Tristan, who was taller and stronger—but these exercises, which resulted in body-on-body contact, made her nervous. Each time Tristan had her pinned or held her closely, she closed her eyes and imagined him holding her for more romantic reasons.

"Tristan?" Hans asked. "Is it okay if I take off? I've got a vampire history test tomorrow morning."

Tristan nodded, and the boy headed out.

Lucette's heart beat even faster at the thought of being alone with Tristan. Maybe tonight was her chance to tell him how she felt.

The fairy queen had told her that she'd know how to prove her love when the time came, so maybe this overwhelming desire to kiss Tristan was a sign. Maybe she could lift the curse before it even took effect and she and Tristan could live happily ever after. Although he was nearly three years older, there were no rules about age where love was concerned, and no way to control when or with whom love happened. How ironic if her father had been right all along. Maybe she *was* old enough for love after all.

She watched Hans leave the room and considered how to tell Tristan she loved him. Slowly, she turned with what she hoped was a seductive smile.

Tristan lunged like a vampire. Lucette's shock vanished and her slayer training kicked in, but she ducked under his arm too late to get a strong hold, and then her leg sweep missed. Before she could adjust her stance, he had one arm pinned behind her back, and he pulled down so that her body was bent back against his—with his teeth on her throat.

She panted, first from the shock and then from the rush of feelings flowing through her. Closing her eyes, she sighed and stretched her head to the side, exposing her neck further.

He dropped her and she fell onto the mat. "Ouch!"

"Ouch?" Tristan glared at her, even more handsome when angry. "Is that all you have to say? If I were a vampire, you'd be bitten. Three bites and you'd be dead. I'm beginning to think you're not serious about this anymore. Maybe we're done. I'm not sure I can teach you much more—not if you're going to be so sloppy."

Her cheeks burned. "You surprised me."

"Oh, sorry." He raised his hands in mock surrender. "If I were a real vampire, I would have said, 'Are you ready, Lucy? Because I'm about to attack you.'"

"Very funny." She got to her feet as gracefully as she could. She stepped toward him with a soft smile on her face. Before she realized what she was doing, she reached out to touch his powerful upper arm.

But before her fingers reached his skin, he pulled his arm away. "What's your story, Lucy? Not many girls want to learn how to be slayers. None that I know of, anyway, other than you."

Her chest heaved as she fought to control her breath and her nerves. He was interested in her, asking personal questions. This was her chance. The fairies had been right: she knew what to do.

She tipped up onto her toes and leaned forward to kiss him. But before their lips met, Tristan jerked back sharply, and the only thing she managed to kiss was air.

"What are you doing?" he demanded.

Undeterred, she reached for him again.

"Lucy, that's highly inappropriate!" His voice was clipped and sharp.

"Why?"

His face turned from shock to pity. He rubbed a hand over his chin. "I don't . . . I mean, I can't . . . You're just a kid."

"I am not." She put her hand on his chest, but he pulled it off. "I'm almost fifteen," she said.

He backed into a leather-topped wooden horse. "Lucy, I'll be eighteen soon. The age difference is too much. I've never met your father, but I'm quite sure he'd kill me."

"No, you're wrong. He wouldn't. In fact, he's been making me date since I was thirteen."

Tristan looked shocked at that, so she stepped forward and cornered him against the horse. Just a few more inches and their bodies would touch. But he slid to the side and rounded the horse to put the large apparatus between them. "I'm sorry if I did something to give you the wrong idea."

Every boy who showed up to her father's Friday-night galas found her appealing, so why wasn't Tristan interested?

Realizing the likely truth, she crossed her arms over her chest and backed up a few steps. Those stupid boys liked her because she was a princess. They were trying to get on the good side of the king. None of them thought she was pretty or really liked *her*; they just pretended to. How humiliating. Her eyes narrowed and she squeezed her lips together, wishing she could erase the entire night.

"My graduation is in a few weeks," Tristan said. "After that, I'll be going home to Judra. If you like, I'll keep training you until I leave, but I understand if you'd rather not." He looked down. "I'm sure Hans would be happy to continue practicing with you."

Her heart pinched, and she turned away to hide the pain she knew was spreading all over her face.

"Just forget it," she snapped. She stomped to the back door, behind which the groom who'd brought her was waiting.

At the door, she turned back. "I'll see you tomorrow night." As hard as it was to imagine training with Tristan after tonight's fiasco, it was even harder to imagine never seeing him again.

"Why so sad?" Her father cupped her face, rubbing her cheek with his thumb like he used to when she was little.

She couldn't tell her father the truth—that she was devastated because her secret slayer trainer had rejected her and had moved home to Judra—and she wondered what she could tell him without lying. Even though she'd been deceiving her father, she avoided outright lies whenever possible.

"Is it boy trouble?" he asked.

Surprised he'd guessed, she nodded as tears filled her eyes. She felt like a total baby, crying in front of her father like this, but ever since Tristan's rejection three weeks ago she'd felt like crying all the time.

Her mother, sensing her sadness was related to her trainer's departure, had offered to find a replacement. Even her mother didn't get it.

Too humiliated to tell her the truth, Lucette had turned down her mother's offer. Her mother was so delicate and pretty, Lucette figured she had probably never been rejected by a boy. How could she have been? She'd met her future husband so young, and gotten married when she was not much older than Lucette was now.

Her father pulled her into his arms. "I'm so sorry. With all your dates chaperoned, I didn't think anything bad would happen. Which one of those boys hurt you?"

She pulled back. "It's not like that, Dad."

"Then what?"

Her lips started to tremble, but she took a deep breath to calm herself. "I like a boy more than he likes me."

"Oh, that's not possible!"

"No, Dad, it's true. And I don't just like him, I love him, but he doesn't love me."

The look of concern in her father's eyes turned to warm sympathy. "Oh, Lucette. I'm so sorry. Tell me who he is and I'll have a word with him."

She pulled back. "No!"

"But if I can help . . ."

She shook her head. "No, Dad. This is one area of my life where you can't help. You can't make a boy love me with a royal decree. Besides, he moved away."

Her father embraced her gently. "If he didn't love you, then he's a very foolish boy, indeed, and not the one you were meant to love. Don't despair, I'll introduce you to more boys at Friday evening's reception. One of them is bound to help you forget this young man."

Lucette buried her face in her father's chest. Even if he was wrong about this, it felt so good to be wrapped up in his arms and, for just a few minutes, to believe that he could keep her safe forever.

Looking into her mirror in her bedroom, Lucette twisted to the side and smoothed her hands down her ribs and over her hips. Just days from her sixteenth birthday, she finally had the womanly figure everyone claimed she would. Dressed in her exercise clothes, the closest thing to a slayer uniform she owned, her new curves were easy to see—even if she was still broader in the shoulders and more solid and muscular than most girls.

Her hair had grown again too, but she kept it cut just below her shoulders. It was long enough to put into a tight braid and out of the way for training, but short enough to keep some spring in her curls when her hair flowed around her face.

Her mother had been right about something else, too. Her oversized blue eyes, sharp cheekbones, and strong brows didn't look so freakish anymore. She finally saw her resemblance to her father, as if she were the softer, more feminine version of his handsome self. Boys had certainly noticed, too. She no longer worried that they were flattering her just to please her father, but so far, not one of them had made her feel even a fraction of what she had for Tristan. Ever since he'd gone back to Judra, she hadn't heard a word from him. Not that she'd expected to. He didn't know where to write her, even if he wanted to. He didn't even know her real name.

Enough about boys, she thought. Now that she was about to turn sixteen, her main priorities were keeping her hands prick-free and her neck bite-free. She picked up a stake and the wood felt secure in her hand, but she looked down at her gloves lying on the bed alongside the dress she'd worn that day. If she wanted to keep handling stakes after her birthday, she should get used to holding them with gloved hands. A splinter would spell disaster.

But before she could put the gloves on, something crashed outside her bedroom door. She spun toward the sound, instinctively moving into a fighting stance. A guard always stood outside her door—one of a group her mother trusted with their secrets—but she heard another crash and knew something was definitely wrong. Still holding her stake, she ran over to the door and then opened it slowly.

According to her father's crazy rules—rules she always followed while at the palace and under his watchful eye—she wasn't supposed to handle doorknobs herself, not even with her gloves on, but she didn't have time to go back for her hand protection. Besides, she had three whole days before she turned sixteen. It didn't really matter yet.

She glanced down the hall, but there was no sign of her guard. She crept into the corridor, moving silently, her senses on high alert, just as Tristan had taught her. From around the corner of the corridor emerged two men locked in combat. One was her guard who fell onto his back, and an impossibly fast male—he had to be a vampire—leaped into view. The vampire bent, picked up the guard by his lapel, and began to bite. Lucette sprang into action, rushing forward, adrenaline pumping though her veins.

Two of the palace slayers leaped for the vampire, but the creature deftly slithered out of their way and headed toward Lucette.

"Princess, back to your room!" one of the slayers commanded. Instead, Lucette planted a perfect side kick into the advancing vampire's chest.

Clearly not expecting that, the vampire staggered backward. But before he could decide whether to attack her or deal with the slayers coming up from behind, she ran, did a round-off to gain power, and then planted her foot in the side of his head. She landed with her stake ready, but couldn't bring herself to plunge it into the dazed creature's flesh. Up close, it looked so human, so alive, so clearly terrified at finding itself at her mercy.

She was still looking into the vampire's eyes when one of the slayers drove a stake into it from behind. She staggered back.

This was nothing like seeing a straw dummy staked, or even watching real slaying from a safe distance. She covered her mouth with her hand, hoping she wouldn't be sick.

The slayers and her guard snapped to attention, and Lucette spun to the side to see why.

She gasped.

"Lucette!" Her father shook with rage. "When, where, and how did you learn to do that?"

"I don't blame her, I blame *you*." Lucette's father glared at her mother.

Lucette cringed. "But, Dad, it was all my idea. I pressured her, I begged her." That wasn't exactly the truth, but if it helped keep the peace, lying was worth it. "I wanted to know a few slayer moves, in case the worst happened."

Listening, her father's face softened, but then his anger returned. "It doesn't matter whose idea this was. If this has been going on behind my back for nearly three years . . ." He shook his head slowly, his eyes narrow and his lips tense. "This is an unforgivable betrayal." He turned to his wife. "You had to know that."

Lucette's mother held her chin high. "I suppose I did."

"Yet you did it anyway."

"I did it to keep our daughter safe." Her mother's voice was calm yet determined.

"To protect her, you thrust her into abject danger?" He looked at her mother with so much scorn it made Lucette's skin crawl.

"You're a fool if you think you can stop this curse." Her mother stomped her foot, losing a bit of her control. "If you had your way, she'd be thrust into the darkness totally unprepared. She'd get bitten the first night." Her mother looked down, as if ashamed by her outburst.

"Mom, Dad," Lucette began. She could fix this. She had to. She might be the reason they were fighting, the reason they always fought, but she could also be the reason they made up. "Can't we put this behind us? I know you both want me to be safe and happy. Dad, I know you want to prevent the curse from happening"—she stared at her ungloved fingers—"and Mom wants that, too. We all do. But if the worst happens, at least I'm prepared for that now. Isn't that a good thing?" She forced a smile onto her face. "I'm so lucky to have you two as parents."

Her father crossed his arms over his chest. "Lucette, please leave the room."

"Why?" Her throat tightened.

"Because I need to have a private word with your mother." His voice was so hard, so sharp. He had never spoken to her in that tone before.

"She can stay if she wants," her mother said. "This concerns her, and she's nearly sixteen. You can't treat her like a child anymore. You've been pushing her to date since she was barely thirteen, and yet you want to shelter her from the very real dangers she faces. You can't have it both ways, Stefan."

"And you can't have it both ways, either. You can't expect me to trust you, when you've deceived me in the most blatant manner. In fact, all of this is a direct result of your betrayal. If you'd just invited her . . . What else have you been lying about? How else have you betrayed me?"

"I have not betrayed you. Ever." Her mother's voice shook.

"All you do is lie."

Lucette felt tears rise in her eyes. She'd seen her parents fight many times, but never with such venom, never with this hate in their eyes. And it was all her fault.

If only she hadn't been so determined to train like a slayer. If only she'd stayed in her room and let the slayers do their jobs. If only she hadn't been cursed. Lucette looked back and forth between her parents, trying to think of something—anything—she could say to make this better.

"This is it," her mother said, calm washing through her voice. "I've had enough."

Lucette let a little hope sink back in. Maybe this was over. Maybe her mother would apologize and the nightmarish argument would end.

Her mother raised her chin. "I'm leaving you, Stefan. I'm moving back to my father's estate, and I'm taking Lucette with me."

Lucette felt as if she were being crushed. She turned to her father. He'd back down now. He wouldn't let this happen.

"Fine," her father said. "You can leave, but you are not taking our daughter."

Lucette felt dizzy. The world felt distorted and upside down. It was now two days until her sixteenth birthday, and she sat on a chair in her bedroom, opposite her mother, faced with another impossible choice.

"Lucette," her mother said, "you know how restricted your life will be if you choose to live with your father. If you think he was overprotective before, just imagine what he has in store after your birthday."

"Why can't you just stay?" Lucette's voice came out high and whiny, and she was embarrassed that she didn't sound more mature.

"That's not an option." Her mother's voice was clipped. "You'll love it on your grandfather's estate. Rolling hills, sheep, and best of all, no vampires."

"But what if I prick my finger?" Although it was horrible to think of being alone at night here in the palace where she'd lived her whole life, to be alone every night in the country—where she knew no one, didn't know the area, and wasn't convinced there wouldn't be vampires—was terrifying.

There was a quick knock, and then the bedroom door opened. Her father strode into the room. "Have you decided, Lucette?"

Her lips trembled, and she fought to keep the rest of her body still. She was trained as a slayer, brave and strong. She could not break down, even though it was clear her parents weren't changing their minds. They'd even refused to let her wait to make this decision until after her birthday.

She had to decide now.

If you were Lucette, what would you do?

OPTION A: Lucette should stay here with her father. Everything in her world is changing. If she stays here, at least one thing will remain constant. Her father might be way too strict with his rules, but with him, she has the best chance of preventing the curse from falling. With his rules, there's no way she'll prick her finger. If you think Lucette should choose option A, go to section 4: Glass Houses (page 113).

OPTION B: Lucette should go live with her mother. If she stays here, her father will have her living in a virtual bubble. The vampire attacks seem centered around the palace, so if she leaves, she might be safer if the curse does start. It feels cowardly to leave, since she'll be the only one awake at night to defend the palace from vampires if the curse falls, but really, no one can expect one person—even one with slayer training—to protect the entire kingdom on her own. Besides, her mother has done so much to support her. If you think Lucette should choose option B, go to section 5: Country Living (page 147).

Section 4

Glass Houses

4

"Tomorrow's your birthday, Lucette." Her father cupped her face in his hand and concern shot from his eyes. "Sixteen." He tucked her duvet more tightly around her legs as she leaned back against the solid gold headboard. Wood splintered; gold didn't.

"I know, Dad." As if she could forget this big day. Unlike most girls' sixteenth birthdays, hers would be anything but sweet. She wiggled her fingers inside her gloves, sick of the feel of the leather on her skin. At least he'd agreed to let her sleep in her room alone now that her mother was leaving. Maybe in time she could figure out a way to sneak from the room at night to do some slayer patrols and keep her skills—and her stakes—sharp.

"Mom is coming to my party, right?" After that horrible talk two days ago, her mother had immediately moved into the summer palace on the far side of the village. She was leaving for the country immediately after Lucette's birthday party.

Her father's smile wavered at the corners, as if he were laboring to hold it. "You do understand we'll have to take some extra precautions after your birthday?"

"Like what? Thicker gloves?" Her father had taken every safety measure imaginable. Sewing needles had been banned from the castle almost since she was born and seamstresses were licensed, the tools of their trade accounted for and locked up each night by armed guards. He'd removed every possible potential finger-pricking tool from the castle grounds, yet still acted as if the curse could fall at any moment.

"Don't worry about it. I'll keep you safe." He ran his hand over her hair, which she'd worn down to please him, and then planted a kiss on her forehead. "Now drink your hot chocolate."

Lucette smiled. She hadn't really liked hot chocolate since she was little—it was too sweet—but her father had brought it into her bedroom himself, so she couldn't refuse it. She took a sip. Tomorrow she'd be sixteen, and something in the pit of her stomach told her nothing would ever be the same again.

Lucette awoke with a start. Something was wrong. She reached out and pounded on the thick glass wall in front of her, but the sound was muffled by the padded gloves strapped over her hands and clamped halfway up her forearms with tight fasteners.

"Hey!" she shouted. "Let me out!" Her heart raced. Was this part of the curse coming true? It was certainly a nightmare. She spotted small holes bored through the glass, and moved her mouth directly in front of the holes. "Let me out of here!"

Her father appeared at the top of what looked like stairs on the other side of the small room about ten feet from the glass partition that divided the room.

"Where am I? What have you done to me?" She felt dizzy.

The last thing she remembered was drinking hot chocolate before bed last night . . .

Suddenly, she shouted, "You drugged me! You drugged me, then locked me up!" The rate of her breaths increased and it felt like she was drowning. Realizing she was hyperventilating, she bent and forced her breathing to slow. Rage and hurt fought inside her and she regretted choosing to stay with her father. "Why would you do this?" she yelled at him.

"You know why, Lucette. Once you calm down, you'll see this is for the best."

"For the best?" She slammed her hand into the glass wall between them. "What good is this, anyway? It's glass! You don't think a vampire can break glass?" She felt sure she knew more about vampires than her father, but decided not to go down that road.

"The glass was enchanted by the fairies," he said. "It won't break. They made it to keep you safe."

"You're lying! Mom told me the fairies said they couldn't get involved, that they couldn't help us anymore."

He drew a deep breath. "Enchanting this glass was the last thing they did for us. I had to promise I'd never ask them for help again."

She backed away from the glass wall and bit at the clasps on her arms, trying to remove the huge padded gloves, but the smooth clasps did not yield to her teeth. She could barely move her hands in these gloves.

"Now, Lucette," her father said as he stepped up to the glass and put his palm on it. "I'm sorry you were frightened when you woke. I'm sorry I wasn't here to reassure you. I stayed all night and only stepped away for a moment."

"That's not the point, Dad." She gave up on her attempts to remove the gloves and walked around her cell. There was a bed with no frame and what looked like a puffy mattress with a duvet on top. A chair constructed in a similar style sat in one corner, and opposite it was another chair cast of heavy iron with padded cushions on the seat. A screen sat in the other corner, behind which she found a bathroom, but all the fixtures were coated with clear rubber.

The walls were made of polished stone, with no edges to climb, and broken only by one bar-covered window high on the far wall. The window had no glass, presumably to let in fresh air, but even if she could figure out a way to climb up to it—an impossible task given the smooth walls, not to mention the thick gloves on her hands—she'd never get through those bars.

"You've locked me in a prison." She strode toward the glass wall and slammed her shoulder against it. "How could you?"

A few hours later, her mother entered the room and her initial shock at seeing her daughter behind the glass turned into rage. She ran to the glass and pressed her hands against it. "Lucette, darling! Are you okay?"

Lucette shook her head. She was not about to pretend she was okay living like this—not even to keep the peace. She held up her thickly gloved hands.

Her mother gasped and then spun toward her father. "Stefan, this is too much! She can't even move her fingers in those things!" She turned back to Lucette. "It's not too late to change your mind. Come away to live with me."

Her father slumped against the stone wall next to the stairs and put his head in his hands. Lucette's heart lurched. She might not agree with everything her father had done, but in her whole life she'd never seen him question himself. Not like this. If she didn't know better, she'd think he was crying.

Her mother approached him and stood just a few feet away. Lucette pressed her ear to the holes in the glass so she could hear what they said.

"Stefan. Those gloves. Really? How is she to wash herself?" Her mother's voice rose with each word. "You've got her in a prison. How could you do this?" She shoved his shoulder. "What were you thinking?"

He straightened and glared, as if her scolding had firmed his resolve. "Unlike you, I will do whatever it takes to keep her safe. To keep our entire kingdom safe. And after what you did . . ." He shook his head. "The lies you told. The danger you put her in. The risks you took." He pushed off the wall and the queen backed up a few steps.

"But, Stefan, the gloves. What can happen to her behind that unbreakable glass? At least give her lighter gloves."

Her father's jaw hardened as he stared at her mother, but he lifted his head and met Lucette's eyes. She held up the confining gloves.

Her father ran his hand over his black hair, and then strode over and crouched in front of a long, narrow slot at the bottom of the glass wall. "Fine. Lie down, reach your hands through this meal slot one at a time, and I'll unlock your gloves."

Happy birthday to me, thought Lucette.

Lucette picked up the latest letter from her mother, who'd written every day since she'd moved to the country. She ran a gloved finger over her mother's signature. There was no sense in risking a paper cut, although she wasn't sure that would count as "pricking" her finger. She'd spent nearly two weeks in the tower, and although her father tried to hide the truth, from the sounds she heard at night, the vampire attacks in and around the palace had increased. Lucette missed her mother, but part of her was glad that she was in the country and away from all this.

Her father had agreed to triple admissions to the vampire slayer academy for the next year, but he had yet to declare war, still believing the Sanguinian ambassador's claim that the majority of their citizens were against drinking human blood.

Lucette set down her mother's letter and climbed the rubber-coated steel ladder her father had finally allowed into the room. If she climbed to the top, she could see out of her tower window and look down over the palace courtyard.

When she reached the top of the ladder she closed her eyes and inhaled. She could almost imagine she was outside. If she climbed up at the right time of day, the sun hit her face for half an hour. Now bathed in moonlight, she looked down the many stories to the palace courtyard below. It was quiet tonight. A team of slayers prowled the roof of the building on the opposite side of the courtyard, and she could occasionally make out the shadow of something moving on the ground, but it seemed as if the vampires were taking the night off. Maybe the slayers were making progress, after all.

She hadn't made much progress herself in finding anything close to true love. Her father had paraded a stream of unappealing young men up to the tower every day to meet her through the glass. In truth, not all of the boys had been horrible, but something was always missing. So far, no boy had come close to making her feel the way Tristan had, even when she'd first met him. Perhaps she was just older and more jaded now. Perhaps Tristan would no longer have that effect on her, either.

Suddenly, from outside the bars of her tower window, a face appeared directly in front of her. Its fangs glinting, its pale iridescent skin, and its yellow-flecked eyes unmistakable, she knew she was face-to-face with a vampire. Heart racing, she slid down the ladder to the floor in panic and scrambled back along the carpet to her bed.

"Hello, Princess." The vampire snapped one of the iron bars off the window as if it were a twig. He stuck his head into the gap and smiled mischievously.

"Help!" Lucette yelled. Someone would surely hear her through the ventilation holes in her glass wall. Guards and slayers were on duty at the bottom of the tower stairs at all times, but she'd begged her father not to station any in her room outside the glass. She needed some privacy.

When her father had worried about the window and threatened to fill it with the unbreakable glass, the slayers had assured him that no vampire other than the queen herself could climb that high, or pull iron bars from stone. Apparently they'd been wrong.

"You smell delicious." The vampire chuckled as he snapped another bar off the window. Lucette heard the bar clatter to the cobblestones far below. Someone had to hear that, even if they missed her cries.

He broke off another bar and then traced his tongue over his fangs. She scanned the room for a weapon, knowing she'd find none. Her father had taken so many precautions to ensure she'd never prick her finger in this room that there was nothing even vaguely resembling a weapon, especially not a wooden one.

The vampire snapped off another bar. One more and he might fit through. "Don't be scared. One bite won't kill you," he said, and then the final bar snapped. "But since I've gone to all this trouble, I might take a very long drink. You have such a beautiful neck."

Lucette grabbed a book from the nightstand and gathered every ounce of strength she had. Taking careful aim, Lucette threw her book directly at the vampire's nose and struck her target. Blood dribbled from his nostrils and shock entered his eyes.

He wiped the blood off his face. "That's no way to greet a visitor."

Holding onto the bottom ledge of the stone-framed window, he pulled himself forward.

She ran to the iron chair, picked up the cushions, and threw them at the vampire. They bounced off his head and shoulders harmlessly.

The vampire pulled through the window and dropped down to the floor. She picked up an unlit candle from the nightstand.

"Nice stake," he said as he rose to his feet. "That wick looks sharp." He stepped around the room slowly, keeping his eyes on her, clearly enjoying her fear and the buildup to his feast. He lunged, hands raised like claws. "Rah!"

She jumped back, and he laughed. Rage rose in her chest. She sprang onto the iron chair and jumped off, kicking. Her foot connected with the vampire's chin and knocked him back a few feet. She landed next to him, and dashed backward, knowing she was vulnerable.

A grappling hook flew through the window. The noise distracted the vampire and Lucette leaped to the other side of her bed. The hook pulled back and snagged the inside of the window. A slayer crew would come up that rope—she hoped—as long as she could hold off the vampire until they arrived.

The vampire leaped across the bed toward her, but she dove under him and rolled over the bed. He roared with anger and lunged again, but Lucette jumped onto the metal chair and launched herself over his head, flipping in the air. She landed before he turned around, and took the opportunity to plant a kick squarely in his back.

He turned, his face twisted. "I didn't plan to kill you, Princess, but now you've made me angry!" He leaped forward, but she rolled down and under him.

Slayers burst into the visitors' area outside the glass and one of them slammed into the glass enclosure.

"The key!" a slayer shouted.

"The king has the only copy."

"Wake him!" the first slayer yelled back to another. "And find glass cutters. Now!"

"Looks like we've got company, Princess," the vampire said. "Normally I like to feed in private, but you might be fun with an audience."

He reached forward and she jumped and twisted, but he caught her in midair, pulling her down and placing her feet on the ground with her back to him. Holding her by the arms, he traced his nose up the side of her neck, but she stomped down hard on his foot.

The vampire howled in pain and let go of his grasp on Lucette's arms. A slayer appeared at the window and pushed his way through. The screech of metal on glass filled the air, but Lucette knew the cutters were no use. If the fairies had enchanted the glass, not even diamonds would cut through it.

The vampire, distracted by the slayer's entrance through the window, had his back to her, so with a quick twist to build momentum, Lucette kicked him hard on the hip, making solid contact. The vampire stumbled.

The slayer bounded down from the window and, with his stake raised high in the air, he lunged at the vampire's chest. The vampire swatted at the stake, knocking it from the slayer's hand. But the slayer was quick, and landed a roundhouse kick to the vampire's ribs, distracting him for a moment.

A second slayer appeared in the window, but Lucette couldn't wait. She rolled across the floor and grabbed the fallen stake. As the vampire prepared to take down the newly arrived slayer, Lucette raised her stake, leaped, and planted the sharp weapon right into the vampire's back.

The creature shrieked and then crumpled to the floor. Lucette rolled off his body. Her chest heaved as she sucked in short, sharp breaths, unable to regulate their speed, unable to draw enough oxygen to fill her lungs.

"Princess, are you all right?" One of the slayers bent down to offer her a hand. She let him pull her up, but had trouble remaining on her feet.

Lucette had been so close to death. The only other time she'd felt real fear was when she'd realized that boy in the forest was a vampire. But that had been nothing compared to this; she'd been like a baby frightened by a fairy-tale witch. This was real and her attacker had been far from friendly. He'd been determined to kill her and, worse, he knew who she was. She wasn't some random throat; he'd been sent to bite *her*.

And she'd killed him. Killed a living, breathing creature. Even if it had been a vampire attacking her, she'd taken a life. Ever since she'd learned about vampires and slayers, she'd been eager to get into the action, but this was far too gruesome, too brutal. Nothing like sticking a straw dummy.

But necessary to save her own life.

Lucette stared straight ahead from a chair in her old bedroom while her father paced in front of her, leaving a flattened trail on the plush carpet. Ever since the attack she'd been trembling, but now, an hour later, she merely felt numb. She'd killed the vampire, draining his life with a single stab. Somehow she could no longer think of a vampire as an "it."

Yes, the creature had threatened her life, but the actual act of killing had been horrific. She wondered if it would have been different if she'd never met a vampire in real life and mistaken him for human. But she couldn't reconcile the boy she'd met in the woods with the monster she'd faced tonight.

"If that tower won't keep you safe"—her father's voice brought her out of her stupor—"we need to send you away."

"To stay with Mom?" she asked hopefully.

"No." Her father stopped pacing and crossed his arms over his chest. "I'll have a bunker built, deep underground, somewhere that vampires can't find you." He nodded and his jaw firmed. "No one can know its location. No one can visit . . ." His voice trailed off as if he was realizing he'd revealed more of his plan than he'd meant to.

Lucette snapped out of her stupor. No chance would she let this happen. At least her glass prison in the tower had daylight and fresh air. She fought to control her terror. Calm reason was the only way to deal with her father.

His skin looked pale and clammy, his eyes rimmed with red from a lack of sleep. He wasn't thinking clearly.

"Dad," she said, "if tonight proved anything, it proved that hiding me is no use. The vampires will find me. But the palace is full of slayers who can keep me safe. Let me out in the world. I was like a sitting duck in that tower." She could fight vampires, too, but there was no use in taking that tack with her father.

"What about pricking your finger?" He looked very grave. "I must protect you."

She put her hand on her father's arm. "I can prick my finger anywhere. No matter where you hide me."

"No!" He grabbed her shoulders. "I won't accept that."

"Can't you see that kind of isolation would be as bad as the curse? I always wear gloves." She held up her hands. "Prick-proof."

"Someone could pull them off. A knife could slice through. Or a fang."

She fought the shiver inside her. She must not let it show on the outside. "Yes, that could happen. And a star could fall from the sky."

"Lucette."

"Dad, if you lock me up in an underground bunker, or put me back in that tower, I will never, ever forgive you."

"Fine." His eyes were glassy. "But if I let you stay in the castle, you have to follow my rules."

"Not if your rules involve that glass cell. If you don't let me sleep in my bedroom, I'll go live with Mom." Her threat felt hollow. Even though he'd given her the choice before, moving to her mother's without his consent now would be difficult. But she knew that reversing her parental choice would stab him where it hurt, and right now she needed to use her strongest emotional weapons. There was no way she would agree to live in an underground cave or a glass cell.

They stared at each other for a few moments, before she broke the impasse. "I'm not a little kid anymore, and if you want me to live with you, there have to be changes. I promise I'll do everything I can to keep from pricking my finger—believe me, I don't want the curse to fall any more than you do—but I won't live like a prisoner. I won't have someone watching me every second of every day."

Her father crossed his arms over his chest. "I'll put slayer guards on your door at night and have a suit fashioned. Something that will disguise you and keep your hands safe."

"Okay." Lucette couldn't help but think a slayer uniform would meet that description very well, but maybe it would be too much to suggest that to her father right now. Even after all he had done, she was willing to give this another try. With more freedom, she might find a way to work with the slayers at night, and even better, if she and her father could get along, she might be able to persuade her mother to come home.

Patrolling the village about half a mile from the palace, Lucette stopped to scan the street for vampires. Over the past three months, she'd managed to convince her father to let her sleep without someone else in her room, but if he ever found out she was helping the slayers, he would surely revoke the privilege. Her door was heavily guarded at night, but she'd made friends with one of the slayers, and he'd given her a uniform, some weapons, a grappling hook, and enough rope so she could sneak out through her bedroom window to do her part to protect the citizens of Xandra from rogue vampires each night. She knew it wasn't logical to blame herself for the increased attacks, but knowing that the vampire who'd broken into the tower had been after her specifically, she couldn't shake the weight of responsibility and guilt.

Lucette adjusted her grip on her stake. Her new gloves were heavy and awkward, like tiny leather prisons, but she considered them her one small concession to her father. No way would she stop slaying just because she'd turned sixteen. It was her duty as a trained slayer to help. Plus, she couldn't let her slayer skills deteriorate; someday, she might be patrolling alone.

Since her sixteenth birthday, twenty-four Xandran citizens had been bitten by vampires, but none more than once. She couldn't imagine the terror of having a vampire feed from her blood, even if it took three bites to transfer enough venom to kill. It had been horrendous even to be threatened.

The sounds of a skirmish drifted over from an adjoining street, and she ran in the direction of the sounds. She jumped up onto the six-foot-high garden wall at the corner, landing in a crouch. Then, after making sure no one had seen her, she walked silently along the top of the stone wall.

Cautiously, stake ready, she approached the sound, but it was only a couple of dogs fighting over a bone.

The tension in her shoulders released, but Lucette decided to maintain her higher vantage point atop the wall. She stepped nimbly onto the next section, which was a few feet higher. This garden wall ended about fifteen feet ahead, at the side of a house. If she took a running leap, she could probably scramble up the house's drainpipe and onto the roof. However, she wasn't positive she could trust the grip of her new heavy gloves. She also couldn't trust the drainpipe to be free from sharp edges or cracks that could cut her if she removed her gloves. But it was either try or lose an even better view of the street, so she took a deep breath and ran.

Her gloved hands slipped on the pipe, but the rubber soles of her shoes held tight and she scrambled until she could grasp the flat roof and pull herself up. Now, about twenty feet above street level, she could see the entire stretch of road.

Farther down, something moved in the shadows. Lucette crouched, then sprang forward, removing a stake from the quiver on her back. She heard a soft giggle, and as she got close enough to the shadow, she saw it was just a young couple. The boy leaned back against the wall and held the girl casually around her waist. The girl pressed against him in a way that made Lucette blush. The boy bent down to kiss the girl.

In a rush of movement, a vampire appeared out of the shadows, pulled the girl away from the boy, and bent his head toward her neck. The terrified boy shouted, but didn't move. Lucette, stake in hand, leaped off the roof and landed with her weapon right against the vampire's back, touching its point just behind his heart, but not penetrating his skin.

The vampire let go of the girl and spun around, a horrified look on his pale face. "Don't kill me. Please. I wanted to know what human blood tasted like, but I couldn't go through with it."

Lucette kept her stake raised and aimed at the vampire. Only shock held her from plunging it into him. She hadn't expected the vampire to plead for his life. Her heart thumped in her chest and she could almost hear the vampire's heart thumping, too. The boy and girl ran off down the street, leaving Lucette alone with the vampire, realizing she could take this one down easily, if she chose to. He might be strong and fast, but he was also scared and didn't have the eyes of a killer.

"What are you doing in Xandra?" she asked.

"I-I . . ." he backed away from her. "I'm starving."

"Liar," she said. "There's blood in Sanguinia. The only reason you have for coming here is to feed off humans." Lucette raised her stake again, and backed the vampire toward the stone wall, keeping the point of the stake aimed at his heart. One strong thrust and he'd be gone.

He knew it, too, and fear filled his eyes. "I just got out of jail," he said. "I got caught sneaking onto a ranch and drinking from the livestock." He licked his lips. "I was hungry and couldn't afford to buy blood at the store."

"You have to pay for blood?" Lucette felt her arm relax, so she tensed it again. She couldn't lose her focus. He might be trying to trick her to gain advantage for his attack.

"Of course blood costs money." He looked confused. "Don't you pay for food?"

"But vampires are hunters, killers who thirst for human blood." At least according to what she'd learned from her training, not to mention her mother.

He shook his head. "Not me. I've never even tasted human blood." He looked down. "I-I couldn't bite that girl, even though it's legal now. I just couldn't. No matter how much money they offered me."

Lucette tensed. "Someone offered you money? Explain—if you want to live."

The vampire's already pale skin became even more white. "I'd been out of jail for a few days and hadn't eaten—not even a drop. A guy approached me and said I could make some easy money if I went to Xandra and drank from a human." He shivered as if the idea were repulsive. "Even more money if I drank the blood of the king, queen, or princess."

Lucette felt a chill shoot down her spine. "Who? Who's behind this?" She suspected it was the vampire queen, but needed proof.

"I-I don't know. The person was in disguise, behind a heavy mask." He clasped his hands together. "Please don't hurt me."

This vampire was clearly no killer, and Lucette's mind reeled with the implications of what he'd told her. What if other vampires roaming Xandra were like this one—just down on his luck and desperate for food? The slayers' policy was to kill first and ask questions later. Were they killing some vampires who didn't deserve it?

Worse, since she had been attacked in the tower, her father had broken off talks with the Sanguinian diplomats and was considering war. At first she'd supported the idea, especially since she knew her vampire-hating mother would too, but now she wasn't so sure. Her father could be making a big mistake if he chose to invade.

Fear for the future bit into her, but one thing was certain. Her father needed to know the truth. She turned to the vampire. "Listen, can you come with me? It would clear up a whole lot of misunderstandings if the king heard this firsthand."

"The king?" Terror flashed onto his face and he slid along the wall as if planning an escape, but Lucette stepped over to cut him off.

"What?" she asked. "Why are you scared?" She'd been sure he'd started to trust her.

He shook his head. "If your king is anything like our queen . . ."

"He's not. Trust me." This vampire clearly feared his monarch. No one feared her father. Did they? Lucette knew all about the cruelty of the horrible vampire queen, but it was way too dangerous to explain that to the vampire. She couldn't let him know who she was. He'd admitted he'd get paid extra for biting her, although it wasn't clear how he'd prove he'd done it.

The vampire looked down. "How do I know I can trust you? You're still pointing that stake at me."

"How do I know I can trust you?" she shot back. "You've still got fangs."

He grinned. "Good point."

Lucette laughed in spite of the tension—or perhaps because of it—and while dropping her stake to her side, she backed away. "Behave—and I won't hurt you, I promise. Assuming you promise the same."

"I promise, but I'm not sure I should go with you," he said warily. His hand trembled as he raised it to scratch his head.

The vampire glanced down at Lucette's stake, then back at her face, as if considering his options. He nodded. "Okay, let's go."

Lucette felt a tiny bit of hope. If her father could find out who was behind the vampire attacks, he might be able to end these hostilities. She gestured for the vampire to follow her down the street, but before they'd taken ten steps, three slayers landed around them, stakes drawn. Horrified, Lucette shouted, "No!" But it was too late. One of the slayers swept the vampire off his feet and another drove a stake into his heart.

She staggered back, not wanting to reveal herself to the other slayers and lose her anonymity. It was bad enough that she'd spoken—the slayers had heard her female voice.

"Got it!" one of the slayers said to the other. "Since I got the kill, you've got to dump his body over the border in the morning."

Lucette ran, hating that the slayers were so cavalier about killing. It was slayer policy to use the dead vampire bodies to send a message to others in Sanguinia to stay away. Clearly it wasn't working, but no one seemed to notice. She couldn't help but think that the slayed vampire corpses might have the opposite effect—inciting anger, rather than building a deterrent.

She didn't stop running until she was back at the palace. Legs burning, they crumpled under her, and she fell back against the outermost wall of the courtyard. Tears sparked in her eyes and she struck her stake against the stone wall. The sound cracked through the night.

She struck the wall again. That vampire's death had been her fault. If not for her, he'd have fled into the night and would be halfway to the border by now. Sobbing, she struck the wall again, and even with her glove on, the vibrations shot through her arm and up to her teeth.

Every time she tried to fix things, they only got worse.

Still shaken from seeing an innocent vampire killed right in front of her, Lucette stuck her stake under her pillow as she did every night. Her father wouldn't approve, but she never slept without some kind of weapon. She no longer believed that every vampire deserved death, but if some had been hired to bite her, she wasn't taking any chances. With any luck, brandishing her stake would be enough to frighten off any would-be finger-prickers or neck-biters.

She stared at her gloves. Many mornings, she woke with deep creases on her face from sleeping with her cheek on the leather seams, but it was worth it to stay safe. For years, her mother had let her sleep without gloves, and out of habit, she sometimes removed them in her sleep, but she'd kept them on all night for the past three weeks.

Moving over to her washbasin, she removed her gloves and carefully washed her hands and face. Staring at her reflection in the mirror, tears rose in her eyes and she swiped them away with the backs of her hands.

Slayers didn't cry. Especially not at the death of a vampire. But the one she'd met tonight hadn't deserved death, and she was sure that if he'd talked to her father, it would have helped. She couldn't tell her father what she'd learned without revealing that she'd been out on patrol.

She put her gloves back on, brushed and braided her hair, then climbed into bed. She double-checked that her stake was in position, even though she no longer felt sure she could use it. She tried to sleep, but instead tossed and turned, haunted by images of the vampire's violent and unnecessary death.

A huge vampire tore into Lucette's throat.

She gasped as she woke with a start, and reached under her pillow for her stake. Just a dream.

She sat and backed up against her headboard to assess any imminent danger. The gloves must have twisted in her sleep, because they were caught between her hand and the stake, pinching the skin on her finger. This wasn't the first time it had happened.

She listened to the darkness of her room. Something had woken her, but the room was quiet. After a few moments, her eyes focused in the dark, and she felt confident she was alone. She let out her breath and fought to slow her rapidly beating heart.

Calmer, she looked down at her hand, and her heart raced again. Her stake. She was holding her stake with a bare hand. One glove lay on the floor next to her bed. She'd removed it in her sleep, and that pinch she'd felt . . .

Panting, she dropped the stake and tried not to panic. Her stakes were all carefully sanded, not a rough spot on them, so it should be impossible for her to get a splinter, even without the added protection of the gloves. She closed her eyes tightly, trying not to think about the pinch, the pinch that had now turned into a sting. Which stake had she put under her pillow? The same one she'd banged on the stone wall in anger and grief? Had it cracked?

Not wanting to use her bare hand to light a candle, she walked to the curtains and used her other hand—still gloved—to pull them back. Moonlight streamed in and she slowly lifted her finger into the light.

A small sliver of wood stuck out of the end of her finger, surrounded by blood. A tiny drop fell to the floor—a small, dark blotch on the pale stone.

"No!"

She staggered back, hoping this was still part of a dream, that she was really still tucked into her bed, still wearing her gloves. Hoping she hadn't cracked one of her stakes. Hoping that cracked stake wasn't the one she'd tucked under her pillow.

Trembling, she stepped back to the window. This was no time to lack courage. As much as she wanted to get back into bed and pretend this hadn't happened, it had, and she had to see if the consequences were as disastrous as she imagined. She looked down into the courtyard. There was no movement, but that wasn't unusual for this time of night. She tried to spot something, even a shadow of a guard, but saw nothing.

She headed for her door, slowly opened it, and gasped. The royal guards and slayers assigned to her bedroom had all collapsed. She shook one and shouted, "Wake up!" She knelt beside another guard and turned his head around. "Wake up, please, wake up!" The guard did not move.

Lucette ran down the halls toward her father's bedroom, gasping for air. The guard in front of her father's door was collapsed on the floor, asleep. She pushed the sleeping guard aside to open her father's door and ran to his bedside. "Wake up, Dad! Please, wake up!" She shook him, but he slept soundly. She slumped to the carpet beside his bed in a heap and began sobbing.

It had happened. Everyone in the kingdom was asleep except her . . . and any vampires who might have escaped the slayers' stakes.

Creeping back to her bedroom, she kept alert to any sound or movement, but heard none. Never before had she heard the castle so silent. Typically, someone—one of the servants, a guard, a slayer—was moving about.

After retrieving a stake from her room, she returned to her father's bedside. As she watched her father in his sleep, guilt plowed through her at how she'd resented his attempts to keep this from happening. Her curse had been the thorn in her parents' relationship, and it hadn't helped that she'd almost always sided with her mother. Lucette stared at her pricked finger. She'd blown everything.

If every citizen of Xandra was sleeping, so too was her mother's entire household, nearly six hours away by carriage and completely vulnerable, with no one to protect them. Wiping away tears, Lucette walked to the end of her father's bed and readied herself to defend him from whatever might come in the night. She knew full well that not every vampire was as timid and well-meaning as the one she'd talked to earlier that evening. And even if she couldn't protect both her parents, given their different locations, tonight she would do her best to protect one.

The next night, Lucette bolted upright from her slumber. She spun her head around to find herself in her father's office, lying on a sofa in the middle of the room and dressed in a white lace gown she'd never have put on without a fight. Her hair was down and brushed out, the curls fluffy and soft.

But worse than being dressed in a way she'd never have agreed to, she realized she was not alone in the room. Her father was slumped over his desk, and six or seven of his advisers, plus several guards and slayers, lay about, having clearly fallen asleep on their feet.

One of the guards had bumped his head on the edge of a table and cut his forehead. A trickle of blood ran down his face, but his breathing was steady.

If they knew they were going to fall asleep when the sun set, why hadn't they prepared and gone to bed? She shook her head, realizing her father must have found her collapsed beside his bed this morning, a stake in her hand.

A stake. If she was the only one awake, she needed weapons She stepped over an adviser and knelt next to a sleeping slayer. She confiscated his quivers of arrows and stakes, but didn't see his crossbow anywhere. No matter, she'd find one.

Feeling slightly more secure, yet somewhat silly with her hair flowing and the leather straps of the quivers across her white gown, she stepped over to make sure her father wasn't hurt. Under his hand was a half-written note. They'd clearly mistimed the sunset—maybe because they had completely blocked all the windows in the room with large boards.

She carefully pulled out the note, and then chided herself for the care she'd taken to pull it away slowly and silently. It wasn't as if she could wake him.

His note told her he loved her, how devastated he was that he hadn't been able to prevent the curse from falling, and that her primary concern should be to keep herself safe and not worry about him or anyone else.

That was one request she couldn't fulfill, especially since she knew vampires were targeting her family. There was nothing she could do about her mother, but she would make sure her father's neck stayed unbitten.

His note also talked of a plan to ensure her safety, but that he needed one more day to prepare. She decided not to think about that part. Her father's last plan, that glass room in the tower, had been a monstrous disaster, but surely he'd learned from that mistake.

After cleaning the cut on the guard's head and bandaging it as best she could, Lucette opened the door to her father's office to peek into the hall. A mouse scurried across the floor and she jumped. Clearly the curse only affected the humans of the kingdom—not that the mice were likely to help her fight off vampires—but it was good to know.

She took out a stake and gripped it in her hand. The smooth wood felt good without gloves, more secure, more like a weapon. And now, well, who cared if she got a splinter? That damage was done.

Her first goal was to change into a more practical outfit, so she started down the hall toward her bedchamber. Halfway there, she heard a thump behind her. She stopped short and spun, stake raised.

A tall vampire with greasy, shaggy brown hair had leaped up to the corridor from the main hall below. He had blood on his chin.

"Excellent. Someone's awake." He licked his lips. "Drinking from sleeping creatures makes me drowsy. Your blood will be much perkier." He strode forward slowly and confidently.

The vampire nodded toward her stake, a smirk on his face. "Don't point that thing at me unless you know how to use it." His underestimation of her abilities rankled her, but she quickly realized that she could use it to her advantage.

She let her arm shake. "P-p-please, d-d-don't k-kill me."

He laughed, stepping forward and walking around her in a tight circle. "I don't want to kill you, I just want a little nibble. You've not been bitten before, have you?"

She shook her head, lowering her chin a little to look up with pouty eyes, but kept her gaze trained on him, snapping her head around as he moved. Maintaining a look of terror was not difficult.

"Don't worry, darling," he said. "The first bite never kills. Sometimes two can, if enough venom is transferred." He reached out one of his long fingers and trailed it along the side of her neck.

Lucette had had enough.

She leaped up and landed a kick squarely in the center of his chest. Her dress tore and the fabric streamed around her as she spun to plant another kick to his head before he recovered.

In a blink, he landed on the other side of her, and caught the fabric of her dress, pulling her close.

"My goodness," he said. "You *are* a surprise. I imagine your blood will be even tastier than I expected. Sweet, yes, but it seems you might be a little spicy, too." His breath heated her neck as he held her stake arm tightly behind her back. However, the vampire left Lucette's other arm free, so she transferred the stake to that hand.

"Oh, please, no!" She tried to sound even more scared than she was as she raised her stake and slammed it into him from behind, careful to pull it back out.

The vampire staggered back. Lucette hadn't had enough leverage to plunge the stake deep enough to kill. It would take a second strike.

His expression darkened. "Now, that wasn't very nice." He reached around to try to cover the wound in his back.

Even injured, the vampire was bigger and stronger and faster than she, and Lucette wasn't confident she could take him down. Her only advantage was that he didn't seem to be a trained fighter.

"Why are you here?" she asked, backing away and glancing over her shoulder to see if there was a sleeping slayer nearby who might have anything she could use as a weapon.

"Thirsty," he said, tracing his tongue over his fangs.

"I thought vampires didn't drink human blood."

He shrugged. "I have a vice. Sue me." He was keeping his distance, as if unsure of his odds against her. He narrowed his eyes and the yellow flecks flared. "Plus, I'm getting paid."

"Leave and I won't kill you," she said.

"Try, and I'll rip your throat out."

Enough of this. She'd wasted too much time and energy on this vampire. Others might be attacking people all over the kingdom. It was time to take him down, but after her first experience killing a vampire, she wasn't sure she could kill again. Not unless her life, or that of someone she loved, was directly in danger. She leaped and planted the stake in his shoulder.

He dove for her neck, flaring his fangs, but she dodged to the side and he struck his head on the wall beside her. He slumped down, rubbing his head and bleeding onto the floor from that wound and the two she'd inflicted. Vampires could heal quickly, but it would certainly take him hours to fully recover.

While he was down, she tore strips off her ripped dress and used the fabric to tightly bind his arms behind his back, then his legs.

"Hey, what are you doing?" he slurred.

"What does it look like?" she answered. "Consider yourself under arrest for trespassing."

He moaned as she tipped him onto his front and tore another strip of fabric to join his bound arms and legs together. Notwithstanding his vampire strength, his confinement—combined with his wounds—would keep him from inflicting any further damage for a while.

She wasn't sure what she'd do with him when he broke his bonds, and she secretly hoped he'd find a way to escape. If he were found in the morning, he'd be staked by a slayer, if sunlight from one of the windows didn't get to him first.

Satisfied that he was secure, she changed into her slayer uniform, hidden in a secret compartment in her wardrobe, and raced back to her father's office. The palace seemed vampire-free, except for her bound catch slumped over in the hall, so she approached her father and placed a kiss on his forehead. Taking his pad of paper and a quill pen, she wrote him a quick note.

Dear Dad,
Don't worry about me. I'm okay, and know how to protect myself. Keep yourself and everyone else in the kingdom safe. Please, don't stay out in the open at night. Barricade yourselves in your bedrooms and block the windows. I'll guard the halls.

Love,
Lucette

P.S. Please ask Mom to come back. I'll feel better knowing you're at least both under one roof.

She felt torn about that last request, but if the vampires were targeting her family, it wouldn't be long before they found the queen at the estate in the country.

Lucette reread her note, sealed it, and then, after locking her father's door, she left to make sure the corridors were empty.

Hours later, Lucette had patrolled the palace and found most doors blocked by furniture and most windows covered by boards. But more than one of the barricades appeared breached. So much for hoping the rest of the night would stay quiet. Apparently her bound friend upstairs wouldn't be the only vampire she'd encounter on her first full night alone.

A window smashed upstairs.

Lucette's heart raced. If she couldn't bring herself to kill one vampire, what was she going to do surrounded by many? From the sounds of it, she'd find out the answer to that question very soon.

Hiding felt cowardly, and she felt bad for the guards and slayers in the halls—she hadn't been able to drag them all into hiding spots before this ruckus started—but now she needed to save herself.

Should she head up or down? Hearing another crash upstairs, she chose down and raced to the stairs at the back of the palace, which led to the maze of corridors and storage rooms in the cellar. Because of her sheltered upbringing, she'd rarely been down there.

She heard the thump of footsteps upstairs. More vampires had broken in, and she had at least four hours before sunrise.

In the first room, she found bins of potatoes, carrots, turnips, and other root vegetables, but nowhere to hide. No place where she felt confident she couldn't be found.

Voices shouted upstairs, and it sounded like chaos up there. How many of the exposed palace staff were being bitten right now? She shivered.

She checked the next room. It was incredibly dark and she blinked her eyes to see. In the far corner was a steel box, the size of a storage space. She lifted its hinged lid and her hopes lifted, too.

Coal.

She could dig herself down into the coal and, as a bonus, it might mask her scent. The voices and footsteps drew nearer. At least one vampire had decided to check the basement.

She climbed into the coal bin, carefully shut the lid, and buried herself as deep as she could. Dust clogged her lungs and stung her eyes, but she choked back the urge to cough or sneeze. She didn't move. It might take three vampire bites to die, but she didn't want to risk even one. And it sounded like there were many more than three bloodsucking monsters in the palace.

As much as she hoped the vampires wouldn't find her, she really hoped someone else would in the morning. The thought of waking in here tomorrow night, after sleeping in coal for a whole day, was too horrible to imagine.

The next night, Lucette's eyes snapped open. She wasn't in the coal bin, but the air around her felt tight and stale. Wherever she was, it was dark. She tried to sit, but her head struck something hard before she was fully upright. She explored with her hands and, as her eyes adjusted to the dim light, she started to make out shapes through the hard, cold surface enclosing her. Whatever surrounded her was transparent. Realization struck her—she was in a glass box.

Exploring its surface, she found a few small holes, then ran her hands down her body and discovered she was dressed in another frilly gown. Her hair was loose. She touched her lips; they were sticky. Lipstick.

She realized that not only was she now trapped in a glass box, she might have been lying there all day, too. A horrible thought flashed through her mind: if she'd been lying there all day, dressed up, had anyone been watching her sleep? It almost felt as if she'd been on display. She shuddered.

Lucette kept feeling around her until her left hand struck what felt like a button. She pressed it and gas lights sparked to life. When she saw where she was, her breaths became shallow as if huge weights were crushing down on her. She was back up in the tower.

Past her feet, she could see the cell where her father had trapped her on her birthday. The glass box she lay in was outside the glass cell and directly against it perpendicularly. And this near-coffin was most likely made of enchanted, unbreakable fairy glass.

So, this was the plan her father had mentioned in his note last night. She was trapped in a coffin of unbreakable glass, barely able to move. Even for her father, this was over the top. Lucette fought to control her panic, as the air suddenly felt even thicker and heavier than it had in the coal bin.

This was crazy. Even if the enchanted glass kept her safe from vampires, was she expected to go through her nights without moving? Without walking around? Without even sitting up? And how would she protect everyone else?

She pounded on the inside of the glass, her heart racing. Then she heard a sound behind her and instantly regretted making so much noise. Craning her neck, she saw light reflecting off the stone wall at the top of the staircase. Someone was coming.

Will Lucette survive the night?

To find out, turn to section 6: In the Dark (page 183).

Section 5

Country Living

5

"Thanks for agreeing to stay until after my birthday party." Lucette hugged her mother. Her father had looked so wounded when she'd decided to live with her mother, but he had kept to his word to let her choose. She and her mother were leaving for the country the day after her sixteenth birthday. The day after tomorrow.

"Get a good night's sleep." Her mother planted a kiss on her forehead. "Tomorrow's a big day!"

Lucette tried not to shiver under her warm covers. Beginning tomorrow, wearing gloves would no longer be merely an annoying rule her father tried to enforce. Starting tomorrow, if she pricked her finger, the curse would fall, and it was her duty to ensure that didn't happen.

Starting tomorrow, she'd follow every rule.

"Wake up!" Her mother's voice pulled Lucette from a deep sleep, one during which she'd been dreaming Tristan had come to her birthday party to declare his undying love. Unfortunately, the vampire queen had arrived too, claiming to have a special gift for the birthday girl and baring her fangs. Just before Lucette woke, Tristan had been poised to drive a stake through the vampire queen's heart, and she wished she'd stayed asleep long enough to see that, even if it was just a dream.

"What is it?" she asked her mother in the darkness. Lucette rubbed the sleep from her eyes and realized she'd pulled her gloves off in her sleep, yet again. She put them back on, looking up to the door to make sure her father hadn't followed her mother into the room. He'd be so angry if he saw her hands unprotected.

"We're leaving," her mother whispered. "Now."

"Leaving? Where to?" Excitement raced through her. Was this some kind of birthday surprise?

"To your grandfather's." Her mother backed away from the bed, turned on the lights, and started rummaging through Lucette's wardrobe, even though most of her clothes were already packed in a trunk.

Lucette's back stiffened. "Leaving? Right now? But Mom, we haven't even had my birthday party yet and it's the middle of the night." She wondered if her parents had gotten into another argument.

Her mother pulled a dress from the wardrobe and clutched it to her chest. "Lucette, I discovered something." Her mother's hands trembled as she helped her out of bed and handed her the dress. "Something horrible. Something for which I'll never forgive your father."

"Mom, calm down. We can't leave in the middle of the night." Plus, it was her birthday and no way would she leave without saying goodbye to her father. He'd be crushed.

Her mother tried to force the dress over Lucette's head, but there was no way Lucette would let herself be dressed like a doll.

"Put on the dress, Lucette. Quickly. And if you promise to be very quiet, I'll show you what I found. When you see what he's done, you'll understand."

Lucette dressed and, a few minutes later, found herself on a winding stone staircase hidden behind a seamless door off the palace's main entrance hall. Lucette had walked through that hallway countless times and had never imagined there was a door there. So many secrets in her own home.

Her mother held a candle, but given the narrow space, the light was mostly blocked by her body, so Lucette held on to her mother's skirt as they wound their way up.

When they reached the top, her mother gestured widely with her arm. "See?"

"See what?" Lucette blinked. It didn't look like much. A small, square room with a wall of glass down the middle.

Her mother pushed a button and gaslights came on to reveal a bedchamber on the far side of the glass. On the near side were a few chairs and some party decorations. Pink and white ribbons were strung in garlands around the room, and a big sign read "Happy Sixteenth, Lucette!"

"We're having my birthday party up here?" It was kind of small, even if her parents hadn't invited any guests.

Her mother slipped her hand into Lucette's. "Your father plans to lock you in there." She pointed toward the glass room.

Her head snapped toward her mother. "What? For my party?"

"No." Her mother had never looked more fierce or angry. "Forever." She pulled Lucette over to the glass and slammed her palm against it. "He means for you to live behind this glass from now on. Alone."

Lucette felt as if her lungs had collapsed, and she struggled to refill them with air. "W-what?" She scanned the small space that contained only one small window high on the stone wall, covered with bars. It was a cell.

"This is his idea of keeping you safe," her mother continued. "He showed it to me earlier this evening, thinking I'd change my mind about taking you with me." She shook her head. "He actually thought I'd be pleased that he'd found a way to keep you from pricking your finger, and that I'd talk you into changing your mind about where you wanted to live."

"But . . ." Lucette's mind swam in what felt like thick soup. "Vampires can easily break glass. So can I. And what if the glass broke and I pricked my finger on a shard?" None of this made any sense.

"Remember when the fairies said they'd made a deal with your father and couldn't help us anymore?"

She nodded.

"Well, *this* was the deal. The glass is enchanted. It won't break. Ever." Her mother's lips squeezed together so tightly her jaw trembled. "Because of this glass, the fairies won't help you after the curse falls. Your father chose preventing the curse over you getting help from the fairies once you're all alone."

A chill that had nothing to do with the night air filled the room, and Lucette hugged herself tightly. She knew her father had done what he thought was best. She knew he thought preventing the curse was more important than any other consideration, including her freedom. But she would not be trapped inside this cage.

"Let's get out of here," her mother said, and Lucette readily agreed.

Lucette slumped against the window of the carriage, angry tears streaming down her face in the moonlight. Her mother reached over to rub her back, but Lucette pulled away. Even though it wasn't her mother's fault, she was hurt and angry, and didn't want to be comforted. Her entire body felt as if it had collapsed in on her. Spikes of pain pinched at her throat and eyes.

"Lucette, darling, I might not agree with him all the time, but your father means well. He loves you and only wants to keep you safe."

Lucette spun so sharply that her mother snapped back in her seat. "Locking me in a cell of enchanted glass? *That's* how he shows love?" Her heart was beating wildly, galloping to match the hooves of the horses pulling their carriage through the night, away from her father, maybe forever. Never again would she question whether she'd made the right choice to go live with her mother. Her chest lurched as she sucked in a few sharp, sobbing breaths.

Her mother stroked her hair. "You'll be happy in the country, I promise."

"Are there really no vampires there?" Lucette wiped away her tears. "I know the mountains are in between, but aren't you just as close to the border there as we are at home?" The only section of the border between Sanguinia and Xandra that wasn't mountainous and treacherous to cross was just ten miles from the palace.

The carriage bounced over a rut in the road and her mother gripped the seat. "I can't say *no* vampires. My father and his farmhands sometimes found bite marks on our livestock." She shuddered and her eyes narrowed.

"Vampires killed your animals?" That would contradict what that vampire boy Alex had told her.

Her mother pulled back a little. "I don't think any of our animals ever died, now that you mention it, but some were certainly bitten."

That was horrid, but it didn't explain why her mother hated vampires so much. "Have you ever met a vampire, Mom?"

"Not until I married your father and met his so-called ally, the vampire king"—her face turned steely—"and his despicable queen who cursed you."

No wonder her mother hated vampires so much. Her entire vampire experience was based on animal bites—it was so cruel to attack defenseless creatures—and on the villain who'd cursed her daughter.

Her mother stiffened and raised her chin. "Why are we even talking about this? Who wouldn't hate vampires? They drink blood. They're murderers. They kill."

Lucette corrected her and said, "Only after three bites."

Her mother shrugged. "Whether it takes one bite or three, murder is murder. Evil is evil." Her mother clearly considered the words "evil" and "murderer" to be synonyms for "vampire."

But Lucette wasn't sure she agreed, and wanted to tell her mother that ever since she'd met that vampire boy in the woods, she'd believed her father was right about vampires—they weren't all evil, perhaps most weren't—but her mother wouldn't be easily convinced. "How are you so sure they're all bad, Mom? I mean, Dad's the one who's spent time with vampires on official court business."

Fire rose on her mother's cheeks. "Your father is so blinded by diplomacy and political correctness, he can't see what's right in front of his face. Ever since you were a baby, those creatures have been attacking Xandrans, yet he still believes their diplomats' lies, and still believes he can stop the attacks by talking peacefully with their so-called government officials."

Lucette's eyes narrowed. Even at the slayer school, where the teachers agreed vampires were killers and taught the students to slay them, they'd also taught that the Sanguinian form of government was more advanced than their own, with less power lying in the hands of the monarch and more in their citizenry. But her mother was so anti-vampire, Lucette wished she'd never brought up the subject. It just reminded her of why her parents fought so much.

Her mother squeezed her hand. "I'm so glad I managed to at least get you some slayer training before you turned sixteen. From the day the curse was laid, I wanted you to be prepared to defend yourself—prepared to kill."

They rode through the night, and after the cold, bouncy carriage ride, Lucette's grandmother's embrace was like a warm blanket. She inhaled the small woman's scent: cinnamon and cut grass and a hint of something else Lucette couldn't quite pinpoint. Perhaps it was home.

She broke away from her grandmother and her grandfather stepped forward, spreading his long arms wide. "Sixteen," he said. "Happy birthday, Lucette. Come, give old Gramps a hug."

She ran into his arms, which were so warm and strong. With his hands firmly on her shoulders, he pushed her back to arms' length. "Let me look at you."

Slightly embarrassed, she felt glad this examination gave her an opportunity to look at him, too. "Old Gramps" was a stretch. She didn't know how old her grandparents were, but he really didn't look that many years older than her father. She knew there was an age difference between her parents, but until this moment, she hadn't realized it was such a big one.

Her grandfather's shoulders were broad and strong, but he was thicker and more solid than her father, plus an entirely different kind of handsome—more rugged and less regal. Under his red hair, which could have used a trim, was a tanned face with a square jaw. A fine layer of lightly colored stubble sprang out from this chin so sharply that Lucette was afraid to touch it in case the hairs were sharp enough to prick her finger. She brushed away the silly thought—after all, she was wearing gloves.

Lucette's mother clearly took after her own mother rather than her tall, red-haired father. And since Lucette took after her own father, she had trouble believing she fit into her mother's family at all.

"I think the occasion calls for birthday cake," he said, and then looked over her shoulder and winked at her grandmother.

"For breakfast?" her grandmother said. "They've been traveling all night. Perhaps Lucette and Catia would like to nap first, or clean up from the road."

Her grandfather ran his strong arm along the back of Lucette's shoulders. "Sleep? On your sixteenth birthday?" He nudged her with his hip. "I vote for cake. How about you?"

A huge grin spread on her face. "I slept a bit in the carriage. Cake sounds great!"

A few hours later, after three slices of birthday cake, a tour of the barn, and a drive over the vast, hilly property on the front bench of an open, horse-drawn cart, Lucette walked around the house, happiness flooding through her. Her grandparents had assured her mother that they'd sanded down every surface on the estate, and had even done their best to remove anything liable to prick Lucette in the barn. Wearing her gloves, Lucette felt safe and comfortable.

As badly as she wished her parents would reconsider their separation, she did think she was going to prefer living out here in the country to living at the palace. The air was so clean and fresh—well, maybe not so fresh in the barn—and in one day here, she'd enjoyed more freedom than she had in her whole life at the palace.

Lucette tested an overstuffed chair in front of the fireplace and her grandmother's cinnamon scent filled the air. She inhaled deeply, then studied the painting above the mantle, trying to figure out why it seemed so strange. It was a portrait of her mother, perhaps at twelve or thirteen, but something seemed lopsided—the painted fabric, draped to the right of her mother's image, hung in an unnatural manner. Perhaps the artist had been having a bad day.

Lucette looked at another portrait, which showed her mother on horseback with a taller horse beside her. Something was off about that painting, too. The coat of the riderless horse and the mountains behind it seemed unevenly painted. Lucette leaned closer, shrugged, and then turned back to the picture over the mantle.

She gasped and then examined the horse painting more closely again. Yes, she was certain. In both of these portraits, someone else had been erased—painted over as if he or she had never been there. Her father once mentioned an aunt who'd died, but he'd been so reluctant to discuss her that Lucette just assumed it had been *his* sister, not her mother's. Was it possible her mother had once had a sister? And if she'd died, why would they have painted her out of all of the portraits?

She ran to the kitchen where her grandmother was stirring a big pot on the wood-burning stove. "Grandma, who's painted out of those portraits? Did I once have an aunt?" As soon as she asked the question, she realized it might not have been very sensitive. If her daughter had died, her grandmother would be sad.

Her grandmother spun toward her, eyes wide, but then they slowly narrowed. Her expression darkened as if a cloud had passed directly overhead. "She's gone. We do not talk about her—ever."

Lucette was startled by her grandmother's reaction. Perhaps she'd ask her mother. But she'd have to find the right time. Clearly this was a touchy subject.

Hours later, Lucette yawned and stretched. "Oh, excuse me."

"Nothing to be excused." Her grandmother reached across the kitchen table where they'd eaten dinner—imagine, eating right in the kitchen!—and squeezed her gloved hand. "You must be very tired, and the sun is setting. Out here in the country, bedtime's never long past sundown."

Lucette smiled, grateful that no one was offended by her dinner-table yawn, but she stiffened at the thought of sunset. She turned to her mother. "We left in such a hurry, I didn't bring any stakes or a crossbow or anything."

Her grandparents didn't look shocked, so Lucette assumed her mother had told them about her slayer training. Her grandmother stood and started to clear the plates from the table. Much to Lucette's surprise, her mother helped.

"You won't be needing weapons up here, Lucette," her grandfather said. "Those vicious creatures are smart enough to stay away from my property. I'll keep all of you safe."

Her grandmother pressed her lips together.

"All the same, Gramps," Lucette said, "I would feel better if I had some weapons." She turned to her mother. "Can we send back for them?"

"Nonsense," her grandfather said. "In the country, a shortage of wood is one thing we don't suffer. Tomorrow morning, I'll make you some stakes."

Lucette smiled, and her eyes soon drifted shut as she relaxed in her chair. The sun hadn't even gone down, but with last night's travel and the excitement of meeting her grandparents and touring their estate, exhaustion was winning.

"May I please be excused?" she asked her grandmother.

"Of course, darling," her grandmother replied. "And no need to be so formal here. You're sixteen, practically a grown-up. You've earned the right to excuse yourself from the table."

Lucette drew a deep breath of nighttime country air. After two weeks at her grandparents' house, she found the freedom of country living exhilarating, and although she missed her father and sent him letters nearly every day, she loved being here. Strolling along the dirt path to the barn, she looked up to take in the stars filling the sky above the distant mountains. They shone so much brighter away from the gaslights and candles in the village that surrounded the palace.

Startled by a noise, she pulled a stake from her quiver and quickly spun toward the sound. A rabbit darted across the path.

She shook her head and stifled a laugh. *Killer bunnies. How scary.* Now that she was living in the relative safety of the country, she needed to learn how to relax. She stashed her stake.

Her mother and grandparents had fallen asleep two hours ago, but Lucette loved taking these short walks at night and saying good night to the barn animals. The only way she'd ever been able to walk alone back at the palace had involved sneaking around, trickery, and often climbing down a rope from her bedroom window. She liked the barn after dark, when the animals were quiet and the only light came from the moonbeams that streamed in between the wooden slats. Besides, if the worst happened and her nights *all* became solitary, wouldn't it be better if she got used to it first?

Lucette pulled the barn door open and followed the moonlight inside. A few pregnant sheep waddled over to their pen's fence, and she reached through the carefully sanded wooden slats to pat their woolly coats. When one nuzzled her hand, she felt a strong urge to pull off her glove to feel its wool, but stopped herself. Whether it was sanded or not, she wasn't so reckless as to put her bare fingers near wood.

Thunder, her grandfather's favorite stallion, neighed, and Lucette left the sheep to see what had upset him. Probably a mouse scurrying through the stall, or maybe the horse was jealous she'd been paying so much attention to the sheep. She smirked. That wasn't likely. In the two weeks she'd been here, Thunder had barely let her get near him, even after her grandfather gave her sugar cubes to tempt him. She'd tried a few times and could only assume the horse was put off by her gloved hands, because he would never accept her sweet gifts.

She stepped in front of Thunder's stall and he reared up, his hooves rising high. Then he walked forward and put his head over the top slat of the gate.

"Thunder," she said softly, "what's wrong?" She spotted the box of sugar cubes and, determined to win the horse's favor, she pulled off her right glove and tucked it into the waistband of her slacks. She could be careful.

The cool night air felt good on her hand, and taking three sugar cubes, she placed them in her bare palm and held the cubes out to Thunder. But he twisted and kicked and backed up, as if he didn't even notice her offering. *Stubborn horse.* She'd seen him gobble sugar from her grandfather's hand.

Weighing the danger, she used her gloved hand to open his gate. The risk of Thunder barging out of his stall and trampling her seemed lower than the risk of sliding her bare hand between two slats of wood, and she hoped that the closer she got to Thunder, the more she showed that she trusted him, the better the chances that he'd trust her back.

Thunder pawed the straw on the barn floor, then slowly clopped closer. Her heart thumped as he nudged his nose and mouth into her hand and gobbled up the sugar. His hot, moist breath tickled her palm and the thrill sent little chills racing through her. With a shock she realized that she'd almost never felt another's touch—human or animal—on her bare hand.

Thunder raised his head sharply and kicked behind him.

Startled, Lucette grabbed the stall door—with her right hand!

As she checked her fingers for splinters, her heart raced even faster and harder than Thunder's hooves when he galloped across an open field, but after finding her fingers prick-free, she replaced her glove, the soft leather suddenly comforting. Thunder kicked again, so she slowly stepped forward, hoping to calm him.

Then she spotted the problem.

A vampire. Thunder reared on his hind legs, and the vampire eyed her from the back wall of the stall. Her heart raced and she pulled out a stake.

The vampire licked his fangs and snarled. "I was planning on horse blood for breakfast, but you will do."

Thunder kicked again, and the vampire ducked to the side, protecting his head with his arms. Lucette marveled that such a strong, vicious creature felt threatened by a horse. Couldn't he take Thunder down if he wanted to? She felt sure that he could, and it was up to her to protect the horse, to protect herself.

"Get out of here!" she shouted.

The vampire bared his fangs. "Not before eating. I'm starved. Now, scat before I change my mind about horse and choose girl."

His words were threatening, but something in his voice sounded less so. But Lucette couldn't be certain and didn't plan to die.

Feeling a rush from the danger, she gripped her stake tightly, every muscle in her body ready for battle. Nearly three years of training and she was finally face-to-face with her first vampire, alone. But right now, getting around Thunder seemed a much bigger obstacle than staking her enemy.

As she advanced down the side of the stall, the vampire kept Thunder between them as he moved along the back of the stall and then started up the other side. "Get lost, or I'll bite you," he said menacingly.

"You're the one trespassing," Lucette said. "Come near me and you'll die."

"Murder?" The vampire looked startled. "That's a bit extreme."

Lucette narrowed her eyes. "You threatened me first."

"Not with death," the vampire said. "I'm just hungry. I haven't eaten for three days."

"That's not my problem." She shivered. "And no excuse to bite me."

The vampire shook his head. "If I wanted human blood I would've headed for the house, not the barn, don't you think?" He moved toward Thunder, licking his lips. "Now let me eat."

"Leave Thunder alone." She drew back her stake. "If you don't want human blood, then go back across the mountains and get your blood in Sanguinia." She didn't fully believe his claims and, as the only one awake, she had to defend her family, these animals, and herself.

"I'd eat at home if I could." He looked down, ashamed. "I lost my job. And when the queen came into power, she canceled the blood stamps program, so I have no money to eat. The farm animals in Sanguinia are guarded at night, and if I get caught stealing blood there, I'll end up in jail. A friend told me if I crossed the mountains it'd be easy to get a free meal in Xandra."

"You cruel, cruel thing, killing defenseless animals."

"I don't *kill* them." The vampire looked genuinely offended. "Why would I kill my food source?" He leaned back against the stall's wall. "If you want cruel, talk to the vampires who drink human blood."

"How do I know you're not one?"

He made a face. "No self-respecting vampire bites humans. I've never even tasted human blood, but"—he leaned forward and flicked his tongue on his fang—"if you don't leave me alone, I might try a taste."

A shiver traced through her, but she refused to show fear. She'd trained to kill vampires, to defend her kingdom, and she wasn't going to back down. "You're lying," she said. "Vampires do drink human blood. Innocent people in my kingdom are attacked every night."

He shrugged. "There's money in drinking Xandran blood. Especially around the palace."

Lucette gasped. "If you want to live, you'd better explain."

"Not unless you lower your stake."

"Not a chance." She raised her stake even higher and she struck her strongest fighting stance.

"Okay, okay." He held up his hands. "Someone in Sanguinia is paying vampires to attack Xandrans, especially around the palace. They pay extra if you prove you've taken blood from a member of the royal family."

Startled, Lucette accidentally banged the back end of her stake against the wall behind her, and Thunder reared up.

Fear raced through her. Her family was in danger—big danger. This vampire claimed he didn't plan to bite her, but he had no idea she was the princess. He'd admitted he needed money. This was not the time to show weakness, so to quell her trembling she gripped her stake harder.

To cleanse the fear from her voice, she drew a deep breath before speaking. "How would vampires prove they've fed from the royal family?"

"They bring back a blood sample. Whoever's behind this knows the royals' scents."

It was the vampire queen. It had to be. Anyone who would curse a small baby must be insane with anger and hatred. And for some unknown reason, all that malice was targeted at her, at her parents. As if the curse weren't enough. The vampire queen wanted to see her dead, too.

Suddenly, Lucette felt sick and she bent over, sucking in air, trying to regain her composure, but the smell of horse urine rose up from the straw and sent her into another round of nausea.

Thunder whinnied, and she straightened. But she was too late. The starving vampire had taken advantage of her distraction and attached itself to the vein in Thunder's neck. Without thinking, she stepped onto an upturned bucket, vaulted over Thunder, and brought her stake down into the vampire's back.

The vampire slumped to the floor. She kept her stake raised in case her first strike hadn't hit the vampire's heart. No chance was this creature going to do any more damage on her grandfather's estate.

From the barn floor, the vampire shrieked and looked up at her with terror in its eyes. Its body shook violently and its eyes turned back in its head. After a few horrifying seconds, it was dead.

Lucette's entire body shook. What had she done? Yes, this vampire had threatened to bite her, had bitten her grandfather's favorite horse, but did that mean it had deserved to die? Had the creature been telling the truth when it claimed it hadn't ever tasted human blood?

She'd never know the answer because she'd killed it.

She'd killed *him*. She'd killed a living, breathing creature.

Lucette backed up a few steps and collapsed onto the straw-covered floor. Somehow taking a vampire's life hadn't yielded the rush of pride she'd always assumed it would. And now, unsure she could ever kill a vampire again, she knew for certain that her family was in grave danger.

When Lucette's grandfather came in from burying the vampire, his hair was damp from rinsing himself under the garden pump. Arms crossed, he stood on the other side of the kitchen table. Lucette pulled her feet up onto the chair and hugged her knees. After the danger she'd faced and the horror of taking the vampire's life, she could deal with whatever scolding she now faced.

Her grandfather spread his large hands on the table. "You should have woken me, Lucette. You should not have taken on that monster by yourself."

Lucette bit her lip. She'd been thinking the exact same thing, but coming out of her grandfather's mouth, the words sounded patronizing, so she straightened her back and squared her shoulders. "I've trained as a slayer. Have you?"

Her grandfather's face remained calm, but his eyebrows drew closer together. "Young lady, princess or not"—his voice was deep and low—"you will not talk back to me. Not while you are living in my house."

Lucette dropped her feet to the floor and her cheeks burned. "I'm sorry." She kept her eyes on the blue and white checks of the tablecloth. Everything about this place had seemed a paradise, and now it was ruined. Ruined by her. Ruined by that vampire. Ruined by the stink of his death.

Her grandfather pulled out a chair and its legs scraped along the stone floor. He sat opposite her. "Sweetheart, even with your training, going outside alone at night was reckless. You might have been bitten or killed."

"I thought you said you didn't get vampires out here."

"Not ones who go after humans," he said. "There's never been a human vampire bite in these parts." He drew a deep breath. "Foolish as it was, what you did was also brave." He pressed his big hands into his knees and leaned forward. "I thank you, and Thunder thanks you, too."

She kept her eyes down. "I don't think he drank much of Thunder's blood, but some venom will have been transferred." Her head snapped up. "Has he been bitten before?"

Her grandfather ran his fingers through his red hair, and a few gray strands sparkled in the early morning light. "No—thankfully. One small mercy is the vampires who attack my animals don't seem intelligent enough to strike the same animals three times."

"Or," Lucette interrupted, "they're intelligent enough not to kill their food source."

"Hogwash." Her grandfather frowned. "Has that father of yours been filling you with his ridiculously liberal ideas about vampires?"

Lucette realized where some of her mother's misconceptions about vampires had come from. She wasn't sure of everything, but she did know vampires weren't dumb creatures. "Gramps, I believe vampires have as much intelligence as we do. In fact, the first time I met one, I mistook him for human."

Her grandfather stood sharply and his chair skidded back on the floor. "You've been cavorting with vampires?"

"Cavorting?" Lucette wasn't even sure she knew what that meant.

His expression darkened. "I should have insisted that Catia bring you here years ago. With all the trouble he caused in this family, I knew Stefan was not a man who could be trusted to keep his family safe—king or not."

Anxiety crept through Lucette. As if causing fights between her parents weren't bad enough, now she was throwing fuel on some feud between Gramps and her father, too. No wonder she hadn't spent much time with her grandparents before now. Still, she felt an overpowering need to defend her father.

"My father has done a lot to keep me safe. You have no idea. If he'd had his way, I'd have never trained with a slayer or met a vampire. I disobeyed him, lied to him. He's very protective and knows how to keep his family safe."

Her grandfather grunted. "Knows how to pit family members against each other is more like it."

Lucette wanted to ask what he meant, but her mother entered the room.

"Isn't it a beautiful morning?" She smiled and stretched. "Lucette, I didn't even hear you get up." She bent over to kiss her head. "Did you sleep well, darling?"

Sunlight streamed down over Lucette, heating her skin. She sat on a big rock in of one of her grandfather's fields and her eyes filled with tears as she reread the latest letter from her father. He was no longer begging her to change her mind and come home. In fact, he said he was glad she was away from the palace. The nightly vampire attacks had increased and intensified.

More and more, she believed what that vampire in the barn had said was true. He'd had no reason to lie. *He.* She shook her head at how she now humanized these creatures. Since that night, she could no longer think of a vampire as an "it." From what she'd seen, vampires were living, breathing, intelligent creatures, and she'd taken a life—*his* life. She'd done it to protect Thunder, but still, it hadn't seemed right. Clearly, she was not cut out to be a real slayer.

She folded the letter and slipped it into the pocket of her loose-fitting slacks. One bonus of living in the country was that no one seemed to mind if she dressed how she wanted, so she chose to dress like the farmhands, keeping her hair in a tight braid. She'd received a few winks and smiles from some of the men who worked on the estate, but even though her mother knew true love might prevent or end the curse, Catia seemed to consider all the men living here unworthy of Lucette. No wonder her mother hadn't married a local boy.

The thought made Lucette realize she'd never heard the story of how her parents met. Tonight she'd ask her mother, and see if maybe she would be more willing to talk about her late sister than her grandmother had been. Right now, Lucette planned to take a long walk up to the hills and visit the shepherds guarding the grazing sheep. She'd been here nearly a month now, and it was time to make friends.

Her breathing grew heavier as she got higher into the hills, and she inhaled deeply the scents of the grasses and wildflowers that grew in the fields. Her grandfather had shown her drawings and pressed versions of every species that had prickles. He'd done his best to remove them all from the property, but as he'd told her, it was impossible to rid the countryside of every raspberry, every thistle, every wild rosebush.

Reaching the top of a hill, Lucette stretched her gloved hands up to the bright blue sky. Not even the horror of killing that vampire, or the reports of attacks in her father's letter, could dampen her fabulous mood on a day like today. She shielded her eyes with her hand and spotted the flock down in the valley, where some of the sheep were drinking from the creek. The shepherds sat atop the hill opposite her, and she waved, but they clearly didn't see her because they didn't wave back.

Filled with fresh air, sunshine, and joy, she started down the hill, then had a wild idea to roll down it. As long as she made sure her gloves were on tightly, what could it hurt? Excitement coursed through her as she stopped and sat on the grass. It might be slightly reckless, but really, what could happen? She tugged on her gloves and tightened the ties that kept them snug around her wrists, then she turned to the side, stretched out, and let herself roll.

"Whee!" The grass rushed past her with each revolution. She bumped her knee on a rock, then another dug into her back, but as long as her fingers remained prick-free, a few small bruises would be worth it for this exhilarating fun.

Slowing near the bottom, she stuck out her arms and legs to stop herself and then sprang to her feet. "That was fabulous!" she yelled at the top of her lungs. The sheep scattered at the startling sound of her voice. Looking up, she saw that the shepherds had spotted her now. She waved at them, and one waved back.

A lamb wandered toward her on wobbly legs, so she crouched down and reached toward it. Another sheep bent to grab a mouthful of grass, and Lucette realized that food might be a good way to lure the lamb. She pulled a handful of grass and clover and held it out for the animal.

She remained patient, and soon the lamb was in front of her, munching. Feeling a smile spread through her entire body, Lucette looked into the lamb's eyes and stroked its wool. Maybe killing that vampire had been justified if she'd protected this sweet animal from bites.

She bent down and buried her nose in the lamb's wool—it was so soft—and another overwhelming desire took hold. She wanted to touch the wool—just once, just for a second—without her gloves. Just for a moment, she wanted to trace her fingers through the wool and pretend she was normal.

Her heart rate increased as she used her teeth to tug on the strap that held her glove tight. Excitement flowed through her as she used her left hand to slowly pull the glove from her right, then set it on her leg, careful not to let a stray piece of grass get inside. It would be ironic if, after removing her glove to pet a sheep, she pricked her finger on a blade of grass that had sneaked inside her glove.

She shook her head—she worried too much—and stretched her fingers toward the lamb, now happily sitting in the grass near her feet. She touched the wool between its ears. It was so soft and almost oily, better than she'd ever imagined it would feel.

She ran her fingers lightly over the animal and the lamb shook as if she'd tickled it, so she grew braver and dug her fingers right down into the wool to the lamb's warm skin.

Her finger struck something hard. The lamb jumped up, and she reached to calm it before looking down at her bleeding finger in horror. It was the last thing she saw.

Lucette woke with a start. Where was she? She spotted a quilt hanging over the end of the bed, woven in a multicolored diamond pattern. At the foot of the bed was a plain chest made of a light wood with big brown knots, and next to it was her own traveling chest, metal covered in leather, the royal crest embossed on top.

She was in her bedroom at her grandparents' house.

A candle burned on the table beside the bed, and her sleeping mother's arm was draped across her. The last thing she remembered was petting that lamb. Foolishly, stupidly petting that lamb—with a bare hand. She wasn't entirely sure what had happened, but there must have been something sharp stuck in its wool—a thistle, perhaps.

She'd done it. She'd brought the curse down, not only on herself but on every citizen of Xandra. Fighting tears, she carefully lifted her mother's arm off of her, and then realized that no matter how rough she was, her mother wouldn't wake up.

After setting her mother's arm under the duvet, she kissed her sleeping face. "I'm so sorry, Mom. So sorry." She got out of bed and spotted a note left for her next to the candle.

Darling Lucette,

The shepherds found you asleep near the creek and carried you home. I don't know how your glove came off, but from your scratches and bruises, I can only assume you fell down the hill. It breaks my heart that you'll be so lonely at night, but I promise to write every day. Will you please write me so I'll know how you're coping? Your grandfather and I agree that it's best for you to stay inside. We've done all we can to protect the house, and your grandfather placed stakes in every room should one of those monsters break through the barriers. Stay strong, my darling.

Love,

Mom

Lucette fought back the tears welling inside her. She would not break down—not on the very first night. But as reality sank in, her insides trembled. At this hour, she was the only person awake in the entire kingdom and vampires might at this very moment be rushing over the border. Her mother and grandparents—and presumably their ranch hands and friends—had been prepared for sundown. Would others in Xandra have collapsed in the streets? Would they wake tomorrow where they fell, some with bites on their necks?

A shiver ran through her as she thought of her father. Her knees crumbled and she dropped to the floor beside the bed. Vampires were targeting the palace specifically, targeting him. How could he possibly survive the night without a bite?

Allowing herself a few moments of despair, she pulled herself off the floor. So far away, there was nothing she could do for her father tonight. She had to hope that he was inside and safe. She picked up the candle and looked around. Someone, presumably her grandmother, had placed strings of garlic bulbs around the room. She shook her head. According to Tristan and what he'd passed on to her from his physiology classes, garlic was not a reliable defense against vampires.

She turned back to her sleeping mother, kissed her cheek, and then left to explore the rest of the house. In the kitchen, she discovered some food left out for her, and all over the house, more of the so-called vampire protection. Garlic was strewn everywhere, and on every windowsill and doorway was a line of what she first thought was sugar, but after tasting it realized was salt. Salt to deter vampires? Even *she* hadn't heard that one and doubted it worked.

The house was quiet save the tick of the mantle clock, so Lucette decided to go out to the barn to make sure the animals were okay, wondering if they'd be asleep, too. She'd been told to stay inside, but the garlic and salt wouldn't keep her any safer than she'd be outside. At least outside she might see what was coming for her before it struck.

She stepped out into the cool night air. The moon hadn't yet risen above the mountains in the distance, and it was so dark that Lucette decided to retrieve a candle from the house before walking to the barn. From the rustling sounds she heard as she approached, and the braying and mooing as she opened the door, she realized that the curse affected only the people of Xandra and not their animals. She shivered, realizing that if more vampires like the one she'd killed in Thunder's stall showed up, without her protection, the poor farm creatures would be exposed to the beasts' undeterred appetites.

She had never heard of a vampire going after anyone's pets or animals back at the village, but she hoped everyone in Xandra had thought to coax their dogs and cats inside before sundown tonight. More likely, it would take a few days—rather, nights—before people developed routines and found ways to keep themselves and their animals safe.

Walking through the barn, the same as ever, her heart rate slowed and calm settled over her. The animals were fine, and better still, they were quiet. They had no idea of the horrible curse that had befallen the kingdom. Lucette set her quiver of stakes beside her, crouched down, and reached out to feel the straw on the barn floor with her bare hands. There was no point in wearing gloves anymore.

After a few hours spent petting and talking to the animals, boredom set in. As much as she loved sheep and horses, they weren't exactly gifted conversationalists, so she returned to the house to make sure it remained vampire-free. After checking on her mother and grandparents, she had a small snack of homemade bread and strawberry jam, then returned to the barn. At least *there* she wasn't the only one awake. Some of the animals were sleeping, but not all, and stroking them, pressing her cheek into their warmth, gave her comfort.

Lucette left the barn door open for light—it seemed safer than candles with all the straw and dry wood scattered about—and she hoped the animals weren't getting cold.

Her instincts snapped to attention as a shadow stretched into the beam of moonlight reaching down the center of the barn floor. Another appeared, and she ducked her head and pulled out a stake. A cow mooed and shifted restlessly.

From inside the cow's pen, Lucette crept along the wall, her back to the barn entrance. Her position gave her the advantage of being hidden from whoever—or whatever—was making those shadows, but the disadvantage of not being able to see back toward the barn door. Was it possible that someone other than vampires was awake? Perhaps a werewolf from Lupinland, or one of the fairies? Had they come to help, after all? Lucette didn't see any wings on the shadows and really had no idea how to spot a werewolf, especially since she knew they could appear in human form.

"She's not in here," a deep voice said.

"Could be hiding," another voice said. "She wasn't in the house."

Lucette held her breath. *They'd been in the house.* Guilt grabbed her and she hoped that her mother and grandparents had remained bite-free while she'd hung out in the barn instead of guarding her family.

"Let's go back and take some blood from the queen, then," the first voice said. "We'll get at least part of our reward."

Vampires. And they were after her and her mother. They'd been found.

Fighting fear, Lucette readied herself to attack.

"I dunno," the second vampire wavered. "I've heard drinking from a sleeping creature makes you tired."

"How would you know?" the other one snapped. "And anyway, if you're worried about it, spit her blood out. We just need to make sure we've transferred some venom and grab a blood sample."

A chill shot down Lucette's spine. From the shape of the shadows, the two vampires weren't far from the cow pen's entrance. If they took another step or two, she'd see them—and they'd see her. It was time to act.

Moving carefully, she stashed her stake in her quiver, grabbed a rope hanging from a beam high on the ceiling, and climbed. Now her shadow appeared, too, but it was on the floor of the opposite stall and the vampire facing that direction seemed not to have noticed it yet.

She climbed until she was above both vampires' heads, then looked up the beam holding the rope. For an instant, she considered continuing her climb; if she hid on that beam, it was possible they'd never spot her. But that was out of the question. She had to get out of the barn before they attacked her sleeping mother.

Holding the rope with one arm, she grabbed a stake and then arched to swing back so her feet touched the top of the stall wall. She pushed off and swung forward, launching into the air. The first vampire spotted her just as Lucette planted a hard kick to the back of his friend's head.

She knocked one into the other and the two vampires landed on the barn floor, one on top of the other, their chests pressed together. Lucette planted her feet on the sprawled arms of the vampire who'd landed on top, pinning them both to the ground, then in one swift move, she plunged her stake through his shoulder.

She chided herself for not going for the kill, but after her first experience, she wasn't sure she could do that again.

"I think you broke my wrists!" the vampire said.

The second vampire started to wriggle out, so Lucette plunged another stake into the dirt next to his neck. "Keep still, or the next one goes in."

"Okay, okay!" The vampire snarled and flashed his fangs. "We're just trying to earn a living! No need to be cruel."

"Cruel? Me?" Her blood started to boil. "I heard what you two were talking about. Who's behind all this? Who's sending you over here to attack us? And why are they targeting the royal family?"

The top vampire groaned as more blood flowed from his shoulder.

"We don't know," the one on the bottom claimed, but something in his face said he was lying.

"Tell me, or this stake goes straight through both of your hearts." She had no idea if she had the strength or the will to follow through on that threat, but from the look on his face, it didn't matter.

"There's rumors, that's all," he insisted.

"What kind of rumors?" Lucette shifted her weight, and the top vampire groaned.

"Some say the queen herself is behind it," the bottom one said. "She's the one who made human blood consumption legal. But I don't know why she's got it in for the royals."

This information tasted like bad medicine. Why was the vampire queen so determined to destroy her?

Lucette pulled out another stake and glared at the vampires. Outside, it was getting lighter. None of them had long. "I'll let you go . . . this time. But one move toward me or the house and you'll both have stakes through your hearts! There isn't a vampire alive I can't take down."

She did a good job of sounding confident and hoped these vampires wouldn't see through her bravado.

"Make her let us go!" the one facing down whined. "It's almost dawn."

"Fine," the one pinned on the bottom said. "Let's get out of here. The money's not worth it."

Lucette jumped off. Walking backward, both stakes up, she moved quickly toward the back of the barn. Thunder reared up and whinnied. "And stay away from our animals, too. Go feed in your own country!" she shouted.

One vampire helped his injured friend to his feet, and they stumbled out of the barn. Lucette advanced behind them, prepared to attack if they went anywhere near the house, but they raced toward the mountains and—she hoped—out of Xandra, forever.

The sky was now tinged with pale pink, and she raced for the house, wondering if she'd get inside before falling asleep on her feet.

A few nights later, Lucette found envelopes addressed to her on the kitchen table, sealed with wax. Her hands trembled, wondering what

her parents would say. The night after the vampires came, she'd written letters to both of her parents.

If they hadn't already figured it out, they had to know that the three of them were the main targets of these vampires. But she'd decided against telling her father that the vampire queen was directly behind the attacks. It wasn't as if he could declare war on Sanguinia while the curse was still upon their country, so what was the point of him knowing? With the curse in effect, the vampire army could wipe out Xandra in one night, while everyone slept.

Perhaps taking over Xandra at night had been the original intent of the curse. It seemed an awfully convoluted way to go about conquering a kingdom—and why keep only her awake? But Lucette wouldn't put that past the vampire queen. From everything she'd heard about the woman, she sounded not only cruel, but also insane.

In the letters to her parents, she'd suggested that she and her mother return to the palace. Hopefully her mother had agreed. At least it would be easier to barricade themselves in there and, if her family were all under one roof, Lucette had some chance of keeping both of her parents safe.

She opened her mother's letter first, and the air rushed out of her lungs. She and her mother would leave for the palace at daybreak. She should be happy that her mother had granted her request, but now she felt the pressure of wondering if she'd been right. The palace would be swarming with vampires and she'd be the only slayer awake.

The next night, Lucette woke with a start and quickly reached her hand to the side to steady herself. It bumped into something hard.

Panicked, she tried to sit upright, but her head also struck something hard, sending a sharp pain through her entire body.

Lucette lay stunned for a few seconds, head throbbing, and then, as her mind cleared, horror filled her heart. She flipped her head to one side, then the other, trying to figure out where she was. She knew that today had been the day her mother had planned to travel back to the palace, but she certainly wasn't in her old bedroom.

She banged on the enclosure, then ran her hands everywhere, trying to make sense of it, wondering if it was just a bad dream. She found a small button and pushed it. Gaslights flickered to life around her, and she discovered she was dressed in a frilly white gown and enclosed in a long box that appeared to be made from glass.

She felt around the virtual coffin, but couldn't find anything to smash the glass with, so she rolled onto one side, braced herself, and kicked one leg back, striking the side of the coffin with the sole of her slippers. Her only reward was a throbbing pain that shot up her leg to her hip.

The enchanted fairy glass! That had to be it. Tears of frustration rose in her eyes. Her mother had brought her home as she'd asked, but then her father had locked her up. Locked her up right in front of the glass prison her mother had shown her before they left for the country. The box she lay inside was perpendicular to the wall of the glass cell, butting right up to the glass. How was she ever going to keep her parents safe from inside a glass box?

She heard a sound and twisted her head to see light climbing toward the room's entrance from the tower staircase. Lucette pushed the button to turn off the gaslights and pretended she was asleep.

Someone was coming.

Will Lucette survive alone in the dark?

To find out, turn to section 6: In the Dark (page 183).

Section 6

In the Dark

6

Unable to sit up straight in her coffin of glass, Lucette craned her neck toward the top of the stairs. A figure appeared in the doorway. She snapped her eyes shut, but then watched the figure through half-closed eyes, pretending to sleep.

As the figure entered and the candlelight grew brighter, she noticed a piece of paper above her on the outside of the coffin, but before she could read it, a face appeared next to the note.

She gasped. Alex! The vampire she'd met in the woods as a kid. His bright red hair and wide, infectious grin were unmistakable. She'd never forget that face.

"Hey," he said, his voice slightly muffled through the glass. "You look a little cramped in there." He picked up the paper and read, "*Dearest Lucette.*" He peeked over the top of the letter. "Sweet opening." He winked and then returned his attention to the letter. "*I'm sorry you had to wake up alone in unfamiliar surroundings, but the idea of my daughter out among vicious vampires is more than I can bear.*"

Alex peeked over the letter again and made a face. "Vicious? Oh, please." He turned back to the note. "*I must keep you safe, my darling daughter. I hope you had a good day's sleep in your case."* Alex looked up again. "Case? Even vampires recognize a coffin when we see one."

"Is that all it says?" she asked. Surely her father didn't expect her to spend all her nights trapped in this case.

"There's more," Alex said, and he continued. *"At your feet you'll find a trapdoor that will let you enter your safe room. Behind the glass partition you'll be protected at night. Once you're in your safe room, make sure you don't close the trapdoor to your sleeping case. It only opens from the case side. It was designed this way so that, if a vampire climbs the tower and comes in through the window, you can escape to your protective sleeping case, shutting the trapdoor behind you."* Alex looked up. "To be clear, when he says case, you known he means coffin, right?"

"Just finish the letter," she said, dread creeping through her. "Or put it back down on the glass so I can read it myself." Her father must have written the letter after trapping her inside.

"Sure thing." He grinned before turning back to the letter. *"For this nightmare to end, you must find true love, so I'll bring every young man in the kingdom up here to see you. I'm confident one of them will love you. I know I do. Your loving father."*

Alex dropped the paper and leaned over, his face near the glass and his fangs glinting in the soft light. "He's parading boys up here to look at you while you sleep? That's messed up."

It *was* messed up and Lucette cringed at the thought, but right now, being face-to-face with a vampire—even through glass—was even messier.

"Do you remember me?" Her voice echoed off the glass.

"Of course. Nice to see you again, Lucette. When we first met, I had no idea you were a princess." He bowed mockingly.

"What are you doing here?" she asked, trying to keep her voice from wavering.

"I heard that everyone in Xandra was asleep except one girl." He backed away from the glass and studied her from head to toe. "Based on the description, I thought it might be you."

"How was I described?" The last time they'd met, she'd been so gangly and awkward.

He shrugged. "Beautiful, tall, big blue eyes, high cheekbones, long curly black hair, alabaster skin . . . You really want me to list it all?"

His grin really was infectious, and if she didn't know better, she'd almost think he was blushing. "I thought you might need some help." He set his candle on the floor. "Looks like I was right."

She twisted in the coffin to keep her eyes on him. "Help? You're a vampire. This glass is supposed to protect me from you."

"Look," he said, "it seems to me like you're trapped in there." He ran his hands over the sides of the coffin. "And that cell you can climb into isn't much better. But if you don't want my help . . ." He turned to leave.

"You can't help," she called out. "You couldn't get me out of here, if you wanted to. The glass is enchanted so it won't break."

"That's harsh," he said as he turned back. Then he studied the coffin, presumably trying to find a way out. "Didn't they even give you lights?"

She hesitated for a second, but then pressed the button and the gaslights flared to life.

He grinned. "Nice." He stepped over to the wall of glass that divided the tower room in two. "There's a door in the glass partition. Any idea where the keys might be?"

She shook her head. If she knew her father, they'd be impossible to locate.

He crouched and stuck his hands through the small slot at the bottom of the glass door. "Doesn't look like you'll fit through here."

"No kidding." The slot was about two inches high and eighteen inches long.

He stepped back to where she lay in her case and pointed at her feet. "Looks like you've got another note down here, inside the case."

Lucette twisted and squirmed in the confined space, which barely fit her when she was tucked up like a ball in the center. After her contortions, she was lying on her front, her head at the opposite end of the box and right against the trapdoor leading into the glass cell. She adjusted the fabric of her gown to make sure she wasn't putting on a show for Alex, then picked up the note. This one was in her mother's handwriting.

Her heart thumped loudly as she read, then she turned toward Alex and blurted, "There's another trapdoor. At that end."

Alex pushed on the end that was now at her feet. "How does it work?"

"It only works from inside," she said, and as she turned back around, she silently thanked her mother for begging the fairy who'd made the case to give her another way out. If she'd had to spend her days in the horrible glass cell after all she'd been through . . . It was too horrible to think about.

And it wasn't just about herself. If she were trapped up here in the tower, who would protect everyone else from the vampires? As her mother advised in her letter, once Lucette got out, she'd have to be careful not to leave any evidence of her nightly escapes and to get back into the glass room or the case before dawn. No sense pushing her father to even more extreme measures. This was bad enough.

Twisted around, and now lying on her belly, she realized if she used the second trapdoor to exit the case, she'd be sliding right into the grasp of a vampire.

But she had to at least see if the trapdoor worked, so she pressed the lower corners of the panel as her mother's note told her to, and it lifted open, swinging up on a springed hinge.

Alex bent down to peer through the open end of the glass case, his face about a foot from hers. "Well, hello there." His fangs rested on his lower lip.

Lucette scrambled toward the coffin's far end, her heart racing.

"Sheesh, I'm not going to hurt you." Offended, he backed away. "Fine, get out of there yourself, if you don't need my help."

Considering her options—semifriendly vampire at one end, prison at the other—Lucette wiggled forward on her stomach until she was out of the box up to her waist. The edge of the glass dug into her hips as she stretched for the floor.

"Sure you don't want some help?" Alex stayed on the other end of the room, leaning against the wall. "'Because I could—you know—help."

She shook her head and pushed her way forward until gravity took over. Her hands hit the ground and the rest of her body followed, rolling into a heap on the floor.

Glancing around the room, Lucette searched for something to use to defend herself. The room was lined with tall wooden cases, each more than six feet tall with slits cut near the top and bottom. Next to one of those cases, she spotted a stake. She took a step toward it, but Alex easily beat her to it.

Her heart almost stopped out of fear, but he passed her the stake, with the sharp end facing his own body. "Stake me if you want, but I wouldn't recommend it."

She grabbed the weapon and raised it, striking a fighting stance. Her heart thumped. "Think I'm not brave enough?"

"Oh, I think you're plenty brave." He didn't move. "But I'm hoping you're also smart, and it looks to me as if I'm the only friend you've got." He lifted his arms and gestured around. "In case you hadn't noticed, all the humans in Xandra are sleeping, and there are vampires roaming everywhere, out for your blood."

Lucette's heart rate slowed as she looked into the vampire boy's eyes. He seemed so sincere, and she wanted so badly to believe him. By trusting him she'd gain the comfort of company, even if it were only the illusion of an ally.

She lowered her stake. "Okay then. First step, I need to find something else to wear."

Lucette sat with her back to the wall and devoured the roasted chicken and potatoes someone had slid through the narrow slot at the bottom of her glass cell back up in the tower. While only one end of the sleeping chamber opened at a time, she'd discovered she could use it like a tunnel to travel in and out of the glass cell.

And she'd found plenty of weapons. The curious wooden cupboards in the tower each held a standing, sleeping slayer armed with weapons. She admired the bravery of those men for volunteering for this duty, especially since it seemed ceremonial at best. What good could they do asleep? At least they'd be there when the curse broke, she thought.

Alex sat cross-legged several feet away, an amused smile on his lips.

"What?" Lucette held up a drumstick. "Would you like some?"

He shook his head quickly and held up a hand. "No way. First, dead flesh is gross. Second, vampires can't digest solids. And third, I already ate."

A shiver prickled along the back of her neck. "What, exactly, did you eat?" She tried to keep her voice even, but if she got even a hint that he'd lunched on a citizen of Xandra, especially someone in the palace, she'd grab her stake and introduce him to its sharp end. All alone, she couldn't take any chances.

"Hmm. What *did* I last eat?" Alex stuck his tongue into the inside of his cheek, as if trying to remember. "I do believe I had a delicious glass of venison."

"A glass of venison?" Lucette wrinkled her nose. "How does that work?"

"I drank deer blood." He made a face as if she were being obtuse.

She shivered. "Did you kill the deer?"

"I thought we already went through this." He crossed his arms over his chest. "The deer who supplied my meal is alive and well and feeling no pain. If you don't believe me, you should come tour one of our ranches. The animals are well treated and are only bled once a week through special stints. The procedure is totally painless—the animals barely seem to notice—and once harvested, the blood is bottled and sold at markets. The stuff at the farmers' markets is always freshest, of course. It has so much flavor." He licked his upper lip.

She took another bite of her chicken and chewed while considering that answer. It was disgusting to think about what Alex consumed in order to survive. But as the only human awake in Xandra, she couldn't afford to be squeamish. "I get what you're saying. Still, I wouldn't want to be bled every week. Poor deer."

Alex nodded toward her dinner. "Poor chicken."

Lucette swallowed her last bite. "Touché. But what about the vampires who've tried to bite me?" She pointed the chicken bone toward him. "And I've witnessed other attacks. You can't claim that everyone in Sanguinia lives off ranched animal blood from the farmers' markets."

Alex paused, then said, "You're right. But it's not in a vampire's nature. Someone's paying those vampires to terrorize Xandra."

"Who?" She wanted to hear someone directly implicate the vampire queen.

"That's what I'm trying to find out." He leaned forward. "I crossed over to figure out who's behind the attacks, and how to stop them."

"I thought you came over to help me."

"That, too." He smiled, and she smiled back. In spite of his blood diet and his fangs, Lucette had to admit that she liked Alex. He was funny and nice and didn't fawn all over her like the boys her father had introduced her to over the years. He didn't seem intimidated by her royalty, either.

But she had to keep her focus. He was the enemy, or at least the queen of his country was. And until this curse was lifted, no one in her kingdom, especially her, was safe. She didn't want to reveal to Alex that she'd heard the vampire queen was behind the nightly attacks. It would be better if she could draw that information out of him as confirmation. "Your queen should do a better job of controlling her people."

His expression darkened, and the yellow flecks in his eyes glowed brighter. "You don't know the first thing about my queen!"

"I know more than you think. She cursed me when I was a baby. This"—she gestured around her—"is all happening because of her curse on me."

Alex's eyes widened, and he leaped to his feet. "How do you know that?"

"My parents told me."

"How do you know they weren't lying? Parents lie to their kids all the time." He emphasized that last part.

Lucette put down the chicken bone. "The facts line up with the story I was told. Your queen laid a curse that would only take affect when I pricked my finger. All my life my parents did everything they could to keep that from happening, but eventually it did, and everyone fell asleep but me." She lifted her arms. "Everything happened exactly the way my parents told me it would. I think that's pretty strong evidence they weren't lying, don't you? I was only a baby, so I can't prove it was your queen, but clearly *someone* put a curse on me."

His face even paler than normal, he reached his hand down to help her up. "I'll see what I can find out," he said. "For now, let's figure out the best way to keep you safe."

She decided to take the risk and his hand. At least she had company, even if it was bloodsucking company.

After Lucette and Alex did a quick walk around the palace and verified that her parents were both barricaded in their respective bedchambers, they stepped into her father's office to look out the window and down to the inner courtyard. Alex easily lifted the huge slabs of wood away from the glass, making her nervous that any vampire could do so if he tried. The barricades would need to be strengthened; she'd leave a note for her father by the slot in her glass cell. No, on second thought, she'd leave the note for her mother. She couldn't explain to her father how she knew about the problem.

Lucette liked the idea that her parents were both under the same roof again, but wished they were sharing a room. At least now they were in the same house, they might speak a few words to each other during the day. Not all of them harsh, she hoped.

She leaned up against the glass and saw a vampire drop the sleeping body of a palace guard to the ground before crossing the courtyard to grab another.

Her breath caught in her chest. Why had the guards stayed outside at dusk?

"We've got to help them." She turned, grabbed her bag of weapons, and headed for the stairs. Alex seized her arm. His grip was stronger than anything she'd imagined, but he wasn't hurting her.

"No," he said. "Not without a plan."

"What plan? Do you have a plan?"

"No, but I saw dozens of other vampires when I crossed the border tonight. Whoever is paying them has doubled or tripled the ranks since your curse fell. There's no point in fighting masses of them all at once. You'll get bitten, and then you'll be too weak to fight."

"Too weak or too dead."

He winced. "Yet another good reason not to dash down there as a solo slayer." He stepped forward. "But most of them aren't killers. And even with three bites, you know I might be able to save you, right?"

She shook her head. "How?"

"If I'm fast enough, a Sanguinian surgeon could convert you into a vampire. Under normal circumstances, the conversion process starts with injections of vampire venom. Bite victims can skip that step."

Lucette shuddered. She'd thought the stories she heard about humans converting to vampirism had been rumors. But even if she could be converted and live as a vampire, she wouldn't want to be bitten. Plus, she liked being human. Imagining drinking blood and living without sunlight—well, right now, she was living that last part.

She looked out the window again. It looked quiet for the moment, but there were guards all around just ready to be bitten. "I need to do something for those innocent people down there."

"You can't take this all on yourself," Alex said. "Those guards will be fine. Sure, they might not be thrilled when they wake up in the morning with a bite mark on their neck, but they'll live."

Lucette ran a hand over her neck, chilled by the idea of even one bite. Maybe by tomorrow night, the guards would be smart enough to stay inside.

"You do have a point," she told Alex. Running out into the night to single-handedly fight off every vampire she spotted was foolish. "Even with your help, the odds will be stacked against us." And if she died before finding true love, the people of Xandra might be trapped by the curse forever. Who knew what might happen if she became a vampire? Xandrans referred to them as the undead.

"Lucette, I need to tell you something else." Alex looked directly into her eyes. "I did come to help you, and I'll do my best to keep you away from danger—they're less likely to attack if I'm with you—but I won't fight other vampires. Not unless it's life or death."

Lucette opened her mouth to protest, then stopped herself. If the situation were reversed, she might warn Alex if slayers were about to attack him, but she wouldn't fight slayers off to save him, either. His terms made sense. "So, what's your plan?" she asked.

He pulled up his hood and approached the window. "I'm not sure I have a plan."

"Are you trying to disguise yourself?" she asked.

"Believe me, one thing I know is that it wouldn't be good for either of us if I were recognized."

"Friends of yours?" She nodded down to the courtyard.

He shook his head. "My face is well known in Sanguinia. I'm sure you understand what that's like, being a princess and all."

"Oh, not that many people in Xandra recognize me. I grew up pretty sheltered." She stopped short. "Why would other vampires recognize you so easily?"

He studied her face intently, and she could tell he was trying to decide whether or not to answer. "People recognize me for the same reason I thought they'd recognize you." He looked down to his feet, then met her gaze. "I'm royalty, crown prince and heir to the throne of Sanguinia."

Alex's revelation slammed into Lucette hard and strong and sucked the air out of her lungs. "You're the crown prince of Sanguinia?" The son of the evil queen who'd cursed her? She staggered back.

He bowed toward her. "At your service."

"Your mother is queen of Sanguinia?" She knew she was repeating herself, but she didn't want to think about the implications. Her brain was having difficulty processing it all. In fact, she could barely breathe, barely form words or coherent thoughts.

"Afraid so," he said. "But I didn't know about the curse—not until you told me. Honest."

She barely knew Alex, yet this felt like a betrayal and like someone had struck her. She backed away, not even trying to hide her terror.

"Don't be scared," Alex said, and raised his hands out toward her. "Just because she's my mother doesn't mean I approve of everything she does. Please believe me."

"But she's—she's evil."

"Your parents aren't exactly perfect." He put his hands on his hips. "Didn't your father put you in that glass coffin?"

She would not be distracted. "Your mother *cursed* me."

"That's nothing compared to what she did to me." Alex approached her slowly and rested his hand gently on her arm.

She pulled back. "What did she do to you?" Warning bells rang in Lucette's mind, yet she really wanted to trust him. If she didn't have Alex, she'd have no help—and no one to talk to.

"I haven't been able to prove it," Alex said as he ran a hand through his hair. "No one has, but . . ." His eyebrows dropped, and yellow specks flashed in his eyes. "When I was just a baby, I think she murdered my father."

By the tenth night, Lucette and Alex had settled into a routine. She'd get up and change into a slayer uniform hidden in the library, and when Alex arrived, they'd meet on the balcony above the main entry hall. The long corridor was the best place to stand guard, since her mother's bedchamber was off to the left and her father's to the right. Not that there weren't other routes that vampires could use to get to either wing, but at least from that spot, Lucette could divide her attention and listen for signs of trouble at either end. Plus, the huge windows in her father's office just behind the balcony looked down over the inner courtyard, and from the balcony, she could see the main entry hall.

"Many Xandrans have already fled the kingdom," Lucette told Alex, based on the information in her mother's last letter. "But how can we help keep the vampires from getting to the people who've stayed?" Her father never shared much information in his letters, but her mother often did. Besides the slayers and the most loyal of the palace staff, nearly half of the population of Xandra had left, especially those who had children. Who could blame them? "My mom says my dad is planning to set up shelters for the people who've stayed, but if everyone gathers in one place and the vampires get in, won't it be like a blood buffet?"

Alex laughed. "You're funny."

She tried not to smile. "There's nothing funny about a gang of vampires sucking on the necks of defenseless people in their sleep."

"I know an easy way to keep vampires away," he said.

"Oh?" Based on her experiences, there weren't too many things that could deter vampires in spite of the old wives' tales.

Alex rubbed his chin with his fingers. "Vampires have a few secrets humans don't know."

"What?" Lucette's hopes lifted. "Is the garlic thing true? Have we just been doing it wrong? Does the garlic have to be roasted, sautéed, finely chopped?"

"No." Alex laughed. "Personally, I can't stand the smell of garlic, but it doesn't have any effect on vampires."

"Then what?"

He leaned onto the railing beside her. "I do want to help you. I really do. But you have to understand that I'm sharing secrets my people have guarded for thousands of years."

She turned to him. "If you're sincere about wanting to maintain peace between our kingdoms, why keep secrets?"

"Don't humans have secrets from us?"

"Here's one. We don't like to have our blood sucked."

"Ha!" He nudged her with his hip. "That's no secret."

She waited patiently. She couldn't force Alex to tell her anything, and sensed that pushing too hard might make him clam up. He was the one who'd offered to help her, after all. And she needed help. In his letters, her father had told her he'd put out calls for assistance to the other kingdoms surrounding Xandra, but apparently there had been no volunteers. At this point, Lucette would even accept aid from the trolls.

"Roses."

She spun toward Alex. "What?"

"That's the secret. Vampires can't be around roses, especially red ones. There's some chemical in the fragrance that sends the vast majority of our population into something like anaphylactic shock."

"Anna-what?"

"A severe allergic reaction. Our throats close up and it's hard to breathe."

"That must feel horrible."

Alex shrugged. "I wouldn't know."

"Is it fatal?" Roses had always been potentially deadly for her, too—the thorns, not the scent.

"Not always, but it really slows us down. Most vampires lose consciousness. Not breathing enough has that effect."

Lucette buried her head in her hands, realizing she'd caused another big problem. "That's just great," she said. "No one in Xandra has *any* roses." She lifted her head and turned to Alex. "Vampires are feeding off defenseless people in their sleep, and it's my fault they don't have the one thing they need to protect themselves!"

"You've got a bit of a complex," Alex said, stepping away from the railing. "Now you're taking responsibility for everyone's taste in gardening?"

She shot him a nasty look. "No one in Xandra is allowed to have roses. My father ordered every rosebush in the kingdom destroyed so I wouldn't prick my finger on a thorn."

"Oh." Alex made a face. "That sucks."

She sighed. "I'll write notes to my parents. They'll send word to the surrounding kingdoms to let them know we need lots of red roses." Not that any of her father's appeals for help had yielded anything, yet. According to her mother's notes, everyone was too afraid of retaliation from the vampire queen.

"I've never even seen a rose," she said. "I suppose you haven't, either."

"Oh, I've seen roses," Alex said.

"But you said . . ."

"I said ninety-nine percent of the population is allergic. I'm part of the one percent." He shrugged. "Probably because my mother was born human."

The vampire queen was born human? Lucette wondered what else she didn't know.

Natasha stepped out onto the balcony high above the gathered crowd as moonlight bathed her subjects. As their glowing white faces gazed up at her, the thrill of her power and the adoration of the throng rushed through Natasha. She leaped onto the balcony's railing, and the noise from the crowd swelled.

Even though they were just a portion of her subjects, the worship emanating from the courtyard below was exhilarating. Soon she'd have all her subjects eating out of her hand. Soon they'd bow at her feet and do her every bidding. Under her rule, vampires would regain their rightful place at the top of the food chain and she, as their sovereign leader, would rule all the known kingdoms. The mere thought of domination over so many buzzed and tingled inside her. As soon as the ranks of her supporters grew, she'd command the Sanguinian armies to invade Xandra, and Stefan and his stupid little wife would pay.

She raised her arms and the crowd quieted. "People of Sanguinia, it is with a heavy heart I must report that our long-held peace with the kingdom of Xandra remains threatened."

Murmurs swelled. With every dead vampire body found near the border at night, the lust for drinking human blood grew, along with support for her. The stupid humans meant the dead bodies as a warning, but the slayers were playing right into her hands. Soon, Natasha wouldn't even need bribes to encourage vampires to help her seek her revenge and claim the throne of Xandra, the throne that should have been hers in the first place. And she didn't plan to stop there. Once she had Xandra, she'd conquer the entire known world.

She placed a hand over her heart and addressed the crowd. "I have just learned of more vampire deaths at Xandran hands. Our citizens who innocently, accidentally, crossed the Xandran border at night have been brutally murdered by vicious killers the Xandrans call . . . vampire slayers." She let the reaction drift through the crowd like a building wave. "Yes, my good people. An army trained with the specific goal of murdering every last one of our race."

Angry shouts rose from the crowd below.

"The evil King Stefan of Xandra is no longer our friend and ally." She jumped down from the railing, turned, and beckoned her son, Prince Alexander, forward. He looked in the other direction. Natasha wondered if it were shyness, as he claimed, or if something else kept him from her side.

She refused to let her disappointment in her son spoil this glorious moment, but if he weren't careful, if he didn't rise up to capture his birthright and start seeing things her way, he'd meet the same fate as his father.

If she did kill her son, she'd need to disguise his death as a casualty of the conflict with Xandra. She grinned. A fabulous idea, but one she'd save as a backup plan. As much as she loved her son and wanted an heir, her people would eagerly rally behind her against King Stefan if they believed Xandrans had killed their crown prince.

"Behind you!" Alex yelled, and Lucette spun and saw a vampire heading toward her, in the courtyard just outside the back entrance to the palace. The vampire lunged, fangs first.

Executing a twisting side-kick, she planted her heavy boot into the vampire's nether regions and he staggered back, bent over in pain.

Raising her stake, she said, "Go back to Sanguinia, or I'll plunge this stake deep into your heart." She'd become better at issuing these threats believably, and so far almost every vampire she encountered cared more about his own life than the money he might earn if he drank from her vein.

She'd had to stake one or two to drive home her point, but no lethal strikes, yet. She hoped her first kill had been her last.

"Boy, I'm glad I'm not that guy." Alex chuckled. "Serves him right, though. No one bites my girl." Alex draped his arm over her shoulders. "Great job."

She ducked out from under his grasp. "Thanks." She tipped her head to the side to stretch her stiff neck. "I hope that's it for tonight."

He reached for her again. "Here, let me rub your shoulders."

"Let's get back inside first." She stepped away from his reach. "No sense in drawing more vampires here on purpose."

They crawled through the tiny, hinged door beside the back entrance that had been used by the royal canines in years gone by to come and go from the palace. When she was a baby, her father had given all of the royal dogs away to ranchers and farmers in the countryside, afraid that boisterous animals in the house might lead to finger pricks.

Once they'd both squeezed through the tiny door, Alex locked it and slipped the key into his pocket. Lucette was so glad she'd discovered that little door that was hard to spot from the outside unless you knew it was there. So far, no other vampires had found that way in, and it provided a great entrance for Alex, without her having to move a barricade from another door, and without Alex having to smash through one, thus opening the way for other vampires to pass through.

As the pair climbed the staircase from the main foyer to the balconied corridor, midway between her parents' bedrooms, Alex's fingers brushed hers. She clasped her hands behind her back, but then turned to smile at him.

"Come on," Alex said. "When are you going to let me hold your hand? We've spent every moment of every night together for more than two weeks now. Don't you trust me yet?" His lips twisted and the skin at the sides of his eyes crinkled. "Don't you *like* me?"

Her heart squeezed at his obvious hurt. "I do like you, Alex. You know I do, but . . ." But she didn't feel that way about him. She didn't want to hold his hand or welcome his arm across her shoulders or around her waist. It felt odd and awkward and wrong. At this rate, she would never find true love.

"But *what*, Lucette?" Alex stopped at the top of the stairs and crossed his arms over his chest. "You need to find true love to break this horrible curse, and I'm sorry, but unless you're falling in love with one of the boys who gawk at you in that display case and fall asleep next to your glass coffin, I'm all you've got."

She walked along the railing that ran the length of the balcony high above the foyer and trailed her fingers on the polished wood. Was Alex right? By resisting his advances, was she prolonging the curse? If Alex was her true love, she'd feel it eventually . . . wouldn't she?

He moved over to the wall opposite the railing, so she turned to face him. She did find Alex attractive. He was certainly handsome. His bright eyes flashed with humor and intelligence under eyelashes that were thick and dark, given his red hair, and his infectious smile never failed to draw out one from her. But it didn't feel right. He felt like a friend, nothing more. Still, wasn't friendship the way true love was supposed to begin?

"Give me time, okay?" she asked. "The curse won't lift if we *pretend* to be in love. It has to be real. I have to prove that it's real." She looked down for a moment. "We can't force it."

Alex leaned back against the wall, crossed one leg over the other, and spread his strong arms to the sides. "Whenever you're ready, here I am."

"Thank you," Lucette said. Alex was right about one thing. He was her only option. All the other boys were either asleep or trying to drink her blood.

Lucette's eyes snapped open in the darkened room. She flipped over onto her belly and pressed the panel to spring herself free from her glass coffin. The twenty-eighth night of the curse, and she still had no idea if her father knew she got out of her cell every night. He had to realize someone was responsible for the wounded vampires, but neither her father nor her mother had mentioned a word in any of their letters. Perhaps her mother was covering some how, or her father was in denial.

She and Alex had become a great team. He might not be willing to fight, but he was good at keeping watch and warning her of danger. Plus, he was super sweet. Almost every night he brought her a small gift. His attention was so flattering, and she realized she needed to try harder to return his affections, especially if she were to find true love.

She rolled out of the long glass compartment and, once on her feet, bent down to stretch out her tight back and legs. Three young men had braved staying in the tower tonight as an expression of their alleged undying love and were sleeping in chairs next to her sleeping case. She turned on the gaslights and looked into the cell to see whether the boys had slid love notes through the slot. She'd stopped reading most of them weeks ago, because they all said the same things: she was beautiful, they loved her, they'd do anything for her. Some even suggested exactly what she should write back to them, in order to prove her love.

If only it were that easy.

Two of tonight's young men she'd seen before. Henry, the one with the dark hair, drooled in his sleep, and, by her count, this was the seventeenth night of his vigil. She admired his persistence and bravery at not locking himself somewhere more secure, instead exposing his neck to whatever might come up the stairs of the tower in the night. He'd already been bitten once, and Lucette had left him a note begging him to take cover, to stop risking himself as a display of his love. But her letter had only encouraged him; his response told her as much. If he was bitten a second time, she'd write to both her parents and insist they force Henry to lock himself up at night.

The second suitor, a pudgy teenager with curly blond hair, was on his third night. She supposed that at some point she should read his love notes to at least find out his name.

The third boy, who looked older and more muscular, was new and wore a slayer uniform. His dark hood and mask covered his face. A slayer was potentially interesting, but off limits: slayers weren't allowed to date, and Lucette couldn't imagine why his commander had allowed him to sleep here. Perhaps he hadn't gotten into his compartment in time? She snagged one of his stakes from the quiver lying on the floor next to him, then checked the eight wooden boxes around the room. All were occupied.

Too curious to leave the room without finding out more about her mysterious new suitor, Lucette turned back to the sleeping slayer.

Had he left her a note? She reached under the slot at the bottom of the cell wall, grabbed the letters left there, and flipped through them quickly. The curly haired boy was named Felix, but there was nothing to indicate that any of the notes were from the slayer.

Time to take a peek under his hood. She thought that was only fair, since he'd been watching her sleep. She stood in front of him, impressed by his broad shoulders, his trim frame, and his considerable height.

She reached for the zipper that fastened his hood to his shirt.

His hand grabbed her wrist.

She gasped, and his other hand came up, holding a stake.

"You're awake," they said together.

She wrenched her arm free and lifted her stake. He had to be a vampire disguised as a slayer. Her heart pounded and she fought to gain control of her thoughts, fought to find an explanation for this person who was awake, other than his being a vampire. She braced herself, stake pointed at his heart, ready to fight should he attack.

"Princess"—he rose slowly, lowering his stake—"I mean you no harm."

"I'll be the judge of that." She lunged, stake forward to show she meant business. Threats frightened most vampires off.

"Hey, careful." He chuckled.

"What's so funny?" Anger rose inside her. Perhaps tonight she'd follow the slayer army code and stake first, ask questions later.

He shook his hooded head. "I didn't mean to offend you. It's just that, watching you sleep this afternoon, I thought you were the most beautiful, delicate creature I'd ever seen. So sweet, so vulnerable."

"Vulnerable?" She drew back her stake. "Guess again."

He backed up a foot. "My mistake. Now you're awake, a better description might be angry and violent." He folded his arms over his chest. "I think I like it."

Her cheeks burned. "How are you here?" It was just minutes after sunset. No vampire could run that fast, and he claimed to have watched her sleep. *Creepy*. Plus, according to everything she'd learned, the only vampire strong enough to withstand sunlight, even on a rainy day, was the vampire queen. "How did you get in here before dark? Do you know Alex?"

"I traveled a long distance," he answered, "but I arrived before dark. And no, I don't know anyone named Alex."

She jabbed the stake with more force, coming closer to him than before, and as if by instinct, he raised his too. But then he took a step back, almost falling into his chair.

"Princess, I'm not a vampire. I'm a human." He thumped his chest as though that proved anything.

"Then how and why are you here?" Something about his voice was familiar, even muffled under the masked hood.

"Stories of the sleeping beauty of Xandra intrigued me," he said. "And I must say, even now, as you're threatening to attack me, your beauty has far exceeded my expectations."

"Do you think my blood will be sweeter if you flatter me first?" She pulled her stake back, ready to strike.

He raised his stake in defense. "I repeat, I am not a vampire."

"Yeah, right. Prove it. Take off your mask and let me see your eyes."

"Sure." He stepped forward. "But only if you drop your weapon. From the look in *your* eyes, I have a feeling I might be mortally wounded before I even get my hood unzipped."

"You put your stake down first." No way would she let herself be tricked.

He set it down and raised his hands.

She considered her options. Alex might arrive at any moment, but some nights he came later, depending on where he'd slept during the day and whether he'd had to head back to Sanguinia to replenish his blood supply. A few nights Alex hadn't come at all, because he'd had to spend time with his mother or she'd get suspicious. But even if he arrived right now, he wouldn't fight a vampire; she was on her own.

It felt dangerous to lower her stake, but she should at least let this guy take off his hood and show his face. One hint of fangs, and she'd move into action.

She lowered her arm. He unzipped the hood and pulled it off.

Tristan.

Lucette froze, unsure of what to say. She was not even sure her tongue would work. Seeing his handsome face, his beautiful blond hair, his lush lips, his strong neck, brought back a flood of memories. At first good ones, sending shivers of attraction racing through her, and then bad ones, piercing her pride and stabbing her chest with the pain and humiliation of his rejection.

"Princess," he bowed, "my name is Tristan of Judra, and I've come to rescue you."

"Is this your idea of a joke?" He was acting as if he didn't know her, had never met her. Given his cruel rejection, he must be setting her up for some kind of humiliation.

"Joke?" He stepped forward. "Princess, I assure you, my intentions in coming here are entirely noble. I heard you were beautiful—which you are. I heard you were alone—which you are. I heard you needed help—

which seems true. And I heard you wanted roses—which I brought."

She gasped. Tristan had answered her father's call for help.

Of course he had. He'd come to rescue her. And he brought roses. Yes, they were intended as defensive weapons, not declarations of love, but still . . . She tried to think straight through the happy thoughts dancing in her mind. Maybe he'd always loved her. Maybe he'd just been waiting for her to be older. Maybe he hadn't meant what he'd told her nearly two years ago.

"You brought roses?" Her voice sounded breathy.

"Yes." He gestured over to the corner where a vase stood, full of red roses on long stems.

She'd only seen drawings of roses, and they were more beautiful than she could have imagined. Their scent was so sweet, too, and she couldn't believe she hadn't noticed the vase the moment she woke.

"I brought these," he said, "and as many bushes as I could carry, too, although I'm not sure I understand the desperate need for flowers. Even a rose would pale against your beauty." He bowed.

She wondered for a moment if he was mocking her, but the gesture seemed real. Suddenly, the truth hit, and she flinched like she'd actually been struck. Tristan didn't recognize her. Not one bit. He had forgotten her that easily.

But perhaps not. *He* looked the same—except his hair was longer and his face had hardened—but *she'd* grown up. She was no longer that little kid he'd so easily dismissed. She wondered how to tell him, but decided not to. Not yet. First, she had to get to the bottom of how and why he was here—and awake. Had Tristan converted to vampirism? She studied his mouth for evidence of fangs, his blue eyes for yellow flecks.

"How are you awake?" she asked, embarrassed that her voice came out so weakly, without the confident tone of a slayer.

He ran a hand over his golden hair that reflected the gaslights. "The curse was on the citizens of Xandra. It appears I'm not affected, since I'm not Xandran."

She nodded. That was possible. "Then why has no one else come to help me? Why only you?"

He looked down for a moment before answering. "Everyone's afraid of getting involved. They think that if they do, vampires will attack their citizens, too."

"So you're *not* a vampire?"

He laughed. "No. Princess, I'm here to defend you from vampires—to slay them. When I heard of your predicament, I came running. I couldn't imagine leaving an innocent young lady here on her own with no way to defend herself."

Lucette narrowed her eyes and crossed her arms over her chest. "I can defend myself just fine, thank you." She dropped her arms to her sides; it was crazy to be so defensive. She might be more capable than he assumed, but that was no excuse to be rude. Help was exactly what she needed, and to chase it away now that it had arrived—especially in the form of Tristan—would be foolish. "Okay then," she said. "Gather your weapons. After I get changed, you can join me on my patrol."

Lucette draped the long, frilly white-and-pink gown she'd been sleeping in over the back of the chair behind the screen in the library, where she hid her slayer uniform each morning before dawn. Her insides were all too aware that Tristan was on the other side of that screen.

She felt insulted that he didn't remember her and that he assumed he could swoop in here and save her. She grabbed the clothes she hid behind a huge atlas, and after she dressed, she pulled on her heavy boots—all the better to kick with.

Suddenly, she heard a loud smash on the other side of the screen.

Tristan had been attacked! Her heart jumped, but she knew not to do anything rash, and she quickly and quietly clasped her belt and grabbed her weapons. The element of surprise would help when she joined in the battle.

"Stay back, Princess!" Tristan called out. "I'll protect you!"

So much for the surprise factor. She grabbed a stake in one hand and a long shaft that doubled as a fighting stick in the other, then slid out from behind the screen, keeping to the shadows. Not that the shadows were much help—vampires could see quite well in the dark.

Only one intruder had come into the library. What a relief.

Tristan leaped up and delivered a kick to the vampire's chest, then the vampire staggered and roared as he sprang back toward Tristan.

Tristan ducked to the side and the vampire fell forward, but recovered quickly and turned around with a horrible, bloodthirsty look on his face. Lucette had never seen a vampire so ugly or crazed. His hair was dirty and matted in patches, and his face was twisted into a horrible grimace.

He lunged for Tristan again, and she made her move. In three long, leaping strides, she stepped onto the back of a chair, then dove toward the vampire, planting her stake in the side of his body. It wasn't a death strike, but it would slow him down and, with any luck, scare him off. He spun toward her, roaring in anger and pain.

He lunged at her with his fangs bared, but she rolled to the side. Tristan leaped up and planted a killing blow in the vampire's back, straight through his heart.

The vampire slumped to the ground, and Tristan ran to her side, his bloody stake still in his hand. "Princess, are you hurt?"

She backed away, her heart hammering in her chest. The vampire was dead. He hadn't had a fair chance to run after a warning.

The door opened and Alex strode in. He froze when he saw the dead body on the floor and the blood dripping from Tristan's stake—not to mention Tristan.

Alex spun toward Lucette. "What's going on here?"

In an instant, Tristan pulled his crossbow off his back and loaded an arrow.

Lucette lunged for Tristan's arm and pushed it aside just as he fired. Alex ducked to the side, and the arrow narrowly missed him, digging into the spine of a book. Tristan grabbed another arrow.

"He's a friend!" She kicked the crossbow from Tristan's hands.

Alex stormed forward, anger hardening his handsome face. "What's your problem? I didn't come near you!"

Tristan ignored Lucette and reached for a stake. She put herself between the two boys. "Stop it!"

Tristan and Alex stepped around her and lunged for each other, but Lucette jumped, twisting in the air and spreading her legs into a side-split jump that struck each of them in the chest with one foot.

She landed between them as they stumbled back.

"That was impressive," Alex said, rubbing his chest. "I've never seen you do that before."

"Lucy?" Tristan said. He stood in shock. "Lucy? You're Princess

Lucette?" He shook his head, as if trying to erase what he'd just realized. "I've never seen anyone else who could do that."

She shrugged. "About time you noticed."

Alex pulled her around by the shoulder. "You know this human? And how is he awake?"

Tristan pulled her back around. "You know this vampire?"

Lucette alternated her gaze between the young men—one human, one vampire—trying to figure out how to respond.

"Of course she knows me." Alex stepped forward and put his arm around her shoulders. "In fact, we're falling in love. And as soon as we prove it, the curse will lift."

"What?" Tristan said, his shock and revulsion intensifying.

Lucette slipped from Alex's grip. He was making it sound as if they were already in love—the last thing she wanted Tristan to hear. "The curse lifts when I prove I've found true love," she told Tristan.

Tristan's nose wrinkled and his nostrils flared with contempt. "And you've chosen . . . you're falling in love with . . . with *that*?"

Alex put his arm around her again and gripped tightly.

"Vampires aren't *things*," Lucette said. "You should say *him*, not *that*." She looked up to Alex, but he kept his gaze forward, so she turned back to Tristan. "We're not in love." She tried to shrug Alex's arm off her shoulders, but he held on to her tightly and she didn't want to struggle, because she knew it would cause even more tension.

Tristan glared at Alex with hate in his eyes. "Let her go. Now."

Alex refused.

So much for preventing more tension. "It's okay," she told Tristan. "Alex and I are friends."

Tristan took step toward Alex and said, "Can't you see that you repulse her? She's trying to get away from you. If you're her friend as you claim, unhand her now."

"Just stop!" Lucette raised her hands. "There's no need to get nasty. If we're going to be spending time together, it'll be a lot more pleasant, not to mention safer, if we can all get along."

Alex stepped back, pulling her with him. "I'm not planning on spending any time with *him*." He narrowed his eyes. "Let him get sucked dry if he won't go back where he came from. I can keep you safer if he stays away."

Lucette looked at Tristan. His arms were tense, as if he were ready to grab a weapon. She couldn't let that happen.

"Listen," she told Tristan, "Alex and I have spent the past twenty-eight nights together, trying to minimize the bites for everyone in and around the palace. I trust him and ask that you trust him, too."

A loud bang sounded from somewhere in the palace, and then another.

Alex released her, and she sprang forward, drawing one of her stakes. "Get the roses!" she shouted.

Tristan grabbed the bouquet of roses, and they ran into the corridor, Lucette's heart thumping hard and fast. The sounds came from her mother's wing, and as they rounded the final corner, she gasped. A group of five vampires, more than she'd seen together at one time, was hacking at her mother's door with an axe.

They'd already made it through the first slab and were moving on to the next. How many doors protected her mother's room now? Everyone who'd stayed in Xandra had made it more difficult for the vampires to break into their houses. All over the kingdom, windows were boarded over and huge pieces of furniture were pushed up against doors each night. But Lucette knew that eventually the vampires would break through.

Tristan dropped the roses, loaded his crossbow, and launched an arrow into the midsection of one of the vampires, just missing his heart. The wounded vampire turned, growled, and charged at Tristan.

Taking a leap of faith, Lucette picked up a rose and ran forward, leaping over Tristan, who was busy reloading his crossbow, and forced the flower into the vampire's face.

"Lucy!" Tristan shouted.

The vampire reacted almost immediately. He clutched at his long pale throat and coughed. Soon he fell to the ground. Lucette stood over him with a stake, her heart racing, hoping she wouldn't have to deliver the death blow. The vampire's convulsions slowed, and he lay there, unmoving.

She turned to Alex. "Did the rose kill him?"

Alex shrugged. "Maybe. I'm not sure. We should tie him up, but he's not your only problem." Alex gestured toward the other vampires and tossed her more roses.

She turned to see Tristan in hand-to-hand combat with a huge vampire. The vampire's fangs were dangerously close to Tristan's neck. Why had she made him take off his hood with its neck protector? Better question, why hadn't he put it back on? And why wasn't *she* wearing one? All their slayer training had gone out the window.

She jumped on the vampire's back and forced one of the roses into his face. He released Tristan, who took advantage of the opportunity and drove a stake into the vampire's chest. He collapsed, twitching in pain, and soon stopped breathing.

"You didn't have to kill him!" Alex yelled at Tristan. "Lucette, the door!"

She looked up just in time to see the feet of the skinniest vampire disappear through a hole that had been hacked into her mother's bedroom door.

She grabbed more roses, stepped onto the back of one of the other vampires—who was bent over to retrieve the axe—then dove into her mother's bedroom.

Blinking against the darkness, Lucette listened for the vampire, but she couldn't hear him over the fighting and shouting in the hall—not to mention her pounding heart. The hole she had come through was blocked by the body of someone following her, but there was no time to see whether it was a friend or foe—her mother was in danger.

Lucette stumbled through the darkness, bumping into a table she'd forgotten was there, and found the button for the room's gaslights. As the lights flickered on, a horrible, piercing scream filled her ears. In the instant that it took to realize that it was her own screaming, Lucette also saw a scene straight out of her worst nightmare: the vampire was feeding off her mother's neck.

"Noooo!" She raced forward, leaping over the bed to land on top of the vampire.

He pulled his fangs out of her mother and turned to her. "Yummy. Just in time for dessert."

"Not likely!" She forced a rose into his face and he moaned, rolling off the bed.

Lucette put her hand over the wounds in her mother's neck, but they were already sealing. It was no use. She'd been infected by vampire venom. Two more bites, and her mother would die unless she converted to vampirism, and she knew her mother would prefer death to conversion.

A shout came from the hole in the door. Tristan was following her into the room, but his shoulders were too wide. He had a twisted, pained expression on his face, and he seemed to be struggling. "Get it off me!" he shouted.

She ran to Tristan. "What's happening?"

Tristan shook his head, a resigned expression on his face. "One of the bloodsuckers just fed off a vein in my leg."

"Got him," Alex's voice came through the thick door. "They're all down and tied up," he called. "The coast is clear."

The next night, the three of them gathered outside the king's office and prepared for the vampires that were sure to attack. Opposite the office door was a railing forming a balcony over the front foyer. This position was strategic because not only could they see the main entry hall below, but the corridor also led off to her mother's wing in one direction, and to her father's in the other.

Tristan crossed the corridor and adjusted the tension on his crossbow as he leaned against the railing above the front foyer. "I think your father was more shaken by your mother's bite than she was. Your mother is exceptionally brave." He grinned. "You come by it naturally."

Pride and hope rose in Lucette's chest. "Did the vampires who had allergic reactions live?" she asked Alex.

"I'm not sure," he replied tightly. "One way or another, they were taken back to Sanguinia."

Lucette grimaced, but realized there wasn't much she could do to control what happened during the day. All she could do was prevent bites at night.

She turned to Tristan. "Did you get any sleep today?"

"Yes." He adjusted his quiver of stakes. "Don't worry about me."

"But I do worry," she said. "I don't think you should stay in Xandra anymore. It's too dangerous."

He tested the trigger on his unloaded crossbow. "You're the one facing danger. You and your whole kingdom. I won't leave you to face this alone."

"She's *not* alone," Alex said from where he sat, leaning against the wall next to her father's office door.

"Please," Tristan spat out. "You won't even help her fight! Coward."

Alex leaped up and charged toward Tristan, but Lucette slipped between them before the face-off turned physical. She touched Tristan's arm. "Even without fighting, Alex has helped me—a lot. And he pulled that vampire off your leg last night, and tied all the unconscious bodies up."

"Still—" Tristan leaned against the railing. "I'm not leaving. Not a chance. If the king dies, Xandra will fall with him. I won't let that happen."

Her heart skipped at the ferocity and concern in Tristan's eyes, but even though she knew it was selfish, she wished that Tristan's concern was for her, not just her kingdom.

Alex bared his fangs. "If you're so concerned about Lucette, where have you been these past weeks?"

"I came as soon as I heard. News of Xandra's predicament was slow to come to Judra." Tristan touched her arm, sending a thrill through her body. "Your father is very grateful and relieved that I've come, and that you're no longer alone."

"She was *never* alone." Alex grabbed her arm. "You need to tell your father how much I've helped you. He needs to know about me, if we're going to get married."

"Married?" Tristan grabbed her other arm, his eyes filled with shock. "You're going to marry this monster?"

Lucette's mouth dried and a million thoughts raced through her mind; she couldn't make them come out as actual words.

Alex's hand slipped down her arm to take her hand. He stepped backward and pulled. "Yes. Someday we will each be the reigning monarchs of our respective countries, and ruling together will bring about everlasting peace."

"Your mother is Queen Natasha?" Tristan grabbed Lucette's other hand so she was strung between them, and Tristan's face was filled with horror and revulsion. "He's a spy, Lucette. We can't trust him. He's probably the one leading the vampires here each night, telling them how to breach the palace barricades."

"It doesn't take inside information to break down doors." Alex said. "Plus, you've got it backward." Alex held firm to her other hand. If either pulled, she'd be torn apart. "I've been giving Lucette inside information. How do you think she knew about the roses?"

Tristan pulled. "Doesn't mean you're not a spy and it doesn't mean she'll marry you. She wouldn't." He turned to look at her. "Would you?"

"Enough!" She lifted her arms, wrenching her hands out of their grasps. "My entire life my parents fought about me as if I weren't even in the room. I won't have you two do it now."

Her cheeks burned as she looked back and forth between Tristan and Alex. Both young men were so handsome, so concerned for her well-being. "I do need to find true love," she said. "It's my duty as future queen of Xandra, and as the one who brought the curse upon my kingdom."

Both boys started to object, but she raised a palm toward each of them and they stopped.

"I am determined to do everything I can to break the curse, but"—she turned toward Alex—"I never agreed to marry you. You know that." She turned back to Tristan. "Still, we can trust him. I'm sure of it. He and I have been through a lot."

But a tiny part of Lucette doubted her statement. There was no way of being certain that Alex wasn't spying for his mother. On the other hand, if he was on his mother's side, why not just kill her? Or kill her parents? What was the point of making sure she never got bitten if he really wanted her dead? It didn't make sense.

Alex paced down the hall and then turned, his long strides conveying his frustration. Glowering, he stopped directly in front of Lucette. "Get rid of him. Make him leave. We don't need him. He's just someone else to take care of. He let himself get bitten on his first night. Two more bites and he'll be no help to us at all."

"One bite," Tristan said. "I only need one more bite." He raised his chin. "I was bitten as a child. It's the main reason I came to Xandra to train as a slayer."

Lucette's stomach dropped. It was so dangerous for Tristan to be here, yet he'd come, and dove through that hole in her mother's door, even knowing the risks. Her admiration for him expanded, as did the flutter in her stomach. But she couldn't get swept up in her fantasies.

He didn't have those same feelings for her. He was only protecting her out of a sense of duty. It wasn't personal.

Alex tugged on her arm. "Send him away. Another human awake in the palace attracts vampires. He makes things more dangerous for you."

"Really?"

Alex looked up and to the side, then said, "Yes. I'm a vampire. I should know how it works." But his expression and body language made her wonder if he didn't have other motives for wanting Tristan gone.

Actually, she knew he did. "Alex," she said, keeping her voice soft and reassuring, "we're stronger as a team of three. He just got here. Give it some time. I'm sure we'll learn to work together." She turned to Tristan. "Given the risks, you probably should leave, but it's your choice." She turned back to Alex. "I won't ask him to go. I can't."

"Yes, you can," Alex said. "And if you don't, then . . ." He pulled her forward until she could see every yellow fleck in his green eyes, "I'll leave and never come back."

She shook her head and her throat pinched. "Don't say that! Don't even joke. You wouldn't." As angry as she felt that Alex was applying this pressure, he'd been her only lifeline through so many nights of darkness and loneliness. Even with Tristan here, she couldn't imagine him gone. She might not get that tingly feeling when she looked into Alex's eyes, but they had a connection, a deep one, one that would rip her apart if she lost it.

"Lucette," Alex said, "it's him or me. You have to choose."

Oh, no! After all those years of being torn between her parents, Lucette now has two boys demanding she choose between them.

If you were Lucette, what would you do?

OPTION A: Lucette should tell Tristan to leave. Alex has been so much help and so loyal. She can't survive this curse without him. Her childhood crush on Tristan hasn't faded, but he rejected her and didn't even recognize her when he showed up last night. Clearly, he hasn't been dreaming of her as she's been dreaming of him. Alex is right. Tristan will just distract her, and with two bites, it's too dangerous for him to be here anyway. Maybe in time her feelings for Alex will grow to true love. If you think Lucette should choose option A, turn to section 7: Friendship Transformed (page 225).

OPTION B: Lucette should refuse to tell Tristan to leave. He was so brave to come here when no one else would. He's especially brave to stay given he'd suffered through two vampire bites. Lucette's childhood crush hasn't faded, and even if he didn't remember her, he called her beautiful the night he arrived. She's not a kid anymore, and although she hates to hurt Alex's feelings, at least she has a chance of finding true love with Tristan. If you think Lucette should choose option B, turn to section 8: A Leap of Faith (page 261).

Section 7

Friendship Transformed

7

Lucette closed her eyes, not wanting to look at either Tristan or Alex. She tried to be strong, but it was hard to hide her breaking heart. She opened her eyes and said, "Tristan, can I speak to you in private?"

Alex put his arm possessively around her shoulders. "Anything you want to say to him, you can say in front of me."

Her mouth suddenly felt dry. Alex shouldn't be putting her in this position, even though she knew his motives were based on affection and truly believing he could help her break the curse. She glared at the young vampire—no one told her what to do, not anymore—but perhaps not talking to Tristan alone was for the best. Alone with Tristan, she might cave in and blurt out that her childish infatuation had morphed into a full-blown crush.

Another rejection from Tristan would be so humiliating, and at least Alex claimed to have feelings for her. Thinking too much about Tristan would just confuse her and hamper her chances of developing a romantic relationship with Alex, or one of the sleeping suitors in the tower.

Even if true love never came to be, as she suspected it wouldn't, she needed Alex's help and inside information on the vampire queen's plans. Tristan wouldn't stick around forever, spending so many waking hours in the dark. Alex might.

"Tristan," she said, forcing herself to look into his eyes, even if it made what she'd decided to say so much harder, "Alex and I have been working together for over four weeks, and, well, we've grown close and become really great friends. I couldn't survive if he left."

Tristan's shoulders shifted sharply back and his expression flickered with hurt, but then hardened so quickly she wasn't sure she'd read it correctly.

"I'll always appreciate your role in training me to slay," she told him, "but things are different for me now. I've learned more about vampires." She looked up to Alex, who beamed down at her, his eyes flashing with the happiness of triumph.

Yes, she was sure she had made the right decision. "Alex is right," she told Tristan. "The two of us were doing fine before you got here. I really appreciate you bringing the roses, but I need to concentrate on falling in love and, well, you're a distraction."

Tristan took a step forward. "That's crazy, Lucette. If you're really in love with this—this vampire—then me being around shouldn't matter."

She knew he was right and secretly hoped Alex would cave on his demand and let Tristan stay. "But you've already been bitten twice," she said to Tristan. "It's such a huge risk for you to be here. You should go back to Judra to keep safe."

Tristan lifted his chin. "Whether or not I go to Judra isn't your decision, Lucette. This isn't just about you. If you die, the curse might never lift, and if your father dies or leaves, Xandra will fall. You need my help. Your kingdom needs my help. I promised your father I'd stay, and I've accepted the risks."

Lucette's throat caught. The truth of his words hurt, and although she selfishly wished his reasons for wanting to stay had more to do with her, she needed Alex's help more. And at least he claimed to love her, even if she had the sneaking suspicion that his ultimatum and love declarations were more about besting Tristan than they were about winning her heart.

"It's all well and good that you're willing to risk a third bite," she told Tristan. "But have you thought about it from my side? What happens if you're bitten? How much help will you be to me then?"

His head snapped back, and she couldn't believe she'd said that herself, but she had to convince him to go. An ache rose in her throat, threatening to close it off and bring tears. But she could not let him see how horrible she felt. What she'd said was true: the thought of him being bitten a third time terrified her. He had to leave. "Tristan, I've made my choice. Please leave."

Tristan looked stricken, but he bowed. "As you wish, Princess." He kept his eyes on her as he backed toward the staircase. It was time for Lucette to let go of her childhood fantasy.

"Keep safe," Tristan said as he disappeared from view.

She stepped toward the balcony to watch him leave, but Alex pulled her back.

"That's better," Alex said. He leaned down to kiss her, but she turned and his lips hit her cheek. Kissing Alex somehow didn't feel right, no matter how much she wished it did.

"We should keep guard," she said as she broke free from his hold, not wanting him near right now. "Which wing do you want to guard tonight, my mother's or my father's?"

"I need a rose!" Lucette shouted to Alex as a vampire appeared, seemingly out of nowhere. She'd just staked another one in the shoulder, but he'd managed to escape by running away from outside her father's bedroom.

Alex, holding extra weapons and his hood pulled down over his eyes, tossed her a rose and she forced it into the vampire's face. He staggered back and collapsed, clutching his throat.

"Leave and I'll let you live." She hoped her threat sounded genuine. It usually worked. The vast majority of the vampires breaking in each night weren't motivated enough to stay in the palace once they realized they faced live opposition.

Lucette heaved a sigh of relief when the vampire ran out, a terrified look on his face.

"That one played rough." She rubbed her arm. The vampire she'd staked had shoved her against a large table at the side of the corridor during their battle.

Alex raced to her side. "Are you okay?"

She still had trouble comprehending how quickly vampires could move, especially since, in so many other ways, Alex seemed perfectly normal—in human terms, anyway.

"I'm fine," she told him, and felt comforted by his concern.

Gathering up her weapons, she realized she also felt something more, but not for Alex—for Tristan. Ever since he'd left, she'd experienced persistent pangs of sadness and longing.

Lucette and Alex looked over the railing as they crossed the center point in the long balconied corridor between her two parents' wings to make sure no vampires were in the entry hall and that the barricades on the main doors were holding tight.

"Let's go check on my mom," she said. Every night they paced back and forth between her parents' two bedchambers.

"Why don't your parents sleep in the same room?" Alex asked.

She shot him a raised eyebrow and stepped away from him. "I don't want to talk about it." It was too sad and too embarrassing to talk about her family's problems.

Alex stepped in front of her and followed her down the hall. "Hey, it's not like I had a model family growing up, either. Mom killed Dad, remember?"

She cast him an empathetic look. "Neither of us had perfect family lives, did we?" Maybe that was why she felt close to Alex, in spite of their differences.

"It would sure make things easier for us if they at least stayed in the same wing," he said.

"Drop it!" She hated how harsh her voice sounded. "Do you think I haven't asked them? They can't even stand to be around each other anymore!" Lucette's attempts to get them to share a room via suggestions in her letters had been met with terse replies, telling her to give up her childish dreams—the marriage was over. Her mother made it clear she was living in the palace for Lucette's sake, not her father's.

Rounding the corner to her mother's corridor, Lucette saw a flash of blond hair as someone ran from her mother's door. "Tristan?" She called after the fleeing figure and then rushed forward, but whoever she'd seen was gone. Had it been a vampire? Her eyes were playing tricks on her.

"Why did you call out 'Tristan'?" Alex asked. His face hardened, and he turned to the hall, stomping in front of her.

"I thought I saw him." Although she knew it was wishful thinking, it had been nice, even for that brief moment, to believe he'd been guarding her mother's door while she and Alex took care of the vampires attacking her father.

"Looks like we're clear here." Alex's voice was gruff. "Shall we go back to the balcony or each take a door?"

"Balcony." She did not want to be alone.

Silence deepened the uncomfortable chill between them, and once at the balcony, Lucette looked over the railing. Alex sat on the floor against the opposite wall and pulled his knees into his chest, a stark contrast to his normally jovial self. She felt bad that she'd been short with him. Her hallucination of Tristan wasn't his fault, nor was the fact that she missed him. Alex had made the ultimatum to ask Tristan to go, but it had been her decision and she had to live with the consequences.

She took the weapons off her back and slid down the wall to sit beside Alex. "Before all this started, my parents were getting a divorce."

"I'm sorry." Alex kept his eyes ahead. "But at least they're both alive."

She put her hand on his forearm. "How did you find out your mom had killed your dad?"

He stretched his legs out. "I heard stuff. I couldn't ask her, of course, so I talked to one of the generals. I figured he'd reassure me that it was all rumors." Alex looked down. "He didn't."

She squeezed his arm. "How old were you when you found out?"

"About nine."

She winced. "That must have been horrible." It was time to stop feeling sorry for herself, or at least to stop complaining about her family to Alex. "How did you face your mother after that? Did you ever confront her?"

He shook his head. "I couldn't. Not without endangering General Adanthas's life and probably my own. He took a huge risk to tell me what he knew, the circumstantial evidence they'd found." He shivered. "The general also told me what my mother did to the vampires who had the guts to accuse her."

She cringed, not wanting the gory details. "I'm so sorry, Alex." She leaned over to wrap an arm over his shoulder. At least her parents weren't murderers.

The next night, Lucette started down the stairs to see if Alex had made it through the dog door yet, and was shocked to find him coming up, a rose in his hand.

He really was so generous and thoughtful, and as he handed the rose to her, she asked, "Did you pick this outside in the garden?" The bushes Tristan brought when he first came were now planted and yielding fresh blooms each day.

Alex looked disappointed. "It was downstairs. I thought you left it for me."

She shook her head, wondering who had left a rose sitting around. It might have been left by anyone, but made her think of Tristan. She missed him so much, she expected to see him around every corner.

As soon as they reached the top of the stairs, Alex leaned over to kiss her on the cheek, but she pulled back.

"You look beautiful this evening, as usual," he said, undeterred.

"Thanks." She smiled, but felt slightly awkward. "You look nice, too."

"Really?" He beamed and ran his hands down his linen shirt.

She nodded.

"Better than Tristan?"

She swallowed, but said nothing.

Alex stiffened and she felt uncomfortable at her unintentional insult. But she couldn't lie. Both of them were handsome, but when she looked at Tristan, her stomach fluttered and her mind went fuzzy. And the thought that he might still be here, still in the palace watching out for her, even though she'd so rudely turned him away—her entire body tingled with the thought. Even if it was just her imagination.

Alex broke the silence. "So, we've been alone again for a few nights. How do you think it's going?"

"Okay. But I still say keeping guard would have been easier with three of us—"

"No," Alex said sharply. "That's not what I was asking. I meant, do you think you're finally falling in love?" His voice lowered and he slipped his arm around her waist. "I'm thinking maybe it's time to take this to the next level."

"The next level?" A lump formed in her throat.

Alex smiled. "How about a kiss?" He turned toward her, but she slipped away.

"I'm not sure." Butterflies raced around inside her—nervous, uncomfortable butterflies. The idea of kissing Alex didn't feel right.

But he continued to look at her, his expression intense. Her heart pounded, and while she didn't feel in danger, she felt decidedly uncomfortable, as she had at age thirteen, the first time her father had dressed her up and introduced her to boys.

It was time to grow up, though. Perhaps she should kiss Alex. If he were right, maybe kissing him would change her feelings. But what about Tristan? The thought of him shot through her with a flush of warmth and she admonished herself for getting distracted.

Tristan had never shown her any romantic interest, whereas Alex was here and interested, and it was her duty to try everything she could to get this curse to lift.

Clearly interpreting her indecision as an invitation, Alex bent forward, but just as he was about to press his mouth against hers, she caught a glimpse of his teeth.

She gasped and pushed him back. "Your fangs."

His eyes widened. "I would never bite you!"

She shook her head. "I know, but . . ." Lucette felt as if her body no longer fit under her skin. Standing here, this close to Alex, was wrong—so wrong—and not fair to him. She simply did not want to kiss Alex.

Her mouth went dry and she backed away. "I made a mistake," she said bluntly.

"What?" Alex's expression fell.

"I miss Tristan." She swallowed. "I think he's the one I'm meant to find love with."

Alex's expression changed from hurt to anger. "That's impossible. You can't love him. He was only here for three nights."

"I knew him before. You know that. It's only because of him that I know how to slay vampires."

Alex's eyes narrowed. "You love him because he taught you how to be a murderer?"

"He taught me how to defend myself." Lucette crossed her arms over her chest. "But it's not just about that."

"What is it about, then?" Alex's expression darkened, and Lucette's fear crept in.

"It's hard to explain," she said. "But the idea of us kissing, it just doesn't feel right." She hated to hurt him, but she had to do this. "Be honest, it doesn't feel right to you, either, does it?"

"But the curse . . ." He scraped the toe of his shoe along the floor, then looked up at her, defiant. "We can work on that."

"I don't think so." She held firm. "Around Tristan I feel—I feel *different*."

Alex's face hardened. "When did you kiss Tristan?"

"I *haven't* kissed him," she said quickly.

In a blink of an eye, Alex was in front of her. "If you've never even kissed him, how can you be so sure he's the right one for you? Kiss me to be sure." He leaned forward, but she pushed back on his chest.

"I'm sorry, Alex. I don't want to kiss you. Not like that."

He backed away, but spots of color appeared on his pale cheeks. "Lucette, if you want the curse to lift, you've got to at least try. I think you're expecting too much from love."

She shook her head and tried to convey with her eyes how sorry she was. "Alex, I like you so much. You're the best friend I've ever had, but I just can't see us ever falling in love." She'd never had a brother, but if she had, she'd want him to be like Alex.

He backed away, then ran down the stairs. "Fine," he called back. "I can take a hint. If you don't want me, I'll go. I know when I'm not wanted." In a flash, he was gone. Sometimes she forgot how quickly he could move.

Her heart heavy, Lucette started down the stairs to make sure Alex had locked the dog door behind him. After checking to see that it was locked, she traced her finger along the nearly invisible crack along the top of the small door. Alex was gone. Tristan was gone. And she was alone, fighting vampires in solitude—with no hope for true love and doomed to a lifetime of darkness.

Lucette woke feeling sad and empty. Alex had been gone two nights, Tristan a week.

She stretched out in her sleeping case, hit the button for the lights, and got ready to turn over and escape the confined space. Above her was a sea of red.

Roses. Someone had left well over a dozen red roses on the top of her glass case. She twisted her head around to see if someone was in the room, but couldn't spot anyone. There weren't even any sleeping suitors in the room as there had been in the past. It appeared her father had given up. Or had the suitors? Probably her father saw the writing on the wall after Tristan left. Love was not in her destiny.

She flipped onto her front to push the trapdoor panel and make her escape from the case onto the floor of the tower room. The roses had likely been placed there by one of her parents. Whoever it had been, she was grateful.

Lifting a rose, she inhaled its sweet scent, marveling that she'd gone her entire life without experiencing such a wonderful smell. Mist clouded her eyes as she thought of the sacrifice her mother had made, having her rose gardens destroyed. A lot of good that had done.

She quickly read tonight's notes from her parents, and it seemed all was much the same. According to her mother's letter, more Xandrans had fled the kingdom—soon the country would be empty except for the palace staff and the army—but it had been more than a week since the last report of a vampire bite. The citizens who'd remained in the kingdom had gotten at barricading themselves in their homes and tricking the vampires into invading empty houses. She was glad to hear that, yet it meant even more vampires would probably focus on the palace.

Lucette ran the end of her finger over a thorn. If she couldn't protect each and every citizen of Xandra, at least she could keep the country's king and queen safe. She had to, and not just because they were her parents. If they died, Xandra would fall under the control of that horrible vampire queen forever.

She shook her head. Standing up here in the tower, sniffing roses, and feeling sorry for herself wouldn't keep anyone safe. It was time to go down to the library and change into her fighting clothes. First, she stuck a rose through the slats of each of the sleeping slayers' cases, careful not to poke them. Keeping the rest of the roses for her own protection, she descended the stairs, alert for signs of trouble. But the palace was quiet.

Lucette checked her parents' doors, ensured they were properly barricaded, and placed one of the roses at each. When she went into the library to change her clothes, she found another dozen red roses lying atop her clothes hidden behind a big atlas. She drew a deep breath that filled her with a thousand smiles.

Lucette spun to check the room, but no one was there. Her stomach fluttered. Tristan and Alex were the only ones who knew where she hid her clothes, and even if Alex had decided to come back, he couldn't have placed the roses there before sunset.

Every part of her body warmed as she thought of how the helpful gift might have come from Tristan, and as she dressed, her mind filled with thoughts of him.

Lucette spent the next three hours searching the palace for Tristan, or more roses, and found neither. Hope vanished from her heart, and returning to her main sentry point on the corridor above the front foyer, she slumped against the wall.

The sun would rise in less than two hours, and at least the night had been vampire-free. On second thought, maybe it would have been better if a vampire had broken into the palace tonight. If Tristan were still here, even if he were still hurt or angry, surely he'd have come out to help fight if she'd been attacked.

Lucette pulled a petal off a rose and pressed it to her nose. She wondered how she was going to cope all alone, never seeing the daytime again. Staring at a gaslight, she tried to remember the feel of sunlight on her face, but couldn't.

A crash rang out from her mother's wing. She sprang to her feet and ran. Her mother had already been bitten once and Lucette could not let it happen again. Heart racing, she rounded the corner to see a mad-looking vampire panting, red-eyed, and scratching at her mother's door.

He was thinner than any vampire she'd seen before, almost emaciated, his eyes hollow, his hair unruly, and his back hunched. He slammed his body against her mother's door, swore loudly, and then lined up for another attempt.

Lucette attacked, rose first. The vampire spun toward her, and she thrust the rose in his face.

"What the hell is that?" He grabbed it out of her hand and one of the thorns pierced her thumb, drawing blood.

Clearly, a rose allergy wasn't one of this vampire's ailments.

He tossed the rose to the floor and lunged, but Lucette ducked and rolled to the side, pulling out a stake at the same time.

"I came for the queen," he sneered, "but the princess will do." His eyes, deep in their dark-ringed circles, turned yellow and glowed in the dim light of the corridor.

"How much are you getting paid?" she asked as she circled around him slowly, watching him, keeping her stake raised and ready. "How much is my blood worth?"

"Wouldn't you like to know?" he snarled like a mad dog.

Lucette leaped to plant a kick in his chest, but he grabbed her foot before she struck him and shoved her back. She flew though the air, but flipped and landed on her feet.

"Impressive," he said.

"Glad I'm keeping you entertained. But why don't you leave before I hurt you?"

He laughed. "As if you could hurt me, little girl. Just for that, I think I'm going to take an extra long drink. Too bad I have orders not to kill you."

She did a twisting leap to the side, hoping to confuse him, and then plunged the stake into his shoulder. He grabbed her arm, so instead of retrieving her stake she braced herself on it and brought her knee sharply up into his groin. He cried out and released her. Lucette staggered back, pulling another stake from the quiver on her back.

Still doubled over, and with the stake sticking out of his shoulder, the vampire panted. His eyes flashed yellow. "Oh, *now* I'm angry. I think I might risk the penalty and kill you."

"What penalty?" She spun around and planted a kick to the side of his head. The vampire staggered, then turned to face her, roaring. Lucette braced as he flew toward her. Luckily, she got her stake out front in time and planted it deep in his chest, but his momentum carried forward and he toppled onto her. She fell back to the floor, him half on top of her, the back end of the stake landing just beside her ribs.

Lucette pulled herself out from under him and scooted along the floor until she felt the wall. Shaking, she looked back to make sure the vampire was still down. Her two stakes were lost. No chance was she going near that creature again. She pulled her legs in and bent forward, hiding her face in her knees. Taking a life, even that of a hideous vampire threatening to kill her, would never get easy.

But so much worse than that—with all the noise they'd made, if Tristan were in the palace he would have come running. He hadn't. He wasn't here. He was gone. And she was alone.

To top things off, she had no way of disposing of that vampire's body. Someone else would have to deal with it in the daylight, and if her father didn't already know she got free every night, he couldn't ignore this. Thinking of daylight, she realized it was nearly dawn and time to get changed and climb back into her sleeping case.

The next night, Lucette woke with sadness for company. She would even have welcomed some of those would-be suitors who used to sleep outside her glass case. After releasing herself from captivity, she checked the letters left under the wall of the cell, but they were both from her parents. None from random suitors. None from Tristan. She read her father's first.

Dearest Lucette,
I hope your days spent in the tower are bearable. At least I know you're safe, although I know Tristan patrols the palace at night and can't stay with you in the tower every moment. I'm glad you have him to talk to. The thought of you alone is so hard to bear. Did you know Tristan killed a vampire last night? Right in front of your mother's room. It gave your mother a real start when she rose, but he apologized for not getting rid of the body.

Lucette's heart raced and her head buzzed. Tristan *was* still here! And from the sounds of it, he'd been lying to her parents to maintain her cover.

Your young man is quite exceptional and brave. I'll be so proud if someday he joins our family. I hope you're giving him a chance. He's got a good head on his shoulders. He even convinced your mother and me that we should sleep in the same bedchamber from now on to make it easier for him to guard us both. He told us how concerned you've been for our safety.

With love,
Dad

Happiness and hope flowed through Lucette. Her parents were sharing a bedchamber! Only the sight of Tristan's face could make her happier. If he were around the palace during the daytime, where was he hiding? Was he spending his nights in the palace, too?

Although she wanted him to be safe from vampires, she was thrilled to hear he hadn't returned to Judra. She knew her feelings were selfish, but she couldn't help how she felt.

Lucette scrambled down the tower stairs, raced to the library, and pulled out the atlas. Another dozen roses sat atop of her clothes. Her heart thumped. They must be from Tristan. Even if he didn't love her, the gesture filled her with giddiness. She changed quickly and then discovered he'd replaced the stakes she'd lost last night, too. Even better, she found a note sticking out of the top of her quiver of stakes.

Dear Lucette,
I tried to stay away, but I can't. I didn't see Alex last night, and I hope he isn't hurt because I know that would cause you pain. I'd like to talk to you, but don't want to intrude on your time with Alex. If you are willing to talk, please give me a sign by dropping one of these roses from the main entry hall balcony before midnight tonight. If you choose not to, I'll understand, and will never bother you again.

Your loyal friend forever,
Tristan

Heart racing, she dashed out of the library down the corridor to the balcony and threw the entire bundle of roses to the foyer below.

She gasped. That had been foolish. Now she didn't have any roses left for defense. She raced for the stairs, intending to retrieve them, and when she was halfway down Tristan appeared at the bottom. Happiness clutched her throat and her chest and her heart. She nearly tripped as she sped down the final stretch, then flung herself into his arms.

"Oh, Tristan, I'm so sorry! I never should have sent you away!"

He led her to the top of the stairs. "Does this mean you're no longer in love with Alex?"

"I never was." She shook her head. "How could I possibly love Alex when—when I know you." She couldn't risk saying the word *love,* although it was what she felt.

Embarrassed and terrified that he was about to reject her again, Lucette wished she could just shrivel up and blow away in the wind. She looked down, but he caught her chin in his fingers and lifted her gaze back to his.

Where she'd expected to see pity, she saw something else. She wasn't entirely sure what it was, but she liked it. The blue in his eyes sparkled in the soft light.

His fingers lightly stroked her cheek and her body trembled with anticipation until he finally bent down to brush his lips against hers. The soft kiss sent a thrill racing through her. Her knees weakened, but Tristan slid his hand around her waist and pressed his lips more firmly against hers.

So many years she'd been dreaming about his kiss, but it was even better than she'd imagined. His lips were firm and demanding, his breath tasted of mint. So giddy, Lucette felt as if her feet had lifted off the ground. Realizing they had, she laughed against his lips. He spun her as they kissed, and she felt as though their bodies had created a vortex into which the entire world might collapse.

Tristan broke away and set her back on the ground. She placed her hand on his cheek. "Is this really happening?"

He smiled. "It is."

"But I thought—" Feeling foolish, she stopped herself, not knowing what to say and not wanting to ruin the moment. This was her first kiss. She had no idea what to do or say.

"You thought what?" His arms felt warm and strong on her waist.

"I thought you didn't like me—not like this." As soon as she said it, she felt presumptuous for assuming his feelings. But then she felt silly for that. After all, he *had* kissed her.

"Oh, Lucette." He bent to capture her lips again. "When we were younger, I admired you more than I should have. You were so bold and determined, plus I thought you were pretty. But I fought my feelings. I had to. I was your mentor. It wasn't right."

He pressed kisses onto her forehead, then her nose. "When I saw you sleeping in that glass case, I didn't make any connection to the girl I'd tried so hard to push from my mind. Now I feel foolish for not recognizing you the second you woke." He shook his head. "The instant I realized it was you, I fell in love. Now my beautiful warrior girl is an even more beautiful warrior woman, and so brave to be facing vampires all on her own." He pulled her into a hug. "I can never lose you."

Lucette felt like she'd burst from joy. Now that she'd found true love, the curse would end.

Standing on the stone balcony outside her bedroom, Queen Natasha turned to Alexander. "Bring the girl back here."

"The princess?" her son asked, sprawling back in his chair as if she'd just asked him to clean up his room.

"Who else would I mean?" she snapped. Natasha forced herself to calm down. Her son was no imbecile, but for some reason, he was being purposefully obtuse, and she was determined to discover why. He might be her son, but she found him hard to trust, even though he'd been crossing into Xandra and reporting back on the work of her bloodsucking minions.

Regardless of all that, the moment Alexander stopped being useful, the moment she suspected treachery, she'd drive a stake through his heart and blame the slayers. The tragic loss of her son would build sympathy and support.

"Why do you want the princess brought here?" he asked as he traced his fingers over a rose embroidered on the arm of her favorite chair.

"Can't you see?" She strode around the back of the chair and leaned over to put her lips next to his ear. "If we take her, Stefan will have no choice. He'll invade, and then our armies will crush Xandra." And then Stefan and Catia would cower at her feet. That idea was most delicious. As was finally sitting on the throne of Xandra as she'd been meant to.

"If you want war"—he pulled out a thread from the chair—"why not invade now?"

"Stop that." She slapped his hand. "You'll ruin the fabric." She circled around to the front. "My darling son, if we attack first, then we'll be the aggressor, and other kingdoms will rise up in Xandra's defense. It would weaken me, spoil my chance to expand my empire later." She wanted the subjects of *all* the kingdoms to bow down before her in adoration and fear. The combination was like the most intoxicating elixir. She'd learned that when she'd aimed a stake at her late husband's heart.

Alexander didn't need to know that the generals still refused to invade unless Xandra declared war. But soon those now-influential generals would bow down before her, too. Soon.

"I get it"—he nodded— "but I can't bring back the princess. They keep her locked in a glass case." He remained nonchalant. "There's no way to get to her."

She leaned down so she could look into his eyes. "Glass? I don't see the problem."

"The glass won't break," he said. "I think it's enchanted."

She flew back from his chair, slammed her fist down on the balcony railing, and the stone cracked. *Those damn fairies, meddling again!* She'd show them. "Have you really done all you can to get to the girl?" she asked her son.

"She's a defenseless beauty in a glass case. I'm a teenaged boy, Mother. Of course I've tried." Alex rolled his eyes, then smiled lasciviously.

She might have scolded her son for his snarky tone, but his words pleased her. "So you've taken a fancy to the sleeping beauty of Xandra?" This was an exciting development. Perhaps she would let her son live after all. Perhaps he would prove useful.

She set her hands on the arms of his chair and leaned toward him. "She'd make a good mate for you, I think." She resisted an urge to rub her hands together in delight. Imagine, Catia's precious daughter converted and married to a vampire, and one day giving birth to vampire children. The idea filled Natasha with vengeful glee.

But she questioned her son's claim. "Others say they've seen the princess roaming the palace." It was beyond frustrating that she couldn't enter Xandra to see for herself.

"That's not possible," Alex said quickly. "If she ever got out of that glass case, I'd be all over her." He shifted in the chair and grinned. "There are humans around the palace some nights—mercenaries from other kingdoms, I assume. Perhaps someone mistook one of them for her?"

Natasha stepped back and narrowed her eyes. It was doubtful, but possible. She wouldn't put it past Catia and Stefan to lure some poor girl from a neighboring kingdom to impersonate their daughter and act as bait. Did they think she'd be so easily fooled?

Alex crossed his legs and rested his elbows on the arms of his chair. "I've always wondered. Why did you do it in the first place? Why curse a baby?"

She studied her handsome son for signs of deceit, but his question seemed sincere. "Because her hateful mother and father betrayed me most egregiously, that's why."

"How?" His expression showed concern for her suffering.

"I was meant to marry King Stefan, not Catia. That horrid, hateful snake stole the man who would be my husband. He was mine and she went behind my back and took him—and my place as the rightful queen of Xandra."

"I understand how that would make you angry. More than you know. Tell me more."

Natasha pulled up a chair beside her son and sat down. "I'll tell you everything." Perhaps Alex did have leadership potential. It was so hard to know with teenagers, but he was maturing, finally showing some promise. Perhaps he wasn't as much like his father as she'd first feared. Perhaps it was time he knew the whole truth.

And if there were no way to capture the sleeping princess, Natasha would order her minions to capture the king and queen themselves. She'd make them pay, and no one would ever know what had happened to the Xandran monarchs. No matter what, it was time to escalate the nightly invasions. From now on, her minions would be ordered to kill.

"Don't ever do that again," Lucette told Tristan as he waited for her to change from her gown into her slaying clothes. "It doesn't seem fair that you watch me sleep." And knowing he was on the other side of the screen right now sent tingles through her body.

These past weeks with Tristan had been wonderful, but although she felt sure she was in love, the curse hadn't lifted.

"But you're so beautiful," he replied from the other side of the screen. "How can you blame me for watching you sleep?"

It *was* kind of romantic. Still . . . "But during the day I'm in a glass case, and can't wake up. It just doesn't feel right. If you watch, it's like you're spying on me."

"That *is* messed up," another male voice said. "Creepy, in fact."

Her boots not yet laced up, Lucette shot out from behind the screen. "Alex!" She ran to hug him. "You came back!" It had been over two weeks.

Tristan stood to the side, and Lucette admired him for remaining calm.

"Do you think I could really stay away?" Alex winked, and then nodded toward Tristan. "I see *he* came out of hiding."

"You knew Tristan hadn't left?" she asked, looking back and forth between the two young men.

Alex shrugged and said, "I never would've left you completely alone. I figured he'd show himself eventually."

"So you're not mad?"

"Nah." Alex took a step back and ran his fingers through his hair. "And I've got big news. Huge."

"What's going on?" Had his mother decided to lift the curse? Her hope vanished when she saw his expression. "Bad news?"

He took a deep breath. "It's not all bad, I guess, depending on your perspective."

Tristan pressed a kiss into her hair. "You two talk. I'll go check on your parents' room."

Lucette watched him leave, her heart nearly bursting with happiness. Alex was back and Tristan trusted her enough, and trusted Alex enough, not to object when she wanted to talk to him alone.

As soon as Tristan left the room, Lucette pulled Alex to a set of leather chairs. "What's your mother done now?" She bent to tie up her boots.

He sat down and crossed one leg, a foot up on his knee. "She wants your dad to invade, so she won't be blamed for starting a war. She's also trying to capture you and your parents and bring you to Sanguinia. And"—he paused and ran his fingers through his hair—"I think I finally understand her grudge against your family."

Lucette raised a questioning eyebrow. "Tell me."

"Well," he leaned forward, "for starters, we're cousins."

"What?" This had to be some kind of a joke.

"Yeah." His cheeks flared red. "Turns out our mothers are sisters."

Lucette felt as if she'd been crushed under a huge stone. The vampire queen was her aunt? Alex, her cousin? No wonder she'd never felt the romantic kind of love for him.

Alex leaned back in the chair. "Crazy, I know. I could barely keep from wanting to strangle my mother when she told me. But I had to make her think I understood why she'd done it."

She looked up. "That must have been so difficult."

He squared his shoulders. "That's just the start. I also found out why my mother laid the curse."

Alex's news was tough to digest, but she didn't have much time to think about it. A crash outside the library and a shout from Tristan drew them both out into the hall.

She rolled and stabbed a stake into the calf of a vampire who had his fangs pointed toward Tristan's throat.

"Ouch!" The vampire twisted as her stake struck, and he let Tristan go. Alex lassoed the vampire with a rope and pulled the attacker's arms in tight.

"Thanks," she said to Alex, still marveling that they were related.

"Look out!" he yelled, and she turned just as a huge vampire, who'd appeared out of nowhere, dove toward her. But before he touched her, his face contorted in pain and he fell to his knees, a stake protruding from his shoulder.

Tristan stood behind the vampire.

"You shouldn't leave your stake in the body," she told him with a cheeky grin. "You might need it for another attack."

"Good advice," Tristan said as pulled out the stake. Then, before the vampire could recover, he wrapped a rope around the vampire's arms. "Whoever taught you that lesson must have wanted to make sure you stayed safe."

She smiled softly, but the sound of splintering wood downstairs pulled her away. She barely had time to talk to either Tristan or Alex for the rest of the night, and for the first time, she felt lucky for the diversion of chasing vampires. They'd come in higher numbers tonight, and they seemed intent on attacking her parents.

Finally, as dawn threatened on the horizon, Lucette bid Alex good morning, so he'd have time to find a safe place to hide for the day. Then she went behind her screen in the library, pulled off her slayer uniform, and slipped into her nightgown.

Walking up to the tower room, Tristan's hand in hers, she knew she had to tell him what she'd learned tonight. He hadn't pumped her for information, and she loved that about him. But she wanted to share it all, every one of her mixed and horrible feelings. He'd help her sort them out.

But there wasn't much time before sunrise. Once they were in the tower, Tristan put his back against the wall and slid down to sit on the floor in what she used to think of as the suitors' gallery. She slid down the wall next to him, and he put an arm around her shoulders.

"Alex upset you," Tristan said. "Do you want to talk about it? Or is there any information I should be passing on to your father?"

Tears welled in Lucette's eyes. "That's the most horrible part. My parents already know most of what Alex told me. They've known it all along, but never said a thing. They lied to me my whole life. At best, they left out some pretty important details."

Tristan pulled her closer, and she buried her face in his neck, inhaling his spicy scent.

"I don't know where to start." Lucette looked into Tristan's bright blue eyes.

"Start wherever you want. But if you don't want your dad to know you've been out of that glass case, you'd better start now." The sky was lightening through the window behind the glass wall.

She nodded, then blurted, "Alex is my cousin."

Tristan opened his eyes wide. "That's not possible. He's a vampire."

"His mother Natasha is my mother's older sister. When she was still human, she wanted to marry my father. But when he chose my mom instead, Natasha went ballistic. She was so eager to get revenge and to sit on a throne—any throne—that she converted herself into a vampire and seduced Alex's dad."

"How would that get her revenge?" Tristan squeezed her hand and Lucette felt warm and safe and loved.

"She figured that as a vampire she could torture my parents—maybe even kill them—and take the throne for herself. My mom hates vampires, and the vampire queen figured that knowing her sister was one would be a form of torture in itself. I guess it was, because my family acts as if she doesn't exist.

"Alex's dad," she continued, "King Vladimir, realized his mistake in his choice of bride. He threatened to divorce her and have her arrested if she didn't give up on her thirst for human blood. So she killed him."

Tristan tensed, but soon relaxed, and nodded. "I'd heard rumors that the vampire queen killed her husband."

"It's never been proven, but Alex is sure. He's even spoken to senior members of the Sanguinian army and they're sure, too. He told me about his father's murder a while ago. It was one of the reasons I first trusted him. Anyway, that's not the worst of it. I found out why she cursed me."

Tears rose, but Lucette blinked to push them back. "All my life, I thought my parents' arguments were my fault. I was all they ever fought about, and I blamed myself. I guess I knew the curse wasn't my fault—I was only a baby—but I figured the curse wasn't *their* fault, either. But it kind of was."

"How?"

"My mom didn't invite her sister to my naming ceremony, and so Natasha cast the curse out of anger and jealousy. She's so petty and cruel. She destroyed my life because she wasn't invited to a party."

"That's horrible. Lucette, I'm so sorry." He hugged her tightly.

As comforting as his hug was, anger and hurt rose inside her. "I wonder if my aunt realized her curse would drive a stake into my parents' marriage, too. Probably. Who would curse their own family?" She drew a deep breath.

Tristan stroked her hair for a few minutes, then whispered into her ear. "If you want to get into that glass case before sunrise, there's not much time."

She started to get up, then stopped. "You know what? If it's okay with you, I think I'd like to fall asleep in your arms this morning."

"But your father—"

She shook her head. "I think there have been enough lies in my family. It will be better if he knows I'm not staying in there at night."

He bent down to kiss her cheek and said, "That is absolutely fine with me."

The next night, Lucette smiled as she watched Alex and Tristan talk. The two young men seemed to have struck a truce. They might not exactly be best friends yet, but they weren't at each other's throats, either.

Since the truth had come out, Lucette had grown even more anxious for the curse to end. And she couldn't figure out why it hadn't. She loved Tristan with all her heart, and felt sure he loved her, but how in the world was she supposed to prove it?

Those cryptic fairies had claimed she'd know what to do when the time came, but the time was here—and she didn't know.

Even with Tristan in her life and Alex as such a good friend—and cousin—she couldn't bear the thought of living the rest of her life in darkness. Plus, if the curse didn't end, Xandra would eventually fall. From what Tristan had told her, fewer than a quarter of the citizens remained in the kingdom. The rest had crossed through the dangerous werewolf territories to live in refugee camps in faraway Judra, with many seeking to immigrate.

But if Alex was right about his mother's ambitions, she wouldn't rest until she ruled every kingdom.

With everyone fleeing, even if her father survived, he'd have no subjects. No real kingdom. It had to be breaking his heart to see Xandra this way.

Breaking away from Alex, Tristan sauntered toward her, a shy look on his face.

"Had enough boy talk?" she teased.

"Definitely." Tristan traced a hand down Lucette's arm. "Actually, I was hoping we could talk alone for a few minutes. Somewhere private. Alex says he'll keep a lookout and shout the alarm if he hears any trouble."

"Great." Her insides stirred at the thought of some alone time with Tristan. Glad as she'd been to see Alex's return, she'd missed the nights she'd had with just the two of them.

He opened the door of the library for her and guided her to a plush upholstered chair. He pulled another over and sat facing her. The formality made her worry about what he wanted to discuss.

Tristan cleared his throat. "Lucette, I love you."

A huge smile spread on her face. "I love you, too." She reached out to take his hand.

"Yes, but . . ." A blush appeared on his cheeks. "The curse. It hasn't lifted."

Her heart dropped. "I know. I've been thinking about that, too, and I'm trying to figure it out. The fairies said I'd know what to do, but I don't."

"Lucette." He took both of her hands in his. "You've got to stop blaming yourself for everything. It's not your fault you were cursed. It's not your fault your parents argued. It's not your fault the fairies were cryptic—they're cryptic with everyone. Fairies love riddles."

"So, what's the answer?" She tried not to sound as defeated as she felt.

He shifted in his chair, the first time she'd ever seen him nervous. "Well, I've been thinking about it and I have an idea—just a theory. It might be wrong. I don't know."

"What?"

He blurted, "I wonder if we're supposed to get married."

Lucette's jaw dropped.

"Or not." Tristan shook his head. "If you're not ready . . . You're only sixteen, and we've got our whole lives . . ." He ran his fingers through his hair. "I thought asking you so soon might be a bad idea, but Alex—"

"You talked about this with Alex?" The blush in Lucette's cheeks rose so ferociously that she wondered if her face might catch on fire.

"I'm sorry." He pulled her hand to his lips and kissed it. "I didn't mean to be disrespectful. And I certainly don't want to be presumptuous. But Alex and I were talking about the curse and it just kind of came up."

Lucette leaned back in her chair. Her mind raced with so many thoughts, it was hard to pin any of them down. Her mother hadn't been much older when she married her father, but look how that had turned out. She knew she loved Tristan, but marriage was such a big step—especially at her age. The future of her kingdom depended on her, but in so many ways she still felt like a kid.

On the other hand, she needed to find some way to prove her love so the curse would lift. It was her duty to try everything she could think of, but this . . . She wasn't sure she was ready for this. The fairies said she'd know how to prove her love, but she didn't feel sure about marriage at all.

She needed to talk to her mother. She shot to her feet, remembering that she'd not read her mother's letter when she got up last evening, or replied. "I've got to go up to the tower. I need to be alone—to think."

"Lucette." Tristan stood and pulled her into a hug. "Forget I brought it up. I'm sorry."

"Don't be sorry." She pulled away. "Really. I understand why you brought it up, I do, and want to marry you . . . someday. Just let me think for a bit." She dried her palms on her slacks. "Come up to the tower in ten minutes and we'll talk again, okay?"

He nodded, and she left the room.

When she stepped into the corridor, Alex turned away quickly and leaned against the balcony railing. It made her think he'd been listening, but she was glad he didn't make eye contact or try to talk to her. Right now, she needed to talk to her mother, and since that was impossible, she'd do the next best thing and read her mother's latest letter.

Lucette shifted quickly through the letters that had been shoved through the slot in the glass cell. Even though everyone knew she no longer lived in the cell, its slot had become a mailbox. In her recent letters to her mother, she'd been asking for ideas about proving her love. Most of the answers so far had been vague, like "Trust yourself" and "The proof will come with time," but Lucette hoped that tonight's letter held more practical advice.

She found the right letter and opened it quickly. But it was no help at all, just more generalities and vague assurances that she should let her love for Tristan develop. Before she fell asleep, she'd write a note to her mother asking her advice about marriage, point-blank. Tristan would have to wait for his answer until tomorrow.

Nerves soured her stomach. She loved Tristan—she did—so why did the idea of marriage make her so nervous? She wanted to be married . . . someday . . . and to Tristan, but not yet.

Suddenly, Lucette heard a noise on the stairs. Someone was coming. Had it been ten minutes already? Would Tristan officially propose? If so, what would he say if she asked him to wait for her answer? Her palms started to sweat.

But instead of Tristan, six hulking vampires burst into the room. Lucette backed toward the glass wall and reached to her back for a stake . . . only then remembering that she'd taken off her weapons and dropped them near the door.

Six vampires? Lucette doesn't have a chance!

To find out what happens next, turn to section 9: At War (page 291).

Section 8

A Leap of Faith

8

Lucette's insides twisted like they had every time her parents wedged her between them. She looked at Alex. He'd helped her so much, but now his behavior felt petulant and demanding, insisting she send Tristan away without any regard to what she wanted and forcing her to choose.

She turned to Tristan, who was leaning back against the balcony railing and didn't look worried at all. He smiled, appearing very sure of himself. The combination of his confidence and grin revived the buzzing in her body, and she knew for sure. Even if Tristan made her nervous, even if he rejected her, even if he'd never love her the way she hoped he would, she couldn't send him away. Not after he'd been so brave and risked his life to come to Xandra. But she didn't want Alex to leave, either, and she hoped his threat had been hollow. It had to be.

"Alex, I can't ask Tristan to leave. With three of us, it will be easier to cover more ground. Besides, even though you've been a huge help—so much—you won't fight vampires, not really. What would I do if vampires attacked both my mother's and father's rooms at the same time? I can't be in two places at once. I need Tristan here." She turned to Tristan. "That is, assuming he wants to stay." She felt a flush rise on her cheeks.

"I would never leave you," Tristan promised.

Lucette heard a thump and turned to see that Alex had kicked his chair over.

"Fine, I'll go then." Alex was breathing quickly and his nostrils flared. "I can see when I'm not wanted." He turned to Lucette, his eyes full of hurt. "I thought we had a real chance." He stepped over the fallen chair. "But if you're not interested in lifting the curse, I guess I'll go tell my mother's generals that I support her now. That I think vampires should drink human blood. That Xandrans are evil murderers slaying innocent vampires. That Sanguinia should invade Xandra." He narrowed his eyes. "We'll conquer you easily."

She sucked in a sharp breath. "You wouldn't do that." Alex was just angry and hurt. Raised by such a cruel mother, it was a wonder he didn't have outbursts like this more often.

Alex shifted slightly and looked to the side for a second, then back to her. "Just watch me."

He ran down the stairs and then, moments later, she heard splintering wood as he broke out of the palace.

Lucette stood, dumbfounded, fighting tears, and Tristan stepped up behind her and put his hands on her shoulders. "We're better off without him."

His hands were so warm and comforting and strong, but she shrugged them off. "Leave me alone."

Alex had been nothing but kind, her only support since the curse had fallen, and because of Tristan, she'd sent him away.

Two nights later, Lucette woke in her glass case to find Tristan bent over the top, looking down at her.

She banged her palms up against the glass and he jumped back.

"Don't do that!" she yelled. "It creeps me out when you watch me sleep."

He nodded, hands behind his back. "I'm sorry. Really." His voice was muted through the glass. "It's just you're so peaceful when you're sleeping, I can't resist." He cleared his throat. "But mostly I feel I can keep you safer if I'm nearby."

She slid down, pushed open the panel at her feet, and slithered out of the display case into the glass cell. Putting her hands on her hips, she turned back to Tristan. "I'm not buying the 'keep me safe' line, so don't even try it. I'm perfectly safe inside that horrid glass coffin. Or back here."

"Out there," she continued, "*you're* the one who's vulnerable after dark. Plus, you've been bitten—twice—so you're taking the bigger risk. Where's your neck protector?"

Lifting a hand to his bare neck, he gestured behind him with his head. "It's not like the vampires can't bite me on another part of my body. We've seen that."

"Yes." She dropped her hands to her sides. "But why make it easy for them to go for their favorite vein?"

A mischievous grin took over his face, and he put his lips against the air holes in the glass separating them. "Why, Princess, if I didn't know better, I might think you cared."

He looked at her with such intensity, her skin burned, and she turned away, yelling back, "I need to get changed. Did you bring my clothes up?"

He nodded and picked up the small pile. They'd decided that since he could smuggle her slayer clothes up here at nightfall, there was no sense in her changing in the library anymore.

"Can you pass them in and turn away, please?" She had a privacy screen behind the glass partition, but didn't like how her body tingled when she knew Tristan was looking in her direction while she changed.

Tristan slipped the clothes through the small opening at the bottom of the glass wall, and then Lucette disappeared behind her screen to change. It had only been two days, but she missed Alex. She'd grown accustomed to his bright, yellow-specked green eyes, his flaming red hair, his pale skin, and his sense of humor.

"Any sign of Alex?" she asked as she changed.

"No," Tristan replied. "Do you think he meant what he said? Do you think he'd betray you to his mother?"

Dressed, she stepped out from behind her screen and was pleased to see that Tristan's back was still turned. "I'm decent," she said.

He turned and smiled. "More than decent, if you ask me."

Blushing, she climbed back through her glass coffin into the outer part of the tower room. As he helped her out, the warmth of his hands on her made her feel dizzy, so she stepped out of his arms to clear her head, and remembered he'd asked her a question about Alex.

She cleared her throat. "I'm sure Alex wouldn't turn on me. Not after all this time." She bit her lip. "He was just upset, don't you think?"

"And jealous of me," Tristan said. "I'd be hurt, too, if you chose him."

She felt herself blush and pulled on her hood so she could hide her pink cheeks. She wanted to press Tristan to say more about how he felt, but lacked the courage. If he rejected her again, she couldn't face him every night, and she certainly didn't want to face being alone.

After picking up her weapons, she motioned for Tristan to follow her down the tower stairs and into the main entry hall of the palace.

"How's the night look?" she asked. "Any action yet?" The entered the foyer and she scanned the large, tiled room with its high vaulted ceiling.

"Quiet, so far." Tristan's eyes looked as if he had a secret. "And I've got a surprise."

"Really? What?"

He pushed a dark rolling screen aside to reveal a meal—roasted duck, vegetables, gravy, and two goblets of wine—set on a table adorned with candles. "I thought we could have a nice dinner together."

"A date?" Lucette's heart raced, and she wanted to gobble the word back. Her cheeks burned.

"Sure," Tristan said. "We can call it a date."

Relief flooded her and her body started to feel a bit like jelly. Then he pulled out a chair for her, and she felt so grown-up. That thought made her laugh to herself. She was responsible for defending herself, defending her parents, defending her entire kingdom against vampire attacks—how could she *not* feel grown-up?

But she often did feel like a kid, and Tristan treating her this way added another whole dimension to adulthood—one she hoped she was ready for. Without true love, the curse wouldn't break.

He poured her a glass of wine before taking his chair, then held his goblet toward her.

She lifted hers, too, but paused. "We shouldn't drink much wine. What if vampires show up?"

"Lucette"—he made and held eye contact—"just for the few minutes it takes us to enjoy this meal, please, let's pretend there are no vampires and no curse. Let's pretend we have nothing to fear."

His voice was comforting, so Lucette nodded and took a tiny sip of the wine. As the flavor filled her mouth, she gazed at Tristan for so long that she grew embarrassed and looked down to her food.

"Thank you," she said as she gestured over the table, "for all this."

"My pleasure." He offered her a duck leg. "You deserve a little something normal in your life."

As he served them, she asked, "What's Judra like? Do you have brothers and sisters? What are your parents like? Before you came here to the academy, where did you go to school?"

He started to laugh.

"Sorry." Lucette smiled. "I just realized that even with all the time we spent together training, I hardly know anything about you. And since you've been back, it's been all about vampires and stakes—and who's covering which of my parents' bedrooms."

Tristan reached across the table, but instead of going for a bread roll as she'd assumed he would, he took her hand.

She fought her first instinct to yank her hand back, and instead drew a long, deep breath. The temperature in the room seemed to have risen several degrees, and she hoped her palm wouldn't start to sweat. That would be embarrassing.

Just then, something crashed in the hall.

They sprang to their feet, grabbed their weapons, and slung crossbows and quivers of arrows and stakes on their backs. As they raced up the stairs, they put on their masks and hoods, and kept close to the wall, alert to any movement in the corridor above them.

Working together silently and confidently, they used the hand signals and nods he'd taught her to determine that Tristan would round the corner at the top of the stairs first.

Lucette followed on Tristan's direction, climbing the stairs and stopping in the open corridor above the foyer. The crash of splintering wood came from the right, where her father's bedchamber lay, and the smash of breaking glass came from the direction of her mother's.

Yet again, she had to choose between her parents, but at least she could decide objectively this time. Tristan was closer to her father's room; she was closer to her mother's.

Before he left, Tristan squeezed her arm and sent her a reassuring look through the slit in his mask.

Lucette's heart pinched. What if he were bitten again tonight? What if this were the last time she saw him? They'd never even discussed what he'd want her to do if he did get that fatal third bite. Would he want her to rush him to Sanguinia so vampire surgeons could convert him? Or would he rather die? She had no idea.

Creeping silently, Lucette approached the bend in the hall that led to her mother's bedchamber and peeked around the corner. In front of her mother's door stood a single vampire, but a big one, and he looked crazed. He slashed and banged at the door with his fingers and fists, as if he thought he could claw through the wood. His fingernails, illuminated by a beam of light, were so long and sharp they looked liked claws. He'd gouged deep scratches in the door, and his fingers were bleeding.

Snarling like a mad dog, he dropped his hands, stepped back, and then rammed his shoulder into the door. "Come on, Queenie!" he snarled. "I know you're in there!"

This particular vampire did not appear to be the brightest candle in the castle, but clearly he'd been told where to find the queen's room, and that thought chilled Lucette. These vampires knew so much about the palace, knew where to find her parents, and she wondered how. But she couldn't believe it was Alex. In spite of his threats, she felt sure he wouldn't side with his evil mother.

Spotting no roses to use as a defense, she took the crossbow off her back, pulled an arrow from her quiver, and then loaded and cocked it. The vampire seemed too unpredictable for her to attack with a stake, or even a rose, if she had one. Better to keep well out of range of those fingernails.

Raising the crossbow, she took aim for the vampire's shoulder, and hoped that if she wounded him, he'd flee. Holding the bow ready, she waited. He pulled away from the door and granted Lucette a clean shot. She fired, and the arrow struck right where she'd aimed.

The vampire screamed a high-pitched screech that had Lucette fighting not to cover her ears. Then he yanked the arrow from his flesh and stared at it, confused about how it had gotten there. He caught a glimpse of Lucette in the shadows, and his confusion turned to anger. With snarling lips, yellow teeth, and sharp fangs, he staggered toward her. No time to load another arrow.

Lucette pulled out a stake and ran toward the vampire. Jumping, she planted her heavy boot into his chest, and the vampire stumbled back.

Roaring in anger, he advanced again. Adrenaline pumped through Lucette as she ducked out of his way, then she spun, jumped onto a table at the side of the corridor, leaped off, and kicked the vampire in the head before landing back on the stone floor.

The vampire clutched the side of his head, but he still wasn't down, and certainly wasn't deterred. Most vampires gave up their quest for blood once they were challenged. Not this one. Baring his fangs, he lunged for her neck. Seeing his fangs up close and personal, she wasn't confident that the metal-threaded fabric of her neck protector was strong enough to stop them, so she dodged under him and rolled to the other side of the corridor.

Patiently, she waited in a crouch, stake ready. He dove for her again, and Lucette stood up, thrust her stake forward, and drove it into his chest.

The vampire wailed. Pain and anguish took control of his face, and then he fell to the floor. Lucette turned to the wall, confident she'd hit his heart and not wanting to watch him die. Even though this vampire had seemed intent on killing her, killing him didn't feel any better than her first kill.

Trembling and panting, she bent over and tried to force his death from her mind. What she wouldn't give to be back at that romantic dinner with Tristan.

A hand landed on her shoulder and, pulling another stake from her quiver, she spun.

Tristan. She dove into his arms, but he grabbed her shoulders and shoved her back. "Never turn your back on a vampire until you're sure it's dead!" He glared at her and then went over to the vampire, studied it, and pulled out her stake. "And never leave your stake behind. You might need it later."

"I killed him," she said, her voice hard and forceful.

Tristan pulled off his hood and handed her the stake. "Yeah, but that doesn't mean you should ignore proper battle protocols. What if you'd missed its heart? What if another vampire arrived? You can't let your guard down after a kill. I taught you better than that."

Her cheeks burned under her masked hood and she fumbled to pull it off. "You're not my teacher anymore." She slammed her hood to the floor. "I have more experience defending myself against vampires than you do. And how can you be so cold about it? That vampire might have been insane, but he was a living, breathing, thinking creature, just like you and me."

Tristan's expression hardened. "Your dad's safe, by the way. I killed my vampire, too. No thanks necessary."

She glared at him. "We don't have to kill them! Not unless there's no other way."

"Was that your idea or Alex's? Ever think he might have been protecting them?"

"Alex had good reasons for not wanting them dead. I already told you that."

Tristan shook his head. "Oh, please. Alex's theory is pretty far-fetched, don't you think? The queen paying vampires to cross the border, knowing some will be slayed, then using the dead vampire bodies as evidence of human cruelty to incite hatred and gain support for her evil cause? You really believe that?"

"Yes, I do. His mother's crazy. She's been trying to get us into a war with Sanguinia ever since I was born."

Tristan put his hand on her shoulder, but she shrugged it off.

"Lucette," he said, "I don't know why she cursed you, but don't you think it's a pretty strange way to start a war? Why would she go after a baby?"

Lucette took a few long breaths before responding. She had to admit, there were still holes in her understanding of the vampire queen's motives. It didn't seem like one nation going after another. It seemed personal.

But what possible reasons could the vampire queen have for a personal vendetta? She turned to Tristan. "No matter what her motives are, unnecessary killing is not okay. Until tonight, nearly every vampire I've found gave up the second he was wounded. Some, even as soon as they saw me coming. We do *not* have to kill them!"

"Fine, fine." Tristan held up his hands. "We'll do it your way. Here's hoping we don't die for your ethics."

He looked away and sighed. After a moment, his expression softened. "I'm disappointed that our date got interrupted."

Lucette relaxed as he approached, but then she trembled as the full realization of what had happened sank in. He put his hands on her shoulders and pulled her into an embrace. "Hey, it's okay. You did what you had to do."

She looked into his eyes, grateful that he understood why she was upset. He pressed a kiss onto her forehead and ran a hand over her hair.

"Lucette," he said, "why don't your parents sleep in the same bedchamber? It would be so much easier to protect them if they were in the same place."

At that, tears filled her eyes, and she blinked rapidly, trying to push them back in. All the emotion and adrenaline that had built during the battle peaked into a rush of grief. A tear dribbled down each cheek and she lifted her hand to brush them away, but Tristan beat her to it, sweeping away her tears.

The tenderness and intimacy of his gesture washed away her thoughts of the battle. His hands on her face were so gentle. She felt at home and safe, as if she'd spent her entire life in his strong arms.

"Come on," he said. "Let's get away from this carnage so we can talk."

She nodded. For the first time in her life, she had someone to confide in. He'd understand about her parents. She just knew he would.

Sitting outside the king's office, Tristan pulled Lucette into his arms and pressed his lips into her hair. "It's not your fault," he said. "When parents divorce, it's never because of the children, even if that's how it feels." They'd finished their meal and were back up on the balcony above the foyer, keeping watch.

"But in my case, it is," Lucette said. "My parents' fights have always been about me. Whether I should be allowed to play with other kids, whether I should be allowed to touch anything without gloves on—heck, even with gloves on—whether I should go to school outside the palace, whether I should start dating boys . . ."

"But it's not your fault that they couldn't agree on these things, or that they let their differing opinions turn into fights instead of working it out. That part's on them."

"But if I hadn't been cursed, none of this would have happened."

He took her by the shoulders and moved her back a few inches so he could look into her eyes. "Lucette, you were a baby when you were cursed, a few weeks old. How in the world can you blame yourself? You couldn't possibly have done anything to make it happen or to change it once it did."

"I know." She took comfort from his eyes, so full of compassion. "But I can't help wondering why Queen Natasha hates me so much that she'd do this."

"It doesn't matter why. All you need to believe is that you couldn't possibly have done anything to stop it."

Conceding his point, she closed her eyes and felt his breath warm her face. She remained still, her eyes closed, and gave in to the moment.

Feeling so close to someone was exciting and new, like something wonderful might happen. Tristan no longer considered her a little girl, she knew that.

The warmth from his breath caressed her lips, and although her eyes remained closed, she could sense how close he was. She wanted him to kiss her, but the wait was delicious, and finally, his lips gently pressed against hers and lingered for a moment. Her first kiss, and she felt it right down to her toes.

Lucette had been waiting for this moment for more than three years, and now that it had arrived, she never wanted it to end. She wrapped her arms around his neck and threaded a hand into his hair to keep his face near. Lucette felt sure, more sure than she'd ever felt about anything in her entire life—she loved Tristan—really loved him. And surely this passionate kiss would prove her love was true. What better proof could the fairies' magic expect? Surely any moment she'd hear the sounds of her parents and members of the palace staff waking up.

He pulled back, and she sighed, reaching up to pull his lips down to hers again. "Tristan, kiss me again. Please."

He smiled softly and kissed her nose. "Come away with me, Lucette. We should leave Xandra tonight and go to Judra. The curse might break if you leave Xandran soil. Perhaps you'll be able to stay awake during the day, and we can be together without constant fear. I know you'll love Judra."

Longing flooded her heart. "What about my parents, my country, everyone here?"

"What about *you*?" Tristan kissed her hand. "All I want is to keep you safe."

The picture he painted was lovely, but for Lucette, it was tinged with despair. "Tristan, I can't," she said. "If I leave Xandra, I can lead a normal life, but everyone else will still have to endure this curse. No citizen of Xandra, or their descendants, will ever be able to stay awake at night on Xandran soil. Not only will the vampire queen rule over the land, she'll be able to use the remaining citizens as food for her people."

She shuddered, thinking of Alex's stories of blood ranches and imagined rows of humans, lined up on beds, tubes in their necks from which they'd be bled each night to satisfy the vampire invaders. Or worse, if the queen were as cruel as she seemed, maybe she'd let the vampires feed on the humans directly, biting them until they died.

Lucette could not sacrifice her entire country and her people just for her own happiness.

"No, Tristan, I'm sorry, I can't go."

He pulled her into his arms. Warm in his embrace, she felt so in love. But how was she supposed to prove it?

Queen Natasha ran her fingers down her throat until they came to rest on the hard, cold weight of the Stone of Supremacy resting above the bodice of her red dress. With this stone, she was the most powerful vampire in Sanguinia, but even though she could change the weather, leap to the top of tall buildings, and crush bodies, it didn't give her the power to attain the one thing she most wanted—adoration. Adoration from all except Catia and Stefan. From them, fear would be enough. She couldn't wait until they groveled before her, begging for their lives—a request she'd be happy to deny.

With each new slayed vampire body crudely dumped over the border, public opinion grew in her favor. Soon all her subjects would rally behind her and willingly pour over into Xandra to feast on humans. Once she controlled Xandra, she could conquer the rest of the world. The thought of every creature bowing before her sent delicious shivers running over her skin.

Impatience growing, she'd now instructed her minions entering Xandra to kill anyone they found—except for Stefan and Catia. She wanted to see their faces before they died.

A knock sounded at the door.

"Enter."

Her son, Alexander, strode into the room, his once-gangly body now that of a fully grown vampire. After spending so much time in Xandra supervising and reporting back on her operations, he'd been around more often these past nights. "Come," she said, gesturing, "tell me everything."

He approached, a cautious smile teasing his lips, and she wondered yet again whether she could trust him. She wanted to, but at the first sign of deceit she'd drive a stake through her son's heart. She'd blame the slayers and use his death to build support. Her son's murder would surely win over all the parents in her kingdom and convince them that the humans of Xandra needed to be punished.

Alexander noticed his mother's distant expression, and embraced her. "Are you okay?"

She forced a smile onto her face. "I'll be better if you have news that the king and queen of Xandra have conceded defeat."

"Defeat?" He raised one eyebrow. "You haven't declared war, but you expect an official surrender?"

"Semantics, dear. Semantics." She turned away. Her skirt rushed around her legs as she walked to the stone balcony to survey the moonlit courtyard. Her back to him, Natasha lifted her hand and beckoned him forward. "What do you have to report?"

Her son grabbed the railing beside her and inhaled deeply. "I do miss the night air of Sanguinia. Xandra smells different."

"Like death?" she asked, hopefully.

He turned to her and smirked. "More like fear."

That would do. "Speaking of fear, tell me, how fares our young princess? She must be living in terror." In truth, she'd expected the girl to have begged her father to surrender the first night the curse fell. The young princess had proven to be of sturdier stock than Natasha could have imagined.

Alex shrugged. "I wouldn't know. She's hidden, locked away."

Natasha snapped her head toward him. "Still? Others say they've seen her, even fought her."

"No way. Your band of minions will tell you anything as long as they get paid. How could they know she's the one they've battled, anyway? The slayers wear hooded masks."

"Who else could it be?" she asked. "The slayers—like all Xandrans—sleep at night."

"Mercenaries have arrived from other kingdoms." Then he added quickly, "They're acting alone. Not under orders of their monarchs."

She tightened her lips. "Is that the only information you have? You must have something more useful. Why else did you come to me tonight?"

"I need to bring information to speak to my own mother?" He looked hurt, but she knew he was insincere.

She'd never coddled the boy and knew he didn't expect it. Still, his devotion was like fuel, enflaming her ambitions. If she had to stake the boy to get ahead, it would be all the more exhilarating knowing she had his adoration. She'd learned that when she killed his father.

She reached out to touch his arm. "Of course not."

"Then tell me something." He leaned back on the railing, his legs crossed in front of him. The casual stance put her at ease. "Why did you lay the curse in the first place? Surely there are easier, more direct ways to invade a country."

Natasha narrowed her eyes. "Why do you ask?"

Alexander shrugged. "If I'm to rule someday, I need to learn strategy. Eventually, you'll be taken from me, and I want to learn as much as I can before that sad fate is thrust upon me."

Pride filled her chest. Perhaps she wouldn't kill him after all. Her son rarely discussed his future role and responsibilities as king of Sanguinia. It was a good sign.

"I did it to punish them," she said.

His head snapped toward her. "Punish Xandra? Why?"

"It wasn't Xandra I wanted to punish at first," she continued, "only Stefan and Catia."

"What did they do to you?" His voice remained cool and even.

"They humiliated me. And Catia took what was mine." Hurt and rage boiled just below the surface. Even after nearly eighteen years, the treachery and her humiliation stung like fresh wounds. Natasha traced the tip of her tongue over her fangs. "I was meant to sit on the throne of Xandra, I'd dreamed of it since I was a little girl. King Stefan was meant to be mine, and he courted me for three years, led me to believe I would be his queen. But my deceitful, traitorous little sister Catia went behind my back and seduced him. Tricked him into marrying her instead."

Alexander kept his eyes on the courtyard, but his back stiffened at her words. He felt her pain and understood, she felt certain.

"But why go after the baby?" he asked. "Why not the couple directly?"

Natasha put a hand on his shoulder. Her long, black fingernails curled over his jacket. "When you're a parent, you'll understand. By threatening their daughter, I wounded them more deeply than I ever could have by attacking them directly."

He nodded slowly, so she continued. "Plus, Catia insulted me. She didn't invite me to her baby's naming ceremony. First, I'm her sister, and second, while I might not sit on the throne of Xandra, I am queen of Sanguinia and deserve their respect." Her teeth pressed together so tightly, she felt pressure at her temples and her fangs dug into her gums. "A simple death will be too easy for those two. They deserve to suffer."

Alex remained quiet a few moments, his gaze forward, his body language impossible to read. "So," he said softly, "Princess Lucette, the sleeping beauty in the glass case, is my cousin. Is that what you're telling me?"

She waved a hand. "Don't let that insignificant connection cloud your judgment. We must control Xandra, and her parents must be punished. If she ends up as collateral damage, so be it." Natasha leaned closer to her son. "But I have another idea." A thrilling trace of anticipation shot through her. "As a final torture for Catia, I'll convert the girl. Make her a vampire. Catia will hate that. Then, if you like, she can be your mate."

He pushed off the railing. "Mother, she's my cousin. My *first* cousin." His face was paler than usual.

Natasha waved him off. "In royal circles, such marriages occur all the time. Especially to forge alliances between kingdoms." She cupped his smooth cheek. "I've heard she is quite a beauty, that she takes after her handsome father and not my insipid little sister."

Her son nodded, but a tendon at his jaw twitched.

Natasha narrowed her eyes. Perhaps she'd stake her son after all.

Lucette woke feeling warm, safe, and happy, but realizing something was very different. She snapped her eyes open to discover that she was lying on a long settee in the tower room, outside the glass wall. Tristan lay beside her, his arm over her waist.

He was asleep and she snuggled against the warm protection of his strong body. How long had they been lying here together? How had he gotten her out? Had he convinced her father to give him the key?

The door at the top of the tower stairs opened, and Lucette lifted her head. Had the curse ended?

"Well, isn't this cozy." Alex strode into the room, a scowl on his face, and at the sound of Alex's voice, Tristan opened his eyes.

"Alex, it's great to see you." Lucette smiled, hopeful. "Has the curse lifted?"

He shook his head, and her heart dropped.

She turned to Tristan. "Does my dad know I'm out of the cell?"

Tristan sat up and grinned. "I convinced him I could keep you safe, and that we'd have a better chance of breaking the curse if there wasn't a glass wall between us. Not that there has been, but he doesn't know that."

Alex's eyes drifted from her to Tristan, then back again. "Lucette, I need to talk to you."

"Sure, what's up?"

"In private."

Lucette sat up. "Whatever you want to say to me, you can say in front of Tristan."

"No." Alex stood his ground. "I can't."

"Alex," she began gently, "I love Tristan. That's not going to change."

"You love me?" Tristan grinned ear to ear. "I love you, too!" He quickly leaned over and enveloped her in his arms.

"Excuse me! I'm right here," Alex said. His expression conveyed his annoyance.

Seeing her in Tristan's arms likely hurt Alex, and Lucette hated that. But she couldn't give Tristan the cold shoulder just because Alex was back. Proving she'd found true love was too important.

Alex groaned. "This is all really sweet and everything, but since your love declarations haven't lifted the curse, can we move on?" Alex drummed the back of one of the viewing gallery chairs and added, "I'm not going to try to get you to love me again, Lucette—believe me—but I do need to talk to you. It's important."

"Then talk," she said. "I'll tell Tristan whatever you say, anyway."

"You might not want to tell him this." Alex turned and started to pace around the room.

"Alex, stop wasting time. My parents' rooms are unguarded, and other vampires might show up soon." She was starting to worry about what Alex might say, but the situation was already so bleak that she found it hard to imagine anything worse. Still, a chill rushed through her. What if the fairy queen's alterations hadn't worked or had been changed? What if the curse would never lift? Maybe true love wouldn't work.

"We're cousins," Alex blurted.

"What?" She waited for Alex to start laughing, but she'd never seen him look so serious. "How?" she asked. "You're a vampire."

He nodded. "I told you my mother converted, right? That she used to be human?"

Lucette nodded.

"Well, she's your mother's older sister. She hates your parents. *Hates* them. And I'm pretty sure the feeling is mutual, because I found out that this whole curse thing started because your mother stole her boyfriend, married him, and then didn't invite my mother to a party."

Lucette's breaths came quickly, making her dizzy. Anger infiltrated her emotions. That the vampire queen was her aunt made her nauseous, but the pettiness of the motivation behind the curse was so much worse.

"How do you know this is true?"

"She told me." Alex grimaced. "She's proud of it and thinks it justifies all she's done. She actually thought it would sway me to her cause."

"I'll give you two some time to talk." Tristan pressed a kiss into Lucette's hair, and she was about to object, but then realized having this talk with Tristan around wasn't fair to Alex. He clearly wanted to talk to her about this in private, and now that she knew they were family . . . no wonder she'd felt a connection to him, but hadn't fallen in love.

Tristan headed for the stairs.

"Wait," she said. "Which of my parents' rooms are you going to guard?"

He grinned. "I don't have to choose."

"Why not?" Her heart rate sped up. Had her mother moved to her grandfather's estate in the country? Or worse, had something happened to one of her parents?

"Because they're in the same room," Tristan said.

Happiness burst inside Lucette. "How did that happen?"

"I talked them into it." He grinned. "They were resistant, but I told them how much harder it was to keep them both safe if they were separated."

"Oh, thank you!" Lucette flung herself into Tristan's arms. "I know it doesn't mean they'll patch things up, but that they're willing to be in the same room, even while sleeping, makes me so happy."

He gave her a squeeze. "I'm glad. Now, let me go check on them." Tristan winked as he left.

Lucette turned to Alex. "It really is good to see you. I missed you." She sat down in one of the chairs, and gestured for him to sit in another.

"I missed you, too." Alex sat down beside her. "I was angry when I left, but I was mostly hurt, and I think deep down I knew that we were never meant to fall in love."

"Especially now that we know we're cousins." She grimaced.

"Yeah, there is that." He let out a short laugh. "Of course, my mother doesn't seem to think that's an obstacle."

"Really?"

"She has this warped idea that after she crushes your parents, she'll bend you to her will, and then suddenly you'll want to be a vampire and join our royal family."

"Why would she think that?"

"Because she's crazy and desperate to have everyone bow down at her feet." He wrinkled his nose. "Once she gains control, she wants to be the sole leader of Sanguinia. She's planning to abolish the democratic council of generals we've had for centuries."

Lucette shuddered. "What does she plan to do to my parents?"

"I'm not sure." He seemed as if he might be hiding something. Still, in spite of Tristan's reservations, she felt sure she could trust Alex.

She put her hand on Alex's arm. "Well, whatever it is, we've got to stop her. You'll help, won't you? I mean, I can understand if you don't want to. She is your mother."

"And your aunt."

Lucette raised an eyebrow and shook her head as she pondered that unwanted reality. To think her own aunt had cursed her to torture her sister and ex-boyfriend. It made the curse so much worse knowing it had started over nothing but petty jealousy and a desire for revenge.

Three nights later, Lucette and Tristan were sitting next to a vase of roses and guarding her parents' room when Alex sauntered down the corridor toward them. Lucette sprang to her feet to hug him.

Tristan shook Alex's hand. "Hey, thanks for coming. Any news from the other side?"

Her joy at seeing the two of them on friendly terms faded quickly. Alex looked grim.

"My mother's gaining support. More and more vampires consider Xandra the enemy now, and she's impatient. She might not need to wait for your dad to declare war. She can't believe that Xandra's"—he turned to Lucette—"that *you've* held out so long. Given all the slayings, more vampires are now out for Xandran blood and she doesn't even need to pay some to risk their lives." He looked down. "Her lust for vengeance scares me."

"It's been quiet tonight," Tristan said. "I know it's early, but not a peep."

"I'll take a walk around the roof to see if I can spot any vampires," Alex said.

"No, I'll go." Tristan reached for his hood.

"No." Lucette took Tristan's hand. "You guard my parents." Because of Alex's no-fighting rule, she felt more comfortable leaving Tristan in charge of protecting her parents. "I'll go with Alex. I could use the fresh air."

Tristan's jaw twitched. He was clearly not happy with the idea.

"I'll be fine," she told him. "Alex and I haven't had much time to talk since he came back and we found out we're cousins."

Tristan paused for a moment, then bent down to kiss her. "Be careful." He looked over to Alex. "Keep her safe."

Alex stepped forward. "I kept her safe for weeks before you even showed up."

Lucette feared they'd start another fight, but Tristan raised his palm toward Alex. "I know. Thank you."

Alex seemed tense. "Are you okay?" she asked. Neither of her parents was perfect by any means, but she couldn't imagine how Alex felt. Even though she sometimes got mad at her parents, she loved them and would be devastated to learn so many horrible things about them. What they'd done paled in comparison to the vampire queen's crimes.

Alex looked around the next corner to check for vampires and then motioned her forward. "I always knew my mom hated Xandra—it's why I snuck over here a few times as a kid. I wanted to see for myself what it was she found so despicable."

"And what was your assessment?" She opened the door that led to the stairs to the roof.

"Other than the fact that you wanted to kill me with a twig?" He grinned and knocked her hip with his. "Seriously, I didn't know what to think. I saw vampires being killed by your slayer army nearly every night." He shook his head. "Even if they were feeding from humans, they didn't deserve that."

"I see that now." She was ashamed at how her country had reacted to the vampires. "But really, it was your mother who started it all."

Alex reached the top of the stairs and turned toward her. "Your mother, too. If she'd just invited her sister to the party." His jaw hardened.

"Do you really think that would have changed things?"

Alex shook his head and squeezed his lips together. "I don't know."

They stepped onto the roof, and the night air felt fabulous on Lucette's skin and in her lungs, and even if it was dangerous to be outside, she was glad she'd joined Alex. She needed to get fresh air more often.

"So, how goes the curse-breaking?" Alex asked.

She shrugged. "I don't get it, I really don't. The fairy queen told me I'd know how to prove my love when the time came, but I don't. I have no idea."

"Maybe you don't really love him," Alex said softly, his eyes trained on the village around them.

She grabbed his wrist. "I do love Tristan! I really do, with all my heart. I've loved him since I was thirteen."

Alex backed away, but he didn't look hurt or angry, just thoughtful and uncomfortable. He jammed both hands into the pockets of his hooded jacket. "Lucette, I hate to suggest this, but maybe it's Tristan who doesn't love you."

She shook her head sharply. "No, he does. I'm sure." But doubt prickled inside her.

Alex tipped his head to the side, and one of his fangs scraped along his lower lip in the way it did when he was deep in thought or not sure what to say. "Has he mentioned marriage?"

She took a step back, dangerously close to the roof's edge. "I'm only sixteen!"

"That's when your mom got married, though, right?" He pulled her away from the edge and put his hand on her shoulder. "What if that's how you're supposed to prove your love?"

Every nerve in Lucette's body tingled, but she wasn't sure if it was in fear or anticipation. Marry Tristan? She wanted that someday, sure, but didn't feel ready *right now*. She was way too young.

But if Alex was right and marriage was the key to proving her love, it might lift the curse and save her kingdom. Maybe it was her duty to marry young. But the fairy queen had said she'd know how to prove her love. If marriage was the answer, why wasn't she certain? Instead, the suggestion made her uncomfortable and nervous.

Her throat closed up and her heart ached. What if she didn't love Tristan enough? What if their love wasn't true?

Alex squeezed her arm. "Listen. I don't see any vampires approaching. Why don't you go back up to your room in the tower?

I'll relieve Tristan and tell him where you are. I promise I won't let any harm come to your parents. You should talk to Tristan, at least see what he thinks."

Lucette's cheeks burned. But if marriage was the way to prove her love, Alex was right. She had to at least discuss it with Tristan, and maybe as they talked, what she should do would become clear.

Lucette paced the space in front of the glass partition dividing the tower room. How could she even raise the subject of marriage with Tristan? Was she supposed to propose?

And what if Alex mentioned his idea to Tristan? It might save her the terror of proposing, but the thought of the two of them discussing her made her feel worse.

The straps from her bow and quiver felt heavy against her chest, as if they were choking her, so she removed her weapons and set them near the door. Hands clammy, she rubbed her palms on her legs and bent over, hoping to gather her composure before Tristan arrived.

Suddenly, the door thudded open behind her. It struck the stone wall, and six hulking vampires burst into the room.

Six vampires? Lucette doesn't have a chance!

To find out what happens next, turn to section 9: At War (page 291).

Section 9

At War

9

Lucette lunged for her weapons, but the vampires were faster. One of them picked up her quiver and brought it down over his leg, snapping all her stakes at once.

Weaponless, she ran at the vampires and leaped into the air. She delivered a kick, striking one vampire in the gut. But as she landed, another grabbed her from behind and ran his fangs down her neck, scraping her skin. "I'll bet you're real tasty," he said menacingly.

Lucette thrashed and squirmed, trying every trick she knew to break free, but the vampire pulled her arms behind her back and lifted her off the ground. Her shoulders burned with pain, but still she kicked, trying her best to make contact with one of the vampires, any one.

"Is this the princess?" a tall, dark-haired vampire asked.

"She's awake. Must be," a blond one replied. "I can't wait for a bite."

"Careful," said the dark-haired one, who seemed to be the leader. "Two bites, max. If we kill her before getting her back to Sanguinia for conversion, the queen will kill us."

The one holding her grazed his fangs along her neck again, and she strained to get away.

"Don't bite now," the leader said. "It's too big a risk. Tie her up, and we'll flip later to decide who gets to drink."

Lucette kicked with all her might, wriggling under the hold of the strong vampire, but she couldn't get free.

They quickly bound her in ropes, securing the knots tightly, and she twisted and pulled against the ropes, but it was no use.

"Let's get going," said the leader. "We can get her back to Sanguinia well before dawn."

The door burst open and Tristan appeared, his slayer hood on, his crossbow cocked and loaded. He pulled the trigger without hesitating. *Thwack!* An arrow punctured the leg of the blond vampire, who fell, groaning in pain.

In an instant, Tristan reloaded the crossbow and aimed at the dark-haired leader, but another vampire swung his arm at Tristan and knocked the crossbow off target. Tristan reached for a stake, but three vampires pounced on him at once. He spun and kicked, landing his boot hard on one vampire's chest.

Lucette struggled against her ropes. They burned and dug into her skin. The dark-haired leader lifted her with one arm and pressed his fangs against her neck.

"Surrender or I'll kill her," he said to Tristan.

"No!" Lucette yelled. "Don't believe him. They won't kill me. They have orders to take me to the queen for conversion." A horrible thought, but it might just save her life and, more importantly, Tristan's. One more bite and he was dead.

The vampire leader laughed. "Doesn't mean I won't take a nice long drink first." He ran his tongue over his yellow fangs. "And my only loyalty to our queen is the money she's paying. If your boyfriend doesn't drop his weapons, I'll rip out both of your throats. Not even our surgeons can save you from that."

Lucette gasped. She heard wood clattering against the stone floor. Tristan had dropped his weapons and lifted his hands in surrender.

The vampires laughed. One of them grabbed Tristan's arms from behind, twisting them up and back. His face distorted in obvious pain, but he didn't cry out.

The dark-haired vampire sauntered around Tristan, bending in to sniff every so often. "You look strong for a human," he said. "I'll bet you taste good. Potent." Tension built as he toyed with Tristan, toyed with her, and Lucette tried to guess what the vampires would do next. It felt as if hours passed, but she knew it had been less than a minute.

The lead vampire lunged, pulling Tristan's head back to expose his throat.

"No!" she yelled. "Don't! Drink from me instead!"

"Lucette, no!" Tristan shouted.

The dark-haired vampire drew his fangs away from Tristan's neck. "What makes you think I won't drink from you both?"

"Drink from me first, then. All of you." She struggled against her bindings. Maybe if she let them all drink, they'd get full and lose interest in Tristan.

"No," Tristan said. "Take me."

The vampire smiled. "Aw, isn't this sweet?" He slammed Tristan's head into the wall, and he fell to the floor in an unconscious heap.

"Tristan!" Lucette tried to see if he was okay, but the five uninjured vampires were blocking her sightline with evil, hungry grins on their faces, while the injured blond one was struggling to pull Tristan's arrow out of his leg.

"Perhaps we should all take a sip of blood, since she's offered us such a polite invitation." The dark-haired one sauntered forward. "What do you think?"

"Just get it over with," Lucette said. If this was the way she'd die, so be it. At least it gave Tristan a chance.

Blood rushed through her head so fast and hard she could hear it, but the knowledge that she was doing the right thing, the only thing, that she was saving Tristan, erased her fear. The vampire's teeth moved to her throat and hovered over the surface, his warm breath moistening her skin.

"Let her go!" Someone shouted from the doorway.

Hope returned as Alex leaped into the room and dove for the vampire who was about to strike. The vampire dropped Lucette, but first his sharp fangs pierced her skin, and twin lines of blood trailed down her neck from the wound.

Just then, one of the doors to the slayers' cases burst open. Then another. And another.

They were awake.

Alex drove a stake through the shoulder of the vampire he'd tackled, and from where he lay on the floor, he turned to kick the leader. The rest of the slayers emerged from their cases, weapons raised, and using quick, practiced motions, they knocked two vampires to the floor.

Lucette's heart burst with joy. They'd done it! By offering their lives for each other, she and Tristan had proven their love, and the curse had lifted. But the battle was far from over, and the slayers and vampires fought ferociously.

Lucette struggled against her bindings. She had to get to Tristan. He drowsily lifted his head from the floor, and her heart swelled. He was alive. The blond vampire, his leg now free of the arrow, lunged for Tristan, fangs forward. But quick as lightning, Alex grabbed one of Tristan's stakes and drove it into the attacking vampire's back—a death stroke to the heart.

All of his team down, the lead vampire raced for the stairs to flee, and one of the recently woken slayers raised his stake over another injured vampire's chest.

"Stop!" Lucette shouted. "Don't kill him! Take him prisoner, arrest him, deport him—but don't kill him."

The slayer paused, and the vampire took advantage and kicked the slayer. But instead of continuing his attack, the vampire raced for the stairs after the leader, holding his wounded shoulder.

The slayers circled Alex and Tristan, clearly confused.

Tristan still looked woozy from his head injury, but he lifted his hand as he pulled himself up to sit. "Guys, you know me." He pulled off his hood. "And this guy is a vampire, but he's also a friend. You saw how he just saved me. Ask the princess."

"He's an ally," Lucette confirmed as a slayer cut her bindings.

She rushed over and dove into Tristan's arms. "I thought they were going to kill you."

"I couldn't die." Tristan kissed her. "That would mean leaving you."

Lucette hugged him, then turned to place a quick kiss on Alex's cheek. "Thank you. You saved Tristan's life."

"No," Alex said. "*You* saved both of your lives by putting him before yourself."

Warmth flooded through her, and she leaned into Tristan, so happy that she could barely speak. But there would be time for hugs later. Right now, she needed to see if her parents were okay.

Queen Natasha struck Ivan across the face and the tall, dark-haired vampire flew into a wall. She smiled at his pain.

Even better, this fool had confirmed that the curse had lifted and she could finally cross into Xandra. But merely killing Catia and Stefan wouldn't do. She wanted to see them suffer, to lose everything they held dear. She'd make them beg to die.

"How did this happen?" Natasha roared.

Ivan shrunk toward the floor. "We were outnumbered."

"You were supposed to be a soldier." He was handsome and dark, but useless, and if she squinted she could almost imagine it was Stefan cowering before her. Ivan was a pathetic excuse for a vampire that she'd sent to Xandra to snatch the royals and bring them back for conversion and torture.

Sneering in disgust, Natasha backed up a few steps. Her ordinary minions had been more efficient than this team of soldiers she'd hired. At least her minions had pierced the occasional throat. At least some of them had been brought back dead, providing evidence of Xandra's aggression. Ivan and his team had failed tonight. Not only had they turned up empty-handed, all but one had lived. And Ivan hadn't even brought back their fallen brother as evidence of Xandran atrocities. Useless.

"My queen," Ivan said, still crouched like a cornered animal, "at first everything was as you'd said it would be. We found the girl alone in a tower, unguarded, awake, while the rest of the kingdom was deserted, most buildings boarded up, only a few with sleeping bodies inside. But then another human arrived, then more came out of the walls, and . . ."

He paused and closed his eyes, his body trembling in fear.

"What?" She strode forward to stand over him. "Tell me everything or your death will be slow and painful."

"It was Prince Alexander."

Natasha sucked in a sharp breath and stepped back, trying to calm herself. "What of him?"

"He was there, too."

"And?"

"It was he who killed our team member. He killed a vampire to save a human's life. Not only that, he attacked me as I was about to drink from the girl's neck."

In a fit of rage, she grabbed Ivan's head and snapped his neck. His body crumpled to the floor. Sometimes messengers simply needed to be killed regardless of their message.

All she'd done for her son, all she'd tried to teach him, all her hopes and dreams for his future—they all burned in a fiery instant. Her own son was a traitor. She didn't know who to kill first, her son or her sister.

Enough with depending on other people. Enough with subtlety and manipulating public opinion. It was time for a direct approach. If she couldn't win her subjects' adoration, she'd settle for fear.

Tonight, she'd kill a large group of Sanguinian citizens herself and dump them near the border. She'd make sure to include plenty of women and small children, and leave enough evidence around—wooden stakes, garlic—to convince whoever found the bodies that the Xandrans had been responsible for the massacre.

If that didn't turn her people against Xandra and send them over the border to feed, nothing would. And this new plan came with insurance. Even if the increased vampire attacks didn't provoke Stefan to act, once the generals learned of the atrocity, they'd feel justified in mounting an invasion. War was imminent. How delightful.

Lucette let the sunlight bathe her as she sat in the courtyard on a wide lounge chair with Tristan, their fingers laced together.

"I hope Alex's okay," she said. "I'll be worried if he doesn't show up tonight."

"Hmm." Tristan turned onto his side toward her. "Do you really think he went to see his mother after the curse lifted?"

Lucette shivered in spite of the warm day. "I hope not." Clearly, family didn't mean much to that horrible queen.

Plus, Lucette wanted to focus on the positive. She ran her palm over Tristan's cheek. How had she become so fortunate? All her life she'd felt cursed, even before learning she actually was cursed, but now she felt like the absolute luckiest girl in the world. Even her parents seemed happy.

"Excuse me, Princess."

She turned to see that Oliver, one of the palace staff, had approached. She sat upright.

"The king and queen would like to speak to you. They're in the king's office."

"Thank you. Tell them I'll be right there." She pushed herself off the lounge chair and turned back to Tristan. "Would you like to come?"

He stood. "If you want me to, I will, but your parents summoned you, not me. And these past weeks, I've seen more of them than you have." He kissed her tenderly before she left.

Lucette stepped into her father's office, and her happiness expanded. Her parents were standing together near the window. They weren't touching, but less than a foot separated them and the vibe wasn't frosty for once.

She cleared her throat and they turned.

"Lucette," her father said and she ran forward, diving into his arms and then hugging her mother, too. It felt so good to be able to hug them again.

"What is it?" Lucette asked. "Not that you need a reason to summon me. I'm so happy all this is over, I'm in love, and you two are here together . . ." She cut herself off, realizing she might be thinking wishfully. Plus, if their newfound closeness was real, her being overeager or presumptuous might stir things up. It was better if they realized, over time, how much they meant to each other. Now that the stress of her curse had lifted, certainly they'd recapture the love they must have felt before she'd been born.

Her father smiled, but then his expression turned stern. "I hate to tell you this, but it's not over."

Of course it was over. "Dad, I'm fine. We won."

"No," her mother said. "Natasha will never consider this over. Not until she's crushed Xandra—or she's dead."

Lucette gasped. "You'd have your own sister killed?" Her mother had always been strong-minded, but this?

The king shook his head. "I hope it won't come to that—but she must be removed from power."

"How?" Lucette asked.

"Your mother has finally convinced me." He turned toward his wife and smiled softly. "Xandra must declare war."

"No!" Lucette shouted. "It's over, let it be over!"

"Lucette," her father said, "I know you went through a lot, which is why we wanted to tell you about this together." He nodded at the queen. "Your mother and I have agreed that it's best if you leave Xandra for a while. I'll ask your young man to take you to Judra."

Lucette's mind spun. On the one hand, going away with Tristan sounded wonderful, plus, her parents were actually in agreement for once. Those two things combined to fulfill her greatest fantasies.

But—her parents were wrong. Lucette stood straight and looked her father in the eye. "Declaring war is exactly what she wants you to do, Dad. She doesn't want to be the aggressor because many of her people aren't on her side. She's hoping you'll invade." And did he really think they'd stand a chance in a war with Sanguinia? Sure, the vampire army only fought at night, but they were faster, stronger, and more bloodthirsty—literally.

Her father frowned, and his tone turned patronizing. "How could you possibly know her motives?"

It was time to come clean, and Lucette took a deep breath. "Because of my cousin, Prince Alexander. He's my friend."

Her father staggered back a few steps and her mother's face paled. "That's impossible," she said.

Lucette shook her head. "When I told you I hadn't been out of the glass cell before Tristan got here . . . I was lying."

Her father's jaw stiffened.

"Alex showed up the first night you put me in that display case. He helped me figure out how to get out. He helped me keep you both safe. He told me about the rose allergy. I wouldn't have survived without Alex."

"Lucette." Looking exasperated, her father ran his hand through his thick, dark hair. "We'll talk about your lying later—not to mention how you put yourself in so much danger." He shook his head. "But how do you know you can trust this Alex? He's a vampire."

She stepped forward and grasped at the fabric of her skirt in frustration. "Because he helped me so much. Plus, I'm a good judge of character, and I like him. You can trust him because *I* trust him."

Her father rubbed his chin. "I was on good terms with his father, the late King Vladimir, but the boy barely met his dad." He tipped his head to the side and pressed a finger to his lips. "How often was he here?"

"Almost every night."

"And he helped you?" her father asked. "He never tried to drink from you?"

"No, Dad. Alex doesn't drink human blood. He never has. He finds the whole idea repulsive, and all he wants is peace between our kingdoms."

"How can you two be so naive?" her mother snapped.

"Naive?" Lucette tried to remain calm, to prevent a fight. "Why do you say that?"

Her mother grabbed Lucette's arm. "Whether or not he's your cousin, he's a vampire, Lucette. Whatever he said was a lie. They use mind control to sway human behavior." She shivered. "If you ever had any doubts about the brutality of these creatures"—she ran her hand over her throat where she'd been bitten—"surely you see the truth now."

"No," Lucette said, terrified that her mother's negative attitude toward vampires would shatter the parental truce. "Vampires don't use mind control, and they aren't repelled by garlic and they are no more murderous than we are."

"If you'd ever met my sister—" Her mother shuddered.

"They aren't all like her, Mom. In fact, *none* are like her. And she paid the ones who came over here to bite people."

"Why would she do that?" her father asked.

"First," Lucette started, "she paid them to harass us, because she was angry that she couldn't cross the border and had to wait sixteen years for her curse to work. Then later she realized she could use the vampire attacks to lure Dad into a war. War is what she wants, Dad."

Her mother wrinkled her forehead as if she were thinking about this, but her father broke in.

"Lucette, what you say ties in with what the Sanguinian ambassador has claimed, but with all that's happened, I think your mother is right. Vampires can't be trusted." He turned to his wife and they smiled softly at each other. "Besides, Alex is the crown prince—her son. Logic suggests he's loyal to her." Her father crossed his arms over his chest. "If he told you Xandra shouldn't invade Sanguinia, I say that's all the more reason we should."

Lucette was breathing so quickly she was nearly hyperventilating. The temptation to cave and simply agree with her parents was huge. It was so rare that they agreed about anything, so she wanted to let this go, but she couldn't.

"Dad, promise me you'll wait. Promise me you'll give me a chance to prove that I'm right. If our armies invade Sanguinia, we'll be crushed and Queen Natasha will win."

Her father waited a few moments before answering. "I'll give it twenty-four hours. No more."

Natasha watched the girl sleep. Lucky for the child, she took after her father and not her insipid little mother. Her niece certainly had inherited her father's dark, striking looks.

She bent down toward the sleeping girl and inhaled. Hunger pumped through her. Even though she'd feasted on a human she'd encountered on the way to the palace, Lucette's scent made her hungry.

But she must resist the temptation to kill the royal family right now. She wanted more time to play with her food.

The girl's eyes opened, and when she saw Natasha, she scrambled away across the mattress. Within seconds the girl was standing on the bed, holding a stake, her thin nightgown blowing in the breeze from the open window.

"Who are you? What do you want?" the girl asked.

"Why, I'm your dear auntie, come for a visit." Natasha nodded her head slightly. "I haven't seen you since you were a babe. It's so nice to finally meet you, Lucette."

"I wish I could say the same." The girl's tone was bitter and angry, but soon she'd bend the child's will. If not, the girl would die.

Natasha raised her hand to her chest and stroked the stone pendant. "Oh, what a cruel thing to say to your long-lost auntie. I mean you no harm. I came to talk."

Lucette eyed a long fabric pull by the side of her bed that would undoubtedly bring servants and guards, and Natasha smiled inwardly. The girl's first instinct had been to go for her stake, rather than sounding the alarm to bring help. She admired Lucette's instinct to act, rather than to rely on others to save her. This girl had potential.

"We have much in common, you and I," Natasha said as she glided along the side of the bed and then toyed with the golden frame at its foot. "While you take after your father in appearance, I do believe, in demeanor, you take after me."

"Never!" the girl shouted.

"Tut, tut." Natasha shook her head. "There's that rudeness again. Apparently you take after my sister, too." She sighed dramatically.

"Why are you here? What do you want?"

"Getting down to business." Natasha smiled. "I like that."

Lucette still held her stake at the ready, her expression fierce and revealing no fear, even though she knew she stood no chance. Natasha liked that, too. "I have a proposition for you, one that's in our mutual best interests."

"I can't imagine how any of our interests are mutual." The girl's stake-holding hand started to shake.

"Now, now," Natasha said and sashayed from the end to the side of the bed. "We're family. Together we can ensure lasting peace between our two kingdoms." She lowered her voice and learned forward. "My sources tell me your father is considering war."

"What sources?"

The girl was smart not to deny or confirm. She gave away nothing. Natasha smiled and said, "I'm hoping you can help me avoid this war, and at the same time mend the horrible rift in our family. It saddens me how these misunderstandings have grown out of proportion."

"*Misunderstandings?*" Lucette drew her stake back. "You cursed me when I was a baby."

Natasha forced her jaw to relax so her expression would appear gentler, friendlier, less threatening to the girl. "You don't know the whole story." She fanned her eyes as if she had tears there. "If only you knew what your mother and father did to me first."

"I do know, and it's no excuse. What you did was unforgivable."

This soon-to-be-dethroned princess was becoming annoying. With one bite Natasha could rip out her throat and eliminate her forever. But that would be hasty. Natasha had new plans for torturing Stefan and Catia. She would use their daughter against them, yet again.

"I do regret my actions that day." She waved her hand. "In hindsight, laying the curse might have been a slight overreaction, and I want to make amends. But because the fairies made it impossible for me to enter Xandra until the curse lifted, I couldn't apologize sooner. If only I'd been able to visit . . . I wanted to lift the curse right from the start, but your parents refused to bring you to me, and I couldn't get here." All lies, but lies the girl might fall for.

The girl frowned and relaxed slightly.

Pleased she'd obviously struck a chord, Natasha continued, "Approach your parents for me, ask them to hear me out, ask them to accept my deepest apologies. Maybe then war can be avoided." She leaned on the mattress toward the girl. "I'm doing all I can to hold my armies back, but my generals are itching to invade to seek revenge for all of our citizens murdered by your slayers." She added a little shiver for effect.

"Why come to me?" Lucette asked. "Why not my father, or the ambassador?"

"You're the perfect person to come to." Natasha held her hands out in mock surrender. "The peacemaker in our clan. After all the misunderstandings in our family, mending the fences is left to you and me." She forced a sad look onto her face. "And now Alex's so angry with you, too, and it's not right for cousins to be fighting, especially when you've just discovered each other."

"Alex's angry with *me?*"

The girl looked stricken and her reaction confirmed that Alex had lied. He *had* talked to the sleeping beauty. Natasha fumed, but tried not to let it show. At least she'd identified the young princess's weakness. The girl might be brave, but she couldn't tolerate conflict, especially among family. As for her traitorous son, when Natasha found him she'd snap his neck, then drive three stakes through his heart.

Natasha forced a sad look onto her face and said, "My sweet son Alexander is jealous of your young man." She put a hand over her heart. "It was Alexander's wish—mine, too—that you and he would one day marry and forge a bond between our two kingdoms that could never again be broken by silly squabbles or misunderstandings."

Lucette shook her head. "Alex doesn't want to marry me. Not since he found out we're cousins, anyway." Her brow furrowed. "And he's not mad or jealous about Tristan. I don't believe you. He saved Tristan's life."

Natasha made her best attempt at an empathic smile. "He didn't do that for your young man, darling. He did it for you."

The girl tipped her head to the side, and satisfied for the moment, Natasha leaped through the window to the courtyard below. Her seeds of doubt had been planted. Hopefully by tomorrow they'd begin to grow.

Lucette crumpled to her mattress. Suddenly, all those days she'd been observed in her sleep by would-be suitors didn't seem quite so creepy. That paled next to being woken by the vampire queen. She pushed her back against her headboard and pulled her duvet up to her chin. Shivering under her warm covers, she considered everything her aunt had said. Mending the rift between her parents and the vampire queen was tempting and fed on all her instincts to keep the peace, but as badly as she wanted to believe that her aunt's desire to prevent war was sincere, she wasn't sure.

The breeze billowed the sheer curtains, and she pulled the duvet around her tighter, wishing she could seek Tristan's advice. But he was staying in another wing, and she knew her father would misunderstand if she got caught sneaking to his room at night. Almost as badly, she wanted to talk to Alex. Was he really hurt and jealous?

Perhaps he hadn't believed she and Tristan had found true love until after the curse lifted, and he'd been holding out hope she'd eventually choose him. But they were cousins. He had to know she'd never marry her cousin.

Lucette rested her chin on the top of her duvet and took a deep breath. The more she thought about it, the more she believed that all the things the vampire queen had told her were lies.

As tempting as it was to think that she could arbitrate peace in their family, and between their two kingdoms, she couldn't believe it. She wouldn't tell her father of her aunt's visit, but she'd do everything she could to convince him that invading Sanguinia was a trap.

For the rest of the night, Lucette couldn't sleep. Partly—perhaps mostly—because of her unwanted visitor, but also she wasn't yet used

to sleeping at night. As much as she'd enjoyed sitting out in the sunlight the past two days, being awake in the night still felt natural.

Three hours before sunrise she gave up, got dressed, and ventured into the halls of the palace. The corridors weren't as silent as they'd been during the curse, and she could hear the occasional clank of a baker's pan from the kitchen on the other side of the palace, as well as the faint voices of patrolling palace guards and slayers.

The two slayers guarding the entrance to her bedchamber's corridor nodded as she passed. It wouldn't do any good to tell them the vampire queen had gotten past them tonight. With that magic stone around her neck, the queen was so much faster, so much stronger than ordinary vampires. The slayers couldn't be held responsible for not spotting her.

And it was better that they hadn't seen her, anyway. If they had, she suspected they wouldn't have survived the encounter.

"Psst." Startled, she stopped in her tracks. "Lucette, over here."

The voice was male but hushed. Was Tristan out of bed, too? She blinked, searching the shadows in the direction from where the voice had come.

Alex stepped out from behind a tapestry hanging at the side of the corridor. Her heart jumped, and she refused to let what the vampire queen had told her eat into her happiness at seeing him.

"We need to talk," he said. "Is there a slayer-free zone in this place? It took me all night to get this far."

Lucette checked over her shoulder, then opened the door to the library just a few feet down the hall. After ensuring that the room was empty, she beckoned Alex and stood watch as he slipped into the room. A guard passed by the end of the corridor, but she quickly followed her cousin inside and closed the door behind them, hoping that if the guard had spotted her, it hadn't raised any alarm on his part.

"I'm glad to see you," she said, watching his reaction. "We were worried about you."

"We?"

"Tristan wants to thank you again for saving his life."

"Oh, yeah. Right." He moved the heavy drapes aside and peeked out the no-longer-barricaded window. "We don't have too long before I have to leave, and I'm not sure I'd survive getting caught."

She leaned onto the back of a leather chair. "You're good at getting past slayers. You did it for years."

He turned. "It's different now. They're out to prove something. Their supposed defense mandate has obviously changed into an offensive strategy. I saw an attack a few hours ago. Six slayers on one young vampire who was totally minding his own business. It was brutal."

Lucette cringed. She didn't like to hear about any deaths, but hearing that slayers had killed without provocation scared her. It would only help the vampire queen gather more support.

"Well, I'm glad you came," she told Alex. "It's great to see you." And even better to see that he didn't seem angry with her as his mother had claimed.

"Good to see you, too." He stepped forward. "But I didn't just come to chat. I've got information."

"Have you seen your mother since the curse lifted?"

He shuddered. "No way. If I go anywhere near her, she'll kill me. In fact, she's put a price on my life."

Lucette gasped. Even for the evil queen, this was beyond horrific. "How do you know?" she asked.

"I overheard other vampires discussing how they'd kill me if they found me."

She squeezed his arm. "Oh, Alex, I'm so sorry. She found out you helped me?"

He nodded. "The vampires who got away from the tower last night must have told her."

She felt more sure than ever that Alex was trustworthy, but how could she convince her father?

"How are things here?" Alex asked. "How did your parents react to the curse lifting?"

"Well obviously, they were glad to see me." For the moment, she kept quiet about the impending invasion. That was a state secret.

Alex stepped forward. "You need to tell your father to brace for war, as soon as tomorrow night. My mother decided not to wait for your father to act. Worse, she did something last night that even our generals believe warrants an invasion."

"What did she do?"

His jaw clenched and the brief hint of pain in his eyes turned to hatred. "My mother arranged the murders of a group of Sanguinian citizens. Her minions killed entire families."

"How horrible!" Lucette reached for his arm and squeezed. "But how does that justify Sanguinia invading Xandra? Won't everyone rise up against her?"

"Her minions used wooden stakes and left garlic lying around. I was there soon after the bodies were discovered, and let me tell you, previously peaceful vampires are now out for human blood."

His words sent a chill down her spine. Every last doubt in her mind about Alex vanished. Every doubt about his mother, too. Natasha had done this horrible deed before visiting her tonight with that false peace offering. It had all been trickery and deceit.

Alex paced across the room, then turned to her, looking stricken. "The police who found the bodies headed straight to the generals, and even though the generals are reasonable, they can't ignore this massacre. Even if they choose to wait for real evidence of who was behind it, the plan was masterful, because now even ordinary citizens are ready to attack."

Lucette cringed. "If the vampire attacks escalate—at all—my father will invade Sanguinia for sure. He's right on the brink."

"You need to tell him not to," Alex said emphatically.

"I'm not sure he'll listen to me." But she had to try. "Stay here." She hugged Alex quickly. "I'm going to wake my father. He needs to hear this."

Lucette's stomach churned with anxiety as Alex stood before her parents in the library. Six slayers flanked the perimeter of the room. She'd tried to object to their presence, telling everyone they had nothing to fear from Alex, but her parents had insisted—both of them.

"Stefan," her mother said, "after all that's happened, I can't believe you've given audience to a vampire, especially her son." The look of revulsion on her mother's face was clear.

Stefan turned to his wife. "He's also our nephew. Let's hear him out."

Her mother shuddered, and her father sighed.

Lucette hated that her mother was being to rude to Alex and that his presence had driven yet another wedge between her parents, but neither of those things could be her main concern at the moment. Not when Xandra and Sanguinia were on the brink of war.

"Dad, please listen to Alex. I trust him completely." Lucette wondered if she should also tell him that Queen Natasha had been in her bedroom just hours ago—even Alex didn't know that—but she decided to keep that information to herself. It might make things worse.

Lucette listened as Alex told her father the same things he'd told her. She tried to gauge her father's expression, and she tried to listen to Alex's story objectively, as though she were hearing it for the first time. He sounded sincere. Her father had to believe him.

"This is some story you're telling," her father said to Alex. "But I can't base a decision that impacts the lives of my soldiers, the safety of my subjects, the very future of my kingdom merely on your word. Can you offer me any evidence? Other witnesses?"

Alex shook his head. "You have to understand, it's not like I can talk to other vampires right now. There's a bounty on my head, so I can't go back to Sanguinia. Not if I want to live."

"That's because he helped Tristan and me," Lucette interjected. "He saved our lives."

Her father ran his fingers over his stubbled chin. "I need to think about this. How long can you stay?"

Alex glanced over to the windows. "Do you have somewhere I can be sheltered from sunlight?"

"Yes, of course," her father said.

"Stefan." Her mother stepped up beside her husband and whispered, but not quietly enough that Lucette and Alex couldn't hear. "I won't have that vampire staying in the palace. It's not safe."

"Your majesty," Alex said politely, "if I stay, it is I who'll be vulnerable.

Your household won't be in danger. Even if I don't come into contact with sunlight—something I'll have to trust you to ensure—vampires are weak while the sun is in the sky. I couldn't hurt you once the sun's up, even if I wanted to."

"Liar." Her mother practically spat the word. "The day your mother cursed my baby, she was plenty strong. She leaped more than thirty feet in one bound."

"That's because she used the Stone of Supremacy," Alex answered. "I assure you, during the day, there's nothing I can do to hurt you. And I wouldn't consider it at night."

Lucette walked up beside him. "Believe him, Mom. He helped save your life."

"I doubt that." Her mother ran her hand over her throat. "How do I know he wasn't the vampire who bit me?"

Lucette blew out an exasperated breath. "Because I saw it happen! Alex helped save you that night and helped me protect you and Dad every other night."

Her mother's cheeks flushed bright red and then she looked directly at Alex for the first time since she'd entered the room. "You helped protect me during the curse?"

He nodded.

"Because I'm your aunt?" She looked perplexed.

"No," he shook his head. "I didn't find out we were related until much later."

Tears rose in her mother's eyes and she clasped her hands in front of the pale blue robe she wore over her night clothes. She stepped forward and took Alex's face in her hands. "Thank you." Her voice was small, but her tone sincere.

"I'd like you to stay," her father said to Alex. "This plan to provoke us sounds like Natasha, so I will hold back on the invasion. With your help and advice, I'll send a diplomatic envoy into Sanguinia to talk directly to the generals—whomever you recommend."

"If the queen finds out," Alex said, "your diplomats won't survive the trip."

"That's why I need your advice," her father said.

Alex nodded. "I'll stay."

The door burst open, and Tristan ran into the room. Lucette's heart did a dance at the sight of him, but he headed straight for her father. "Your Majesty, I've got horrible news."

"What?" her father asked.

"It doesn't matter what you decide about invading Sanguinia. The Xandran refugees have returned and have taken up arms. They're planning to invade Sanguinia on their own."

Lucette paced around the library. "We've got to do something," she said to Tristan.

He rose from a leather chair and put his hands on her shoulders. "Your father is handling it. He's talking to the ambassadors right now."

She shook her head. "*We* have to do something to stop it." She admired her father, but there was no time to talk. "We should go to the border," she said. "We can stop the refugees before they cross into Sanguinia. I'm sure I can reason with them."

Tristan's jaw firmed and he remained silent for so long that Lucette started to worry, but finally, he nodded. "Your bravery astounds me. It's why I fell in love with you, and if this is what you think you should do, I can't stop you. But what about him?" He nodded toward Alex, who was sleeping under a canopy of dark fabric they'd strung between some of the bookcases in the corner.

Lucette thought for a second, then crossed over to the black velvet tent and opened it. "Alex, are you awake?"

He stretched his arms. "I am now."

"We need to talk."

Lucette clung to Tristan as they drove the funereal carriage toward the border. Alex was in the back, tightly sealed into the only thing she could think of to safely transport him during daylight hours—a coffin. When he'd heard her plan, Alex insisted he come along to talk to the vampire villagers on the other side of the border. She and Alex agreed that talking to diplomats and generals wasn't the answer. Stopping the bands of ordinary citizens was key to preventing all-out chaos.

The carriage rounded a bend and the Xandran border village came into view. All the windows and doors in the village were boarded over, and there was no sign of life on the streets. Were they too late?

Arriving in the town square, Lucette's worst fears were confirmed. It was filled with men and women sharpening stakes. She climbed down off the carriage and ran to the closest man. "Who's in charge here?"

He shrugged. "No one, really, but we're of one mind. Stake as many of those monsters as we can before nightfall."

"But the sun sets in four hours."

The villager narrowed his eyes and said, "Then we'll finish them off tomorrow."

"But as soon as night falls, they'll come over here to retaliate. You might not live to fight a second day."

"So be it." He ran his ax along a stake. "We've got to try. After what they did, making us sleep every night so they could do with us as they wanted, we need to exact our revenge."

Lucette grabbed his arm. "It wasn't ordinary vampires who did that—it was their queen. They didn't have anything to do with it. Just like you, they were innocent victims."

"Victims?" The villager laughed harshly and went back to sharpening his stake.

Lucette caught sight of Tristan having a similar conversation with another villager, but he did not seem to be making any progress, either. It wouldn't work to talk to these people one at a time, so she raced to the center of the square and climbed to the top of her father's statue. It was more than twenty feet high, and by the time she reached the top she had the attention of the entire crowd.

"Look!" voices shouted. "It's the princess!" Soon everyone in the square was paying attention.

For her first sixteen years, barely anyone in the kingdom had known her face, and now so many did. Lucette fought off the horrible realization that many of her countrymen had visited her while she slept, like an animal on display at a zoo.

She went through the same arguments she'd made to the first man, and slowly she felt as if some of the crowd were seeing her point.

A tall, broad man stepped forward. "But what if we do nothing today and they attack us tonight, anyway?"

"We hope to prevent that," Lucette replied. "As soon as night falls, the vampire prince and I will make the same appeal to the vampires across the border. They believe *you* were responsible for a horrible massacre last night—families and children were murdered." A roar rose in the crowd, so she raised one hand to quiet them. "Their own queen did it to frame you, to incite war. She wants Xandra to attack." She shook her head. "We must prevent war."

"But they cursed us," the same man said. "They cursed you."

Lucette realized this man was the closest thing this group had to a leader. Convince him and she'd win over the crowd. "*They* didn't curse us," she told him. "Their queen did. It was a personal vendetta against my parents, designed to torture them by hurting me, and all of you. If you attack, you're playing into her hands. Right now, she doesn't have the support of her people, and she doesn't want to appear the aggressor. But if Xandra invades first, she'll win."

The noise in the crowed swelled as they discussed what Lucette had told them. She looked down to Tristan, who smiled. If these people weren't yet convinced, she'd just have to keep trying. At least every moment she held them back was another moment they weren't crossing the border to stake sleeping vampires.

Finally, the man she'd been talking to stepped up onto the back of a cart. He raised his hands and the crowd quieted. "What the princess has told us makes sense. I propose we give her the chance to stop the vampires from attacking. But if they come across the border tonight, we will retaliate at dawn. Stay safe tonight. Board up your houses. Put roses on your doors."

One side down. Hopefully, Alex would have equal luck over the border.

When darkness fell, Lucette and Tristan let Alex out of the coffin. Tristan returned to the palace to tell King Stefan what they'd accomplished. All this would be for nothing if the Xandran army suddenly arrived at the border crossing with orders to invade.

Alex and Lucette entered Sanguinia and, as expected, they immediately found a group of vampires discussing how and when they'd enter Xandra to exact revenge for the massacre.

At first, the villagers didn't believe Alex, but Lucette spoke to them, too, and explained how she'd been cursed. It turned out that most of the people weren't even aware that the Xandrans had been unable to wake at night for the past two and a half months. When Lucette told them how all these troubles had begun because of the vampire queen's jealousy, the villagers started calling for their queen's death.

Alex and Lucette stood together, trying to figure out what to do next. They'd stopped the ordinary citizens of both kingdoms from attacking, but still had to deal with the armies. If the Sanguinian army now believed they were justified in invading because of the massacre, the vampire queen would get want she wanted.

A low rumbling sound rose in the distance, and Lucette strained to make it out.

Alex tensed beside her. "The vampire army. It's coming." He ran into the village road and took up a place in its center. Lucette remained at the edge of the road, in the shadows. Moving faster than a team of horses, the marching vampire army progressed toward Alex. Lucette worried he'd be trampled to death.

But Alex raised his hands, and they stopped.

"Prince Alexander, what are you doing here?" A vampire dressed in a uniform of red and black with bars of gleaming silver on his chest approached Alex. "I know you've never supported your mother's stance on Xandra, but after that massacre last night, the public demands we invade."

Alex lowered his voice as he continued to talk to the vampire, who must be a general. He was so tall and broad that he looked as if he could knock Alex off his feet with the flick of a wrist.

Suddenly, Lucette felt a whoosh of air and spun to see the vampire queen had landed beside her.

"Lucette," Queen Natasha said, smiling. "So nice to see you on Sanguinian soil. Welcome."

Lucette fought the urge to run. "Do you always bring your army to greet visitors?"

The vampire queen bent toward her ear. "We can stop this, you and I."

Lucette pulled her head away, but she decided to stand her ground. What was the point of running? Any vampire could outrun her, and her aunt, it seemed, could practically fly.

She braced herself and stood up to the vampire queen. "Alex and I are doing just fine stopping this ourselves," Lucette told her. "And don't pretend that you want to end it. You're trying to provoke it. This is all your fault."

The queen shook her mane of red hair. "No, darling. It's your fault."

A shiver traced through Lucette, but she stayed strong. "It is *not* my fault."

"Oh, but it is. If you'd never been born, if you hadn't pricked your finger, if you'd been more obedient, none of this would have happened."

This was exactly what Lucette thought, but hearing the words coming from the evil queen's mouth, she realized the line of reasoning was ridiculous. She couldn't control other people's actions, even if their battles involved her.

"Lucette," the vampire queen hissed, "I admire your courage and strength." She ran a hand down the girl's arm. "You're like the daughter I never had, and together we can put a stop to all this. My son is weak, but with you at his side, he'll turn into a strong king someday."

She raised her hand to the stone hanging around her neck. "If you convert, as I did, you'll have unimaginable power and this can be yours someday." She tapped the Stone of Supremacy. "In fact, if you convert, I'll share my power with you."

Lucette wanted to scream "No!" but she kept quiet. Seeing an opportunity, she pretended to consider the queen's offer. "How does the stone work?" she asked.

"Infused by magic, its holder has great powers," the queen answered, still fingering the stone. "And as a vampire, my powers are already superior to those I had as a human."

Lucette nodded, trying to infuse her eyes with awe. "It must feel wonderful."

"You have no idea." The queen's lips drew into a wide smile, baring her sharp white fangs.

Hiding her fear, Lucette instead did her best to convey adoration. "You're very beautiful." Lucette hoped she sounded sincere. Lying had never been her strong suit. "Your skin is so smooth and pale and your very presence exudes power." She reached forward, but dropped her arm before touching her aunt's bare forearm. She wanted the queen to think she was curious, but also shy and respectful.

"Why, thank you, dear." The queen traced her long-nailed fingers down Lucette's cheek, leaving an icy trail in their wake. She gripped Lucette's chin between her fingers. "You're quite beautiful, too. You're very lucky to take after your father, but you'll be even more ravishing after you convert." She released her and stepped back. "Your skin will become luminescent, your hair will shine more brightly, and your teeth . . ." She smiled, again flashing her fangs to emphasize her point.

"It's so tempting." Lucette looked the queen directly in the eyes. "And after I convert, you'll let me share your power?"

The queen's excitement was obvious, it showed in her eyes and she answered, "Yes, I promise."

Lucette didn't trust her evil aunt's promise at all, but hoped the vampire was falling for her act. "Can I"—she broke off purposefully and smiled—"can I hold the stone? Just for a second? I want to feel the power for myself before I decide."

The queen looked over her shoulder to where Alex was still talking to the general.

"Alex doesn't understand," Lucette said. "He doesn't see how lucky he is to be a vampire, to be your son. And he certainly doesn't understand that it's natural for vampires to rule over lesser creatures, like humans." She laid the lies on thick, and her aunt turned back, smiling.

"You're so right." She reached behind her head to unclasp the chain that held the stone, and Lucette nearly burst with anticipation, every muscle in her body ready to battle the queen. Once that stone was removed, the queen would still be strong, but just a vampire, and Lucette had taken on her share of vampires.

To hide how eager she was to snatch the stone, Lucette clasped her hands behind her back, and said, "Since your visit to my bedroom, converting is all I can think of." She pretended to shiver with excitement. "I'm sorry if I was rude that night. It was a shock to see you, but I realized later how what you said made sense."

"You're really willing to convert?" Her aunt asked.

Lucette nodded eagerly. "My mom will be upset once it's done, but I'm sixteen and old enough to make my own decisions. Plus, I don't care what my mom thinks. It's her fault we had a rift in our family in the first place, and I never had the chance to know you until now."

A huge smile spread on the vampire queen's face, and she lifted the Stone of Supremacy off her neck and held it forward. "Here, my lovely niece. I choose you, instead of my deceitful son, to be my heir. Touch the stone to see what awaits you."

Lucette carefully took the stone from her aunt's hands, and an instant later, she spun and delivered a twisting kick straight to her aunt's stomach. Then, while Natasha was distracted, Lucette slipped the stone into her pocket, sensing its power was too dangerous to harness.

"You horrid little girl." Her aunt sprang forward, mouth open and fangs bared, but Lucette dodged her and planted a side-kick into the evil vampire's ribs.

Her aunt stumbled and then roared with anger. "You tricked me! No one tricks me!"

Lucette pulled out a stake and thrust it toward her aunt, but the vampire was too quick and leaped away.

"Give me my stone!" the queen screamed. "I killed to get that stone once, and I'll do it again! Hand it over now, before I change my mind. Join with me and we'll rule the entire world."

Lucette realized that her aunt's screams had attracted the attention of the soldiers on the road.

"Never," Lucette said. "You're petty and jealous and vengeful. You murdered your husband, ordered your son's murder. You're despicable, and I will never join forces with you."

The queen's face filled with rage, and Lucette braced herself, fearing that the words she'd just uttered were her last.

Her aunt charged forward, but Lucette was ready. She ducked under the attack, then quickly turned and jabbed the sharp stake into the vampire queen's back, purposefully missing her heart. *Better she stand trial for her crimes,* thought Lucette.

Suddenly, the entire vampire army moved toward them as one force. Alex rushed over, scooped Lucette into his arms, and ran, moving more quickly than the wind.

When they were far enough away, he set her down and they looked back. The army had easily overpowered the vampire queen, now that she lacked her magic stone. They bound her and then raised her above them. She struggled, but was unable to get away.

The general broke out of the pack and ran toward them. He bowed in front of Alex. "Prince Alexander, your mother has been removed from the throne and will be tried for her crimes. You are her rightful heir."

Lucette's heart pounded and she felt so happy, but also nervous, for her cousin. Imagine being a king when he was barely seventeen.

"Alex," she said as she pulled the Stone of Supremacy from her pocket, "as the future king of Sanguinia, this is rightfully yours."

Alex stared at the Stone of Supremacy. "No. That thing should be locked away in the royal treasury, or given back to the fairies. No single vampire, no single creature of any kind, should ever hold all the control and power it allows." He took the stone, but instead of putting it on, he wrapped it in a handkerchief and handed it over to the general.

The general smiled, patted Alex on the back, and said, "So wise, even at your young age. I will be proud to serve under you, King Alexander."

Alex balked. "I'm not king yet."

The general clapped Alex on the shoulder. "Merely a technicality."

Lucette hugged her cousin. "Congratulations, Alex! This is so great, really, but is it okay if I don't stick around to celebrate? I've got to get home." She couldn't wait to tell everyone the good news.

Lucette and Tristan stepped out of the Sanguinian palace into the fresh night air, and he draped his arm around her shoulders.

"He'll make a good king," Tristan said. "And now that his mother is locked up in prison, and drinking human blood is illegal again, lasting peace between all the kingdoms seems assured."

Lucette's heart swelled with so much love and pride. "Alex is so young to be ruling, I can't imagine . . ."

Tristan squeezed her shoulders. "Oh, come on now. If you were suddenly thrust upon the throne of Xandra, you'd do just fine."

She looked into his eyes and smiled. "Maybe, if I had you at my side."

"Nothing would make me happier," Tristan said, and then bent to kiss her.

They walked through the crowd of vampires and dignitaries from other kingdoms who'd assembled for King Alexander's coronation, until they found a quiet place under a tree, near the edge of the stone-paved courtyard.

"Lucette"—Tristan took her hands—"there's something we need to discuss."

She nodded. "What is it?"

"I need to return to Judra."

Her heart seized. "What? No. Really?" She couldn't think, couldn't breathe. The idea of being separated from Tristan, even for a day, tore at her heart like she'd been staked. "Why?"

"As a member of the royal family—"

"What?" Her breath caught in her chest. "You're a prince?"

He nodded. "I didn't tell you before, because I worried it was just another complication in your life, and not really that important."

"Not important?" Fear surged inside her. "Do you need to live in Judra? Are you going to be king one day? Because I think I need to stay here, and my parents are just starting to get along again, and—" How could she possibly choose between their two kingdoms?

"Lucette." He leaned forward and kissed her. "Slow down. I didn't say any of that." He smiled broadly. "I have four older brothers, so it's unlikely I'll ever be king, and I want to live in Xandra, with you. I know you need time with your family, but I do need to go home for my father's birthday. I was hoping you'd come."

"Oh." Air filled her lungs again and she felt as if she were floating.

Tristan cupped Lucette's face tenderly with his palms. "Do you think you could come to Judra for a visit? I'd love for you to meet my family, and even if we're both too young to get married right now, my greatest hope is that someday you'll be my wife and, well, I want you to see my homeland."

"Yes," she said, breathlessly.

"Yes, to what?" he asked.

"All of it. I'd love to go to your dad's birthday party, and someday, yes, I would love to be your wife."

"Lucette? Tristan?" her father's voice called out from across the courtyard, and she turned to see both her parents approaching—holding hands.

Lucette beckoned for them to join her and Tristan. Joy filled her heart. Her family was together, she'd found true love, she was no longer cursed, and—she turned to look into Tristan's handsome eyes—she had truly found her happily ever after.

Answers

There are eight possible routes through this book:

1, 2, 4, 6, 7, 9

1, 2, 4, 6, 8, 9

1, 3, 4, 6, 7, 9

1, 3, 4, 6, 8, 9

1, 2, 5, 6, 7, 9

1, 2, 5, 6, 8, 9

1, 3, 5, 6, 7, 9

1, 3, 5, 6, 8, 9

Become enchanted again with another title in the Twisted Tales series!
Will Cinderella ever escape her stepmother's spells and become the warrior she was meant to be?
A thrilling twist on a classic!

sneak preview

Cinderella ◆ Ninja Warrior

Cinderella's shoulders quivered with fatigue as she tipped the twenty-seventh wooden bucket of fresh water into her stepmother's bath. The water, laced with sweet-smelling oils, sloshed up the tub's sides, threatening to spill over the edges and onto the pristine floor that she'd have to mop again if the hot water escaped.

She brushed stray blonde hairs off her lightly freckled face, and then crouched to stoke the fire, which crackled as it heated the tub. Stretching her aching fingers toward the warmth, she rubbed the calluses on her palms and fingers. Along with her many other chores, the countless trips from the cellar to the upstairs bathrooms to fill three tubs twice a day had taken their toll on her body.

Cinderella had just turned eighteen, but her hands looked much older. Her real mother, one of the most powerful wizards in the kingdom, had died at her birth, and five years later her father died too, only days after he remarried. Her stepmother, also a wizard, treated Cinderella more like a servant than a daughter.

Cinderella often wished she were a ninja warrior—no, make that a ninja and a wizard. A wizard could break her stepmother's entrapment spells, and a ninja, well, a ninja could give her stepmother what she deserved.

But hard work and determination carried more power than if-onlys and wishes. Her stepmother's magic was powerful, and it seemed as if she'd thought of everything to keep Cinderella trapped. That was no excuse for Cinderella to sit back and do nothing, though. It was better to practice the few innate magic skills she had inherited from her mother, and to develop her self-taught ninja training. Sometimes the best offense was a good defense.

Enough of this whining, thought Cinderella. There would be no time for training if she lazed about staring at the fire and daydreaming. If captured, real ninja warriors didn't sit around thinking about escaping—they took action. She sprang to her feet and grabbed the empty buckets, ready to make the much easier trip down the three long flights of stairs to her cellar room. Her stepmother had used black magic to cast entrapment spells that kept her confined to the cellar, except to do chores during the day and to garden at night.

Twisting sideways, she squeezed through the tiny entrance at the top of the servants' stairs that were dark and narrow in places.

On reaching the bottom, she gripped her buckets and moved into a crane stance to prepare for a side kick. "Ha-ya!" she shouted, and then her bare foot struck cleanly against the heavy wooden door.

The door swung open, hitting the stone wall with a bang, to reveal the cold room that doubled as a bedroom for her and storage space for everyone else in the house. She'd moved into the cellar at age five, right after her father died. The damp, chilly room no longer scared Cinderella; she had much scarier things to face every day—like her evil stepmother.

Turning to the cupboard on the wall opposite the fireplace, Cinderella reached a hand toward her pewter goblet on the top shelf, above the beautiful crystal and bone china dishes that were reserved for the rest of her family.

Concentrating, she focused on connecting her hand to the goblet. *Come to me, goblet.*

Her fingers tingled and the goblet wobbled, but it didn't move off the shelf. She dropped her arm in defeat.

Who was she kidding? Her magic wasn't that strong. To do something that purposeful, she needed a wand and instructions.

She carried her stool from the side of the planked table to the cupboard and, after tucking the bottom hem of her torn skirt into the waistband of her pantaloons, climbed onto the stool's scratched seat. Balancing barefoot on the wobbly stool, she stretched up to reach her goblet.

She snagged it, the stool tipped, and she shot one leg and her arms to the sides to catch her balance. Still on one leg, she let the stool tip to one side, then the other, as her body stretched out in all directions.

Striving to keep her balance, she found her center, brought her limbs in, leaped high into the air, tucked her knees into her chest, and executed a perfect somersault, landing on her toes without a sound.

Holding the goblet in front of her, Cinderella bent her legs to lower herself into a crouch, and then spun and leaped, kicking and chopping at an imaginary foe as she crossed the room to reach the pump. Once there, she pushed down on the handle until fresh water flowed from its spout, and then eagerly set her goblet under the stream to catch the crisp, ice-cold water from deep in the well, her reward for the past twelve hours of grueling work.

Not seeing her stepmother or her stepsisters for four hours had been a fine reward, too. It was unusual for them to leave her alone for so long. She glanced at the single window of thick glass that she'd long ago given up trying to break. The pane was too thick and probably enchanted to give it extra strength. Given the angle of the shadows on this long spring evening, she figured there was less than two hours before darkness set in, the back door opened, and the wolves came out.

But what if something had happened to her stepmother? She had been gone a long time. Would the entrapment spells be broken if her stepmother was killed? Maybe one of the doors out of the house would open before nighttime arrived.

Cinderella set down the goblet and dashed to the cellar door that led up the steep, damp stone staircase into the garden. Taking a deep breath, she pulled on the iron handle.

It didn't move an inch—not even a wiggle. The garden door was sealed as it always was when the sun was up, just like every other exit from the house. She slumped against the door. As impossible as it seemed, she believed that someday she'd find a way to escape.